BELLEVUE

By IVANA DOBRAKOVOVÁ

Translated by Julia and Peter Sherwood

JANTAR PUBLISHING

London 2019

First published in Great Britain in 2019 by
Jantar Publishing Ltd
www.jantarpublishing.com

First published in 2009 in Bratislava as *Bellevue*

A CIP catalogue record for this book is available from the British Library
ISBN 978-0-9934467-7-1

This translation was made possible by a grant from SLOLIA committee,
the Centre for Information on Literature in Bratislava, Slovakia

LITERÁRNE
INFORMAČNÉ
CENTRUM

BELLEVUE

Slovak writer and translator Ivana Dobrakovová first attracted attention in 2008 when her story *Žiť s Petrom* [*Living with Peter*] won the short story competition *Poviedka*, organised by Koloman Kertész Bagala, the maverick publisher of Slovak literature with an uncanny nose for new talent. This story was subsequently included in her first collection, *Prvá smrť v rodine* [*The First Death in the Family*], 2009, which was shortlisted for Slovakia's most prestigious literary prize, Anasoft Litera, as was *Bellevue*, Dobrakovová's first novel, the following year. Her most recent collection of interlinked short stories, *Matky a kamionisti* [*Mothers and Truckers*], appeared in 2018, for which she received the European Union Prize for Literature in 2019. Based in Turin, Dobrakovová also has a number of translations of French and Italian literature into Slovak to her credit, including two novels by Emmanuel Carrère and, notably, Elena Ferrante's worldwide hit, the Neapolitan saga. Her perceptive and lively translation has helped to spread the 'Ferrante Fever' to Slovakia.

Dobrakovová is widely regarded as one of the most gifted authors of the generation that came to the fore in the new millennium as well as part of the great flowering of women writers whose emergence has been a distinctive feature of contemporary Slovak literature. Her books reflect the experience of living abroad, which has gained her the label of "expat writer" alongside other authors such as Zuska Kepplová,

Svetlana Žuchová and Michaela Rosová. However, in addition, Dobrakovová also focuses on motherhood, dysfunctional family relations and traumas. In this respect, her writing shows parallels with contemporary British and American female writers, such as Rachel Cusk in *Kudos*, Deborah Levy in *Hot Milk*, or Karen Roupenian's short stories.

Dobrakovová's protagonists are plagued by existential fear, anxieties, and mental disorders, the main themes of *Bellevue*. The novel builds on and expands a story from her first collection: both feature as their main character a student who takes a summer job at a centre for people with physical disabilities in the French city of Marseille, where her encounter with their severe conditions triggers a nervous breakdown, with *Bellevue* delving deeper into the state of mind of the narrator, Blanka.

The Slovak literary critic Ivana Taranenková has pointed out that the novel 'can be read as an initiation novel with a disastrous ending, a tragic report on a young woman's failed pursuit of excitement, adulthood and a new life. At the same time, it is a pessimistic novel about egotism, the inability to escape "our own private cages", where we have been imprisoned by fear, anxiety and mistrust, no less than indifference to others.' What begins as a coming-of-age novel, leading one to expect a young woman's holiday adventure in the idyllic environment of the picturesque tourist destination that the institution's name suggests, turns ironically into an unflinching account of a descent into mental illness. What at the outset appears to be an irritating lack of empathy on the part of Blanka is gradually revealed to be a symptom of her illness. The progressive deterioration of her state of mind is depicted without frills or flights of fantasy, pulling the reader inexorably into her growing paranoia, an obsession with her own body and sexuality no less than those of the centre's residents.

Her fear of losing control over her bodily functions are realised as she succumbs to illness and ends up helpless and hospitalised.

'The relation between physical and mental dependency is chiastically inverted – Blanka ends up turning from carer into someone who needs to be cared for, dependent on the help of others,' as Slovak literature scholar Peter Zajac puts it. He continues: 'The meaning of the word Bellevue is upended, turning from "beautiful view", a place of refined relaxation, recreation and the recharging of batteries, into a site of decline, decay, destruction (and self-destruction), as well as a place of re-presentation: Bellevue as the popular name of mountain and seaside resorts turns into a place of suffering and excessive violence against oneself and others.'

Dobrakovová shows how frighteningly easy it is to lose one's grip on reality and how thin the line between sanity and insanity can be. In writing about mental illness, Dobrakovová has tackled a subject that is still largely a taboo in Slovak society and that has rarely – if at all – been tackled in Slovak fiction, although there are many examples in world literature. The works Dobrakovová has acknowledged as her inspiration include Sylvia Plath's *The Bell Jar* and Elena Ferrante's *The Days of Abandonment*. In an interview on the *Asymptote* blog, she told me:

'*The Days of Abandonment* […] bowled me over and I have ever since cited Elena Ferrante as evidence that what really matters is not what you write about but how you write about it. For what could be more banal and "ordinary" than the story of a woman who suffers a breakdown after her husband leaves her for a younger woman… However, Ferrante was able to portray this stereotypical situation in a way that draws the reader more and more deeply into Olga's hallucinatory states, a kind of feverish accumulation of increasingly dread-filled situations, until the reader feels like shouting "Stop it, I can't take this anymore!" Later I re-read the novel because as a writer I was interested in the linguistic devices Elena Employed to achieve this effect, for example the vulgarisms that begin to pervade Olga's vocabulary as she imagines what her husband is up to with his mistress, the terrifying honesty of unfiltered writing, without any self-censorship.'

Dobrakovová has certainly found her own stylistic way of depicting her character's mental decline: as Blanka's condition worsens, the narration becomes fragmented and breathless and normal rules of punctuation are abandoned. Sentences, or rather: clusters of thoughts, end with commas or question marks rather than full stops mirroring her relentlessly and obsessively racing thoughts. The narration changes from the past tense to the present, creating a sense of immediacy; direct speech is no longer marked, erasing the difference between Blanka's utterances and her feverish thoughts. The urgency is increased even further once Blanka is hospitalised and the perspective shifts from 'I' to an uncomfortable 'you'. As the narrator veers from depression through states of paranoia to mania, her perception of the world is distorted, making it increasingly difficult to distinguish what is happening in reality from what is just a figment of her imagination. The readers are skilfully drawn into her nightmare and while that may not be exactly a fun place to be, they gain insight into, as well as developing compassion and understanding for, the state of mind of someone afflicted by mental illness. Not least, the skill and incisiveness of Dobrakovová's writing is sure to heighten, in the words of the Slovak critic Martin Kasarda, 'the reader's relief at not living in Blanka's world.'

Julia Sherwood, London 2019

BELLEVUE

By IVANA DOBRAKOVOVÁ

For months I had tried to talk my boyfriend into travelling to the US in the summer after our end of term exams – *Work & Travel USA* like everyone else, make a few dollars, see the country – but by Christmas Peter swore that he wouldn't set foot outside of Košice all summer and instead would stay home, reading the set books for his finals (we were both in our second year), revising his Spanish and working through the phrasal verb exercises. I had to give up on the idea of America, it's too far anyway, what with the Atlantic and being all alone in a strange country and all that jazz, never mind, I told myself, I might as well spend the first part of July in Košice with Peter, on the Ťahanovce housing estate, then go and temp in Prague for a couple of weeks, and then later in August take off somewhere on my own.

One day after class I dropped into Inex, leafed through their international exchange catalogue and picked a sort of summer camp in a care centre for people with physical disabilities in Marseille: volunteering six hours a day, free board and lodging, minimum age eighteen and, most importantly, fluent French essential – great, I thought, at last a place where only French is spoken, a chance to become fluent! The Bellevue Centre is located on a hill, has a family atmosphere and takes only eight volunteers a year.

Back at home I dashed off a motivation letter, full of platitudes: I was the ideal person for this job, I've always yearned to help the physically disabled, when my dad was sick I used to visit him in hospital every day; only right at the end did I come clean and admitted that, unfortunately, I didn't have much practical experience.

In June a letter came from Marseille informing me that I'd been accepted. I showed it to my classmate Svetlana as we sat on the low wall by the Danube outside the university waiting for the results of the French grammar test. Svetlana read through it, took a drag on her cigarette and commented: 'Well, sounds better than au pairing for some French people: at least you won't be stuck with a godawful French family and have to pretend you're grateful that they let you eat at their table, demeaning yourself like I had to last year.'

On the whole I didn't have a bad time in Košice with Peter. We spent most of the days in Lúčky where his parents had been building a house for over twenty years. I would hang around vats of concrete and piles of sand, pick blackberries in the garden, feed the feral cats and occasionally walk to the other end of village, to the embankment where the Zemplínska Šírava dam began; there I would sit on a rock with my face turned to the sun, quite the perfect idyll, if only I didn't have to spend the whole time swatting the mosquitoes that kept landing on me even though my whole body was slathered in insect repellent. Peter and I would go for walks, I would pick sunflowers, crack their hulls with my teeth, spit out the skins and crush beetles hiding among the leaves.

Early in the evening we'd pile into the Lada with Peter's parents and drive back to their flat in Ťahanovce, making sure we got there in time for the seven o'clock news, earnest conversations about the future with my prospective mother-in-law and evasive glances from Peter's siblings whenever we happened to bump into each other in the narrow hallway. Peter would immerse himself for hours in Borges, Cervantes and Bolaño, and I had to walk around on tiptoe, or he'd go: 'Do you really have to make so much noise? Blanka, please…' so I would just lie on the bed getting bored, listening to my discman and waiting for night to fall.

Because at night, after everyone had gone to sleep, Peter would lock the door and slip into the small bed that was hardly big enough for one, and whisper: 'Shush, we don't want them to hear us, my father is a light sleeper'. Afterwards I would spit the sperm out of the window, onto the pavement in front of the block as I didn't want to risk meeting some bleary-eyed family member with my mouth still full of the yucky stuff, that's why the window, I can take anything but that I'm not going to swallow.

Two weeks later I was passing City Park on my way to catch the night train to Prague, a seventy-litre rucksack on my back, Peter tagging along to see me off. He seemed to be in high spirits, cracking jokes, almost relieved to see me leave at last. He put me on the train, gave me a kiss and said, sounding as if he meant it, 'Take care down there in Marseille, I've heard the place is full of Arabs so make sure you don't end up in some harem.' I burst out laughing and gave him a thump on the back, 'Yeah, right, a harem! You'd better go back to your Argentinian novels, or you won't finish in time for finals,' and as I took my seat in the compartment I was still mumbling to myself, a harem, really, the things he comes up with.

My sister found me a temping job with an organisation helping Holocaust victims and their families to receive compensation, and since I'd got in through connections, all the Czech temps looked daggers at me the whole time. Every morning I was handed a pile of documents to photocopy and for the rest of the day I'd stand by the copier, sorting papers and reading letters explaining why their writers should get compensation. I spent hours reading about fathers who'd been taken away, never to be seen again, about the harsh winter of 1942, about starvation, fears and dashed hopes.

Every lunchtime I made myself a cup of tea in the kitchen and took an apple out of my bag, and one of the temps, Ondra, would tease me, 'Let's see what's for lunch today – surprise, surprise – an apple with its own peel as garnish… you'd better watch it, you might put some weight on!' In fact, I was quite fond of Ondra, he was the only one who would talk to me at all. My Slovak made him laugh, especially the fact that we say *hej* for yes and one day, as I stood on a ladder looking for a file, he asked, 'Is it true that *kokot* is the worst swearword in Slovak?'

I would finish work at four o'clock and take the underground from I.P. Pavlova straight to my sister's house. Prague held no attraction for me, I would spend the evenings with my sister and her family, surreptitiously reading expert opinions written by my brother-in-law, a forensic psychiatrist. I was particularly fascinated by the case of a homeless man who had attacked another man; he kept pounding his head with a rock until a hole opened in his skull and when he spotted 'something white' inside, he knew for sure that this man wasn't a human being but an alien from outer space.

By the time I was due to leave Prague I had had enough. I was irritable and grumpy at work, I couldn't wait to go to France, the silent hostility of the other temps was beginning to wear me down; although, admittedly, I didn't make a huge effort either. On my last day an email was doing the rounds of the office. One of those crass jokes, people printed it out and shared it, laughing, frowning with disgust and amusement, and around lunchtime Ondra passed it on to me as well, 'There you go, have a look.' I was appalled to discover it contained definitions of various kinds of shit, things like shit-a-boo, Napoleo-shit, and other supposedly funny stuff of that kind. I read the whole thing, but it didn't make me laugh, it was too disgusting and besides, there are certain things you shouldn't talk about.

That night, thoroughly fed up with my temp job, I told my sister I was looking forward to the camp and hoping I would finally get fluent in French. Hearing that, my brother-in-law chuckled, 'Oh yeah, those basket cases are all just waiting to talk to you,' then he twisted his body into various unnatural positions and emitted odd sounds, 'ooohyyy, mhaaaa, gheeaaaa.' I laughed, 'You must be joking, why would anyone talk like that? I can't believe you just did that.'

The Eurolines coach was full of Poles talking loudly, unpacking their sandwiches, schnitzels, bottles of vodka and shot glasses, the aisle was already full of rubbish by the time I got on, Bratislava was just one stop on the Kraków – Nice line. I sat next to a tongue-tied young man, who spoke only once in the course of the many hours we spent side by side, *'przepraszam bardzo,'* excuse me, when he had to wake me up to go to the toilet. The journey took fifteen hours, overnight from Saturday to Sunday, and when we arrived in Nice in the early morning, I was quietly envious to see an old lady meeting him at the bus station because nobody would be coming to meet me, I was sure of that.

I changed to a bus marked Marseille – Toulon, it was much emptier, no more Poles with their *'dawaj kielicha,'* give us a drink, or *'chodźmy się narąbać,'* let's go and get pissed. I was sitting on my own at last and could look out of the window. I exchanged a few text messages with Peter, *how's Marquez doing? finished 100 years of boredom yet?* and as we approached Marseille, I grew anxious about the very idea of having to make a phone call and explaining where they had to meet me, total strangers, in a totally strange city.

It had been raining, and the countryside outside the windows looked sodden in the semi-darkness. During a thirty-minute stop at a petrol station I huddled under the awning of a bar munching crumbly Bebe biscuits and gazing at the forest and the black clouds above it, but as we neared Marseille, the sun came out and the skies were clear again. We drove along a three-lane motorway lined with oleander trees, passing gigantic blocks of flats in the suburbs. At some point a sign for the airport flashed up on the right. Then we reached the centre, I saw a park, an arc de triomphe and we pulled up at the coach station in Victor

Hugo Square. I got out feeling shattered, waited for the driver to haul out my huge backpack, it was the last one of course, then bought a phone card at a kiosk and called the Bellevue Centre from a phone box, *je suis place Victor Hugo, vous pouvez venir me chercher?*

Two women in headscarves came to meet me, they could have been mother and daughter, they spoke Arabic in the car and laughed heartily at something, ignoring me, didn't ask how my trip was and why I'd arrived a day late, they evidently didn't care and that was fine by me, in a way. As I listened to their incomprehensible jabbering I couldn't help thinking of Peter, what he had said about Arabs and a harem and I laughed inwardly, for all I knew they could be taking me there now, to a harem. I took out my mobile and texted my mother, so she wouldn't worry, *arrived OK, Marseille is beautiful.*

The Bellevue care home was situated on a hill above the city, and as we drove through the main entrance, we passed some kind of park with trees, bushes, flowers whose names I didn't know, a bamboo grove to the left, plus the obligatory oleanders. We parked in front of a grey, three-storey building, the Arab women pointed me to a room behind reception and left me to my own devices, disappearing down a corridor somewhere in the bowels of the building.

I hung around the door for a while gathering strength, and when I finally plucked up the courage to go in, I froze in the doorway. There were some fifteen people inside and thirty pairs of eyes were fixed on me instantly. Feeling very uneasy, I said I was Blanka from Slovakia, I'd just arrived and… then I seized up and didn't know what else to say.

Someone brought me a chair from the dining room, everyone shifted a little to make room for me at a round table, and they all introduced themselves. I just let their names drift by without even trying to remember, glad I could just about register their nationalities: a woman from Algeria, one from Sweden, another from Algeria, one from Romania, two guys, an Italian and a Slovene, and a Czech girl! Czech! I was so happy to see someone from my part of the world, plus the girl looked about my age, unlike the Romanian, who must have been at least fifty. After I sat down, an older man with a beard introduced himself as the director of the centre, 'So, where was I? Oh yes, the morning wash and the rota…'

I didn't really listen to what he was saying and eyed the other volunteers instead, the two swarthy Algerians, one in a headscarf, the blonde Swede, thirtyish, with a slightly crumpled face, the curly-haired Romanian who referred to herself as the camp leader, a young Italian, terribly nice, all smiles, wild gestures, sickeningly stereotypical Italian, and the Slovene guy, whose French was apparently not good enough, as the Italian was translating everything into English for him, with the Slovene listening, head bowed, nodding from time to time, and finally the Czech girl, a slim, blue-eyed blonde, who gave me a warm smile whenever our eyes met.

Suddenly everyone burst out laughing, the bearded chap stopped mid-sentence and started shouting at the Italian: 'Luca, pur-lease! I was saying that we're inundated with photos of perfect people, we're used to seeing all these perfect bodies, and that some of you might find it shocking to be in a place like this, where none of the bodies is perfect. But what you're translating for this poor chap is something about your divine body. What's all that gibberish you're telling him?' Luca, the Italian, roared with laughter and threw up his arms, gesticulating wildly, 'I just can't help it, Michel! It's not my fault that I have a divine body. So why should I keep it a secret?' he justified himself, pretending to be upset but now everyone was rolling about with laughter, except for the poor Slovene guy, who looked rather confused.

Finally, we were all given maps, bus tickets, the rota, and as people started getting up from the table and chatting in small groups, the Czech girl elbowed her way over to me and offered to show me around, take me to 'the place where you'll be staying, our cute little house'. I heaved the backpack onto my shoulders, quickly glanced at the Italian who was pointing something out to the Swede on the map on the wall, and followed Martina, *'jo, já jsem Martina,'* hi, I'm Martina, across the dining room and out of the building.

We passed an empty swimming pool and some people in wheelchairs parked in the shade of the trees, then went downhill to a low building by a bamboo grove. On the way Martina explained that she'd arrived three days ago and was quite settled in by now, there would be just three of us sharing the little house, the Romanian Elena, Martina herself and me, everyone else was staying in the main building, in a room behind the kitchen, but moving to the annexe today. I listened to her, quietly envious that she could navigate the compound so confidently, she obviously knew her way around the place.

When we reached the little house, Martina went around the corner, fetched some kind of a remote, pressed a button, the door began to creak open and an orange bulb flashed above the door, stopping only when the door came to a halt. She showed me around, the kitchenette, the bathroom, the back room with two beds where she and Elena had already moved in with their stuff, and the front room where I would be sleeping, with a mattress on the floor instead of a bed. I dumped my backpack on the floor, looked out of the window at a big yellow dog snooping around the bamboo grove, and just then the Romanian Elena arrived – 'hi, girls, everything all right?' – and disappeared into the bathroom without waiting for a reply. Martina whispered to me that she wasn't too keen on Elena, and then turned on her heels, 'I'm off to see Patrick, I promised I'd stop by.'

I slumped down on the mattress, not sure if I should start unpacking, I didn't really feel like it and there wasn't anywhere to put my stuff anyway, not a single chair, bedside table or a wardrobe in sight. That didn't bother me too much, what intrigued me more was who this Patrick that Martina mentioned could be, a male nurse, or maybe even one of the locals, it wouldn't have surprised me if she'd already made some friends in town. Martina impressed me instantly with her easy manner, she seemed the kind of person who could fit in anywhere, she was happy to chat to me even though we'd never met before, and she sounded so nice and natural, too, in short, she was the exact opposite of me who had barely strung three sentences together in the two weeks I spent temping in Prague.

The door opened with a loud bang and Elena appeared, a towel wrapped around her head in a turban, she walked from the bathroom to the back room humming a tune, I heard the rustling of bags and my thumb inadvertently crushed an ant crawling onto the mattress, and soon I spotted another. Then another, and another, and another. I got up, pushed the mattress aside and spotted what looked like a regular anthill, a heap of teeming black dots and a path leading all the way to the door.

As I stood in the middle of the room wondering where to move the mattress so that it wouldn't be right in their path, I heard someone knock, raised my head and saw Luca the Italian making faces at me through the window and gesturing for me to open the door, but by the time I figured out how to operate the automatic door from the inside, he stopped smiling and was hovering tensely, and as soon as he came in, he went, *'Ma che cazzo fai? ragazza, che cazzo fai?'*, and when I stared at him in bewilderment he switched to French and asked if I could help them move, it would be really nice of me, they would all appreciate it.

There were five sleeping bags on the floor, and holdalls, pillows, handbags, bath towels, cosmetics, sunscreen, bits of clothing, books lay scattered all around the place, a complete mess. I helped to carry the stuff to a two-bedroom flat in the annexe reached through the main building, past a big drainpipe and a flowerbed, across a short metal bridge above some kind of crater filled with gravel and finally down a long balcony, the second door on the left. The flat was very clean, light, with a view of the building opposite, a bathroom, a toilet, one room for the guys, the Slovene and the Italian, the other for the girls, the two Algerians and the Swede. Unlike our little house the flat was fully furnished, but I didn't feel hard done by, the view from my mattress was much nicer, a bamboo grove outside my window, and Martina in the room next door as a bonus.

The Swede tried to get us organised to bring some sort of order into the aimless running around, but she soon had to give up as no one paid her any attention, Luca did basically nothing, just cracked jokes which made the younger of the two Algerians crack up, she nearly split her sides laughing, slapped her knees and hooted, *'Mais arrête, Luca!'*, the older Algerian woman just sat on the bed with a careworn expression, wiping sweat from her brow and muttering, *'mes enfants, mes enfants,'* so between us the Swede and I ended up doing most of the moving on our own.

I was walking down the ground floor corridor, it was early afternoon, siesta time, not a soul anywhere, looking for the computer room and telling myself, it's supposed to be somewhere near the stairs if I understood right, the stairs are here, so... when Martina suddenly appeared from around the corner with a carafe of wine, smiled at me, put her free arm around my waist and led me to the lift, *'pojď, seznámím tě s Patrickem,'* come, I want you to meet Patrick. We went up to the first floor, down another long hospital corridor, unsticking our feet from the linoleum, the third door on the right, Martina opened it and we walked in.

This was the first resident's room I'd seen, it had a fantastic view of the sea, the Frioul islands and the Chateau d'If. It was an ordinary room, except for a mobile hoist in the middle. In a wheelchair by the window sat a man of around thirty, quite good-looking, slim, short black hair, brown eyes, he actually looked like a normal guy who'd just sat down for a moment to have a rest, and I said to myself, this is a completely normal guy, but only until he opened his mouth. Martina introduced us, 'this is my darling Patrick, my sweetie,' and the man in the wheelchair looked at me as if about to say something, his mouth contorted into a terrible grimace, you could see he was making a huge effort and eventually he managed something like *cheuté*. He reached out his right arm, which jerked up and down in a scary way, I muttered an embarrassed *enchantée* and tried to get hold of his hand, clasping it firmly in mine, squeezing to stop it jerking to make the scene slightly less grotesque, but I couldn't help myself, it felt like a fish in its last throes was thrashing about in my hand. Just then Martina spoke again, *'no a tam v rohu je Drago, ale toho už přece znáš,'* that's Drago over there, in the corner, but you've met him already.

Surprised, I turned around and indeed, there was the Slovene, sitting in the corner of the room silently watching me, he must have witnessed it all from the start, the whole scene with Patrick in the wheelchair but when our eyes met, he just gave a noncommittal nod. Martina bent down to me and whispered, 'I don't know what to do about him, he won't leave us alone, and give Patrick and me some privacy,' then she placed the carafe on the table and poured everyone a drink. We drank 'to our camp', but I suddenly had this overwhelming urge to get the hell out of there, that very minute.

I ran down the stairs to the ground floor, stopped for a moment in amazement in front of some sort of barricade, then it dawned on me, of course, it's a barrier to prevent those in wheelchairs falling off the stairs. As I walked along the corridor and out of the building wheelchairs kept buzzing by, siesta time was over, dinner would be served soon, lively traffic, I moved between them like a giant, tactfully averting my gaze, it seemed inappropriate to gawp and just as inappropriate not to look, I tried to appear natural at all costs, like there's nothing strange about the fact that both your legs are missing, that your head is twice the size of a normal one, that your arms are like matchsticks, spindly and contorted, that you're drooling, reek of stale urine and faeces, and your face is frozen in a permanent grimace.

I soon found the exit and continued down the corridor. Suddenly it seemed terribly crude to have two legs, both in working order, like I was flaunting it, don't be absurd, I said to myself, how can there be anything offensive or immoral about having two legs, or even something I should feel guilty about. For a moment I almost wished I were like them, wheelchair-bound, or at least not sticking out like a sore thumb.

By the time I reached the dining room, dinner was in full swing, I saw Martina feeding Patrick at one of the tables, she held a napkin under his chin and a glass of water to his mouth, at the other end sat the two Algerians women, nurses also in normal life as I learned during the move. It wasn't my shift, so I headed for the first empty seat I saw; there were two guys in wheelchairs and a nurse, who didn't so much as look at me when I joined them. I took some bread from the basket, poured myself some water from a carafe but didn't feel like eating, just nibbled at some bread and watched the nurse and her skilled movements as she gave mouthfuls to the residents, wiped the sauce off their chin with a napkin and still managed somehow to eat herself. Apart from the clinking of cutlery the room was relatively quiet, hardly anything was said, except for questions like 'more water?', 'have you had enough?', 'would you like some more?' but most people managed just with gestures.

I watched Martina and Patrick and suddenly recalled the afternoon, the room with the view of the sea, and heard Martina's words again, *'můj Patriček, mé zlatíčko,'* my darling Patrick, my sweetie-pie, and only then did it dawn on me: she spoke about him as if he was her boyfriend! as if they were an item! but just then the chap in the wheelchair to my right gave me a nudge, he was a shrivelled up old man who'd been sitting there the whole time with his chin jutting out unnaturally and spitting into his plate every now and them, as if inadvertently. I pretended that it was nothing – it really wasn't – that I didn't take any notice, I just moved a little further to the side to get out of his way, but he gave me another nudge, more forcefully this time. That's when the nurse laughed and I finally plucked up the courage to raise my eyes from the table.

The little old man was pointing to my plate, rolling his eyes heavenwards and saying something like *'mege, mege'*. I sat there perplexed, unable to say anything, so eventually the nurse spoke, first turning to the old man, 'If you want the young lady to understand you, you have to speak more clearly', then to me, 'Don't worry about it, sometimes we don't understand them either, he just wants you to eat up, he's concerned that you haven't been eating your dinner.' She pointed her fork at the bowls with meat and pasta in the middle of the table, 'Have some, don't be shy', so I quickly helped myself to a piece of meat because for a moment I was scared that she would serve me.

In the middle of the night I opened my eyes into the darkness, roused by some noise, a creaking, I sat up and in the flashing light of the bulb saw Martina come in through the automatic door, wearing a bikini and carrying a towel. Totally confused, I asked, 'What's going on?' Martina quickly bent down to me and stroked my head, 'Don't worry, Blanka, go back to sleep, I've just gone for a swim with the boys.' Then she straightened up and quietly walked over to the other room, I heard the bed groan as she lay down and thought I heard Elena mutter something in Romanian in her sleep, but by then my eyes had closed again, and I was drifting off.

The communal lounge was full of sprightly nurses and bleary-eyed volunteers, on the round table there perched a coffee pot, a sugar bowl and two cartons of milk. Shifts were being assigned, the rota was being drawn up: a resident's name was read out, followed by a brief discussion: 'No, I'm definitely not taking Jean today, yesterday was quite enough', 'OK, I'll take Gérard then', 'François and Sophie need a bath today, who'll do them?' 'By the way, has the doctor seen to Valentina's foot, the one that swelled up yesterday?' Martina was the only one to volunteer, yes, she'd be happy to look after Patrick again today, as always, the rest of just sat there waiting for our assignment and hoping the coffee would revive us.

We weren't expected to work unaccompanied on our first day, so the nurses divided us up and I was assigned to Isabelle, a black nurse, who led me down the ground floor corridor before knocking on a door next to the lift and walking into a dark room without waiting for a response. She opened the blinds and I saw the little old man who had nudged me at dinner the night before, lying in his bed huddled under the sheets, blinking in the light and rasping quietly. Isabelle shook him, *'Bonjour, Thomas, vous avez bien dormi?'* and although the old man didn't reply, Isabelle started to talk, another sunny day was dawning, not a cloud in the sky and she would definitely go for a swim at the Plage de prophète in the afternoon after her shift, last night there was some shooting again in La Canebière, must have been some mafiosi settling scores, terrible, you almost had to be scared of going for a walk in town, and this here is Blanka, our new nurse from Slovakia, so be a good boy, Thomas. As she talked she washed the old man, showing me which washcloth to use on his face, which on his body, where the nappies were stored, how to hoist him into his wheelchair, 'you have to secure him in this sling, otherwise he'll topple over.' I watched in silence as she brushed his teeth, put his clothes and shoes on, shaved and combed him, trimmed the hairs in his nostrils, smiling all the while, like it was all a breeze.

The wash took less than twenty minutes. She showed me how to operate the wheelchair, the gearstick and the wheel brakes, and all three of us headed for the dining room. Martina, Patrick and Drago were already there, as was Luca with a woman in a wheelchair who must have weighed about a hundred kilos, and the nurses, everyone with a baguette, cutting, spreading it with butter, helping themselves to jam and honey pots from the basket, pouring coffee and tea as if they'd been doing it all their lives.

Isabelle told me to eat up and not worry, she would take care of Thomas, and besides, there was another resident, Serge, waiting for us, so I cut off a piece of baguette and spread it with some butter and jam. I had to smile because it made me think of Peter, he lives on bread and butter and jam all year round, he's too lazy to cook when he's in hall, plus it costs money, so he buys bread, margarine and jam, 'Tesco Everyday Value', of course.

Serge was a plump man in his forties, frowning at the sun that shone in his eyes and grumbling, Isabelle should have warned him before she opened the bloody blinds, he needed more sleep, we should give him at least another thirty minutes, and this, that, and the other, but Isabelle ignored his whining, rolled him vigorously over from one side to the other and washed him, the same routine as with Thomas. As she hoisted him onto his wheelchair, she told me that Serge was the grandson of the woman who founded Bellevue, 'Aren't you, Serge, tell mademoiselle who you are so she knows who she has the honour of looking after,' and that's how I learned that not only had Mme F. founded dozens of similar centres around the country, but she was also the first woman minister to have served in a French government.

Under Isabelle's supervision I brushed Serge's teeth and combed the five long hairs he was clearly very proud of, shaved him and put his glasses on. Serge smiled benevolently throughout the procedure, yawned with boredom and even cooperated while I shaved him, holding out one cheek then another, puffing out his upper lip, sticking out his chin and turning his head as necessary. I took to him straight away, not least because he spoke quite normally and had no tics. As I cut his nails, I thought to myself that washing an unproblematic patient like this was almost a pleasure, fun almost, that Serge was someone who just needed a little help but was fine otherwise. 'Well, that's it,' Isabelle said with a contented smile when I finished washing him and told me to take Serge down to the dining room for breakfast, 'Give him whatever he asks for, he's on a diet and knows best what he's allowed to eat and what he isn't.'

I wheeled him towards the lift. We bumped into Luca who was there, waiting with someone in a wheelchair, the sight of whom made me immediately look away, he had long, skinny, insect-like arms and legs in constant motion and an unnaturally square head. The man sat in his wheelchair drooling, clearly trying to say something, pointing to an alphabet board attached to the front of his armrest, pointing to the letters and emitting inarticulate noises. The minute I saw him I felt worse, but Luca didn't mind at all, he laughed and gestured, 'Listen, Adam, I can't understand you, let's try again, shall we?' The man in the wheelchair started to bang on the board, Luca bent down to him trying to work it out, reading out the letters the disabled guy was pointing to. 'A … R … A … N … G … ARANG?!!' Luca laughed again, patted Adam's shoulder, and looked at me, 'I bet his own mother can't understand him!' I didn't know what to say so I just gave a vague smile. Luca turned to the man again, 'You know what, let's forget it, the lift is here.' It was a large lift that easily accommodated all four of us.

In the dining room I pushed Serge towards a table and sat down on a chair, took a quick look at the baskets of food and the thermos flasks and started asking what he would like for breakfast, but Serge said yes to everything, absolutely everything, yes to coffee, yes to tea, yes to milk, yes to honey, yes to jam, yes to Nutella, whatever I pointed to, he wanted it, so in the end, at a loss, I said 'But Serge, Isabelle said you're on a diet, she said you know what you're allowed to eat?' but he remained stubbornly silent. I wondered if I should go and look for Isabelle, explain the situation and ask her what to do, what to give him, but it would have been foolish of me to embarrass myself like that on my first day, useless, unable to take decisions, so I just put some butter on a baguette and poured him some coffee and when he started demanding Nutella I pretended that I was deaf and didn't understand.

Early in the afternoon Martina went to town 'with the guys', I saw them walking down the tarmac road to the main gate, she, Luca and Drago, the sun was baking, just shorts, T-shirts, sandals or trainers, a bottle of mineral water, I watched them leave and felt a bit jealous that it was so easy for her to charm the guys.

The Swede, the Romanian and the Algerians were resting in their rooms after the morning shift, the nurses sat around the pool chatting, their feet up on plastic chairs, a few residents were watching TV in the communal lounge. I walked past them and headed for the computer room, four computers, one of them in use, a young guy in a wheelchair, an Arab, playing some computer game, firing missiles from a cannon at boats trying to approach the shore, it looked pretty simple, basic rules, basic graphics but he obviously didn't mind, firing at everything that moved with a beatific smile. I sat down in front of the computer next to him and he turned his head towards me, watched me for a moment and then, a very slow, *'sa-lut-je-suis-Ah-mad,'* came out of him. I introduced myself as well, wondering if I should shake hands with him but decided against it – what if he has convulsions, I typed in freemail.com trying to look busy, but he kept staring at me, I was slightly put out, shifted in my chair and turned to him with a smile, 'At least five boats have docked now, you'll lose the game if you're not careful.'

I opened my mailbox, read my emails and started to write a reply to my mum, *it's very hot here, we haven't been to the seaside yet but I'm sure we will, we'll visit Count Monte Cristo's island too, don't worry about me, I'm sharing a little house with Elena from Romania and Martina, a Czech girl, there's a wonderful bamboo grove next to the house,* and at some point I noticed that Ahmad was leaning out of his wheelchair to get a closer look, he was quite shamelessly peering at my email over my shoulder, *the work isn't hard, the disabled people are OK, I've almost stopped taking notice and it doesn't bother me that they're drooling all over the place and that food keeps falling out of their mouths, I suppose it doesn't look very different when I eat,* just then Ahmad smiled and suddenly I was gripped by an absurd feeling that he knew Slovak and could read what was writing. All of a sudden, a ghastly jingle announced the end of his game, he must have realised that he'd lost, turned back to his computer, switched it off and buzzed out of the room. Only then did I breathe a sigh of relief, now I could finally write to Cédric.

Cédric was my friend from last year's camp, a guy from Bordeaux, I was desperate to meet him while in Marseille, *Cédric, s'il te plaît, viens, je veux te voir, on trouvera sûrement une place pour toi ici, viens, je t'en prie,* suddenly I regretted I was in Marseille on my own, without Cédric, without someone I could have a normal conversation with.

I lay on the mattress reading a text message from Peter that had just arrived, *only 5 Spanish lit books left, but no reading today, played computer games all day, you'd have told me off if you'd been here, miss you my darling, Peter.* I was just about to write back when Elena suddenly appeared in the doorway carrying a huge plastic bag. She asked, 'Blanka, you are Blanka, right?... ever been to Romania, Bucharest?', 'No, I haven't,' I said, and added, just as a courtesy, 'I'm sorry to say, but I'm sure it's a lovely country.' Elena nodded earnestly, 'it's a beautiful country, come, let me show you,' and she took me to the other room, emptied the plastic bag onto the table, and out came a bucketful of postcards, maps, photos, tourist brochures and picture books.

I was horrified but it was too late to back out, I couldn't get out of it by claiming I had some urgent chore (except maybe a sudden indisposition), so I sat with her at the table for over an hour listening to a lecture on Romania, the huge square in the middle of Bucharest, Romanian Moldavia, the country's natural beauty and the wonders of its modern architecture. I nodded dutifully at everything she said, throwing in the odd 'oh, I didn't know that', 'really?', 'who would have thought', desperately wishing someone would come to my rescue. When we got to the end, Elena was all smiles, happy to have done such a brilliant job of presenting her country, then she laid a hand on my shoulder, 'now you tell me all about Slovakia.'

The acceptance letter had said we should bring some brochures on our home country to show the residents, who'd be very interested (as if!), and I remembered that while packing I did bury at the bottom of my backpack some pictures of Bratislava's Old Town, its four streets and five historic buildings, so I went over and started to throw out my clothes looking for them. This time the Romanian sat down at the table and I handed her the postcards one by one, 'this is St Michael's Gate, this is the Main Square and this is the National Theatre,' and as expected, Elena jumped for joy at every new picture, shouting with fake enthusiasm, 'oh, Bratislava is beautiful! I hope to see it one day!' I felt awkward and nauseated that some Romanian woman should pretend to be interested even though she didn't give a shit about my home town, just like I didn't about her Bucharest.

That's when Martina came back from town with Luca and Drago, sweaty faces and T-shirts knotted above their bellies, they stood there astonished – I was holding a pop-up book showing the monuments of Bratislava, the materials on Romania lay scattered around the table – Martina turned to me and asked: 'Blanka, did you see any suspicious characters hanging around the neighbourhood? Someone stole Luca's money while we were in town!'

For my first shift I signed up for Serge, I was sure it wouldn't be difficult, I had managed to wash him in Isabelle's presence, I'd manage on my own as well. As I entered, I shouted a cheery *'Bonjour, monsieur Serge,'* but there was no response, so I walked over to the far side of the room, opened the blinds and picked up two washcloths from the basin. I tried to talk to him, asked if he had slept well and how he was, it didn't really bother me that he didn't respond to my questions, I gave him a thorough wash from head to toe, but when I tried to roll him over to his side to wash his back, I realised he was too heavy. I stopped jabbering for a moment, leaned into him properly, 'Let's do it, here we go!', I shouted to spur myself on and when I finally managed to turn him over to his stomach, I saw that his nappy was full.

I stared at it in puzzlement, this wasn't a scenario I had imagined, I wondered what might be the best… technical way… to deal with it, and just then I heard Serge mutter something into his pillow, 'What? What is it?' I bent down to him and realised he was protesting because he was extremely uncomfortable lying on his stomach. I whispered, 'just hang on a minute, I'll be right back,' and ran to the nearest toilet, returning with an armful of toilet paper.

Eventually, after I heaved Serge onto his back again, he looked at me with slight horror and I realised I didn't quite know what to say to him, it was rather awkward, the incident with the nappy seemed to have humiliated both of us, I made a few more feeble attempts at communication, 'Which T-shirt would you like?' and 'Where's your shaver?' but Serge didn't respond, he just watched me making a mess and looking alarmed. I was getting more and more troubled and spooked, Serge's lack of cooperation didn't help, I couldn't remember what I was supposed to do, in what order, how to operate the hoist and what it was that I absolutely mustn't forget.

After thirty minutes of struggling I wheeled him down to the dining room, parked him at the nearest table, 'wait here, I'll be right back' and dashed back to his room to give it a quick clean up, rinse the hairs and toothpaste from the washbasin, pick up the towels that lay scattered about and smooth down the bedsheets. On returning to the dining room I found Isabelle feeding Serge. When I joined them, she reproached me, 'how could you have left him here without breakfast? you know he can't put jam on his bread on his own …' I tried to stammer out an explanation, but Isabelle wasn't listening, she just dismissed it with a wave of her hand, 'Don't worry about it, Blanka, but take more care next time. Go and see to Laurence now, she's been waiting for you.'

Laurence was a girl roughly my age, a slim brunette with regular features, desperately trying to communicate, constantly emitting moans, shrieks, wails, at least that's what it sounded like to me, she flailed her arms around furiously and kicked out in every direction, she wasn't able to control her body or keep it still, and at first I was frightened that she might harm herself with those violent movements. I couldn't understand her disjointed French so I just kept nodding with a lump in my throat, washed her, dressed her and combed her hair saying, *oui, oui … oui, oui*, but that apparently just wound her up, she contorted her face and bared her teeth in an attempt to articulate, to get through to me and make herself understood, by turns smiling and sounding conciliatory, then again fuming and spitting about.

I felt awful, literally paralysed by horror and helplessness, all I could think of was how to get the hell out of there as soon as possible, I guess her displays of affection terrified me more than her show of defiance, but what I found most difficult was the sight of the thick curly hairs in her crotch, which forced me to admit that her genitals looked exactly like those of any other woman, that despite the shrieking and jerking she was still a woman with a vagina between her legs. I couldn't help feeling revolted, but at the same time I felt a kind of kinship, a closeness, an oppressive sense that there but for the grace of God…

Once she was seated in her wheelchair, she indicated that she needed a pee, I didn't know what to do so I ran out into the corridor and grabbed Martina, who was just coming out of the lift pushing a wheelchair, 'please come and help me, I can't manage on my own.' Martina went in and the first thing she did was peck Laurence on both cheeks, *'salut, ça va, chérie?'* stroking her hair and giving her a kind smile. She showed me what to do in this kind of situation, found a bedpan in the wardrobe, together we placed it under Laurence and waited for her to finish her noisy peeing. Martina wiped her with some napkins, threw them into the bedpan and handed the whole thing to me, 'here, go and empty it in the toilet while I strap her in.'

At lunch I sat next to Oscar, a portly man with a voracious appetite. I kept stuffing him, dipping the fork into his mouth at regular intervals, he kept asking for more, he couldn't get enough, gave disgruntled snorts and kept urging me, *'encore, encore'*. I ate very little, there were onions in the spaghetti sauce, I can't stand onions, so I just stirred the pasta on the plate every now and then, shifted it around and ate mostly the baguette and breadsticks.

But all of a sudden, as I was giving Oscar his dessert, tears welled up in my eyes and my throat tightened with anxiety. It came abruptly like a wave sweeping over my head, suddenly I had difficulty breathing and everything went blurry. Without thinking I leapt to my feet and ran out of the dining room, locked myself in the first room that I found open and tried to calm down, mildly nauseated, my head pounding in panic.

When I returned to the dining room, Oscar looked at me reproachfully, the unfinished dessert on the table in front of him, the arms that couldn't hold the spoon hanging limp by his sides. I sat down quickly and started to feed him, no one must notice anything, just pretend nothing's happened, I told myself but at the same time, I felt certain they must have noticed my sudden flight from the dining room, they must have figured it all out.

The plan was to go out in the evening, visit the Vieux Port, the harbour, admire the Madonna on the hill, get some ice cream and just walk around eating it without thinking of the residents for a while, like on a holiday, but Martina insisted that we take Patrick along, she wouldn't go anywhere without him, and if Martina didn't go, neither would Drago, and if Drago and Martina didn't go, neither would Luca, so we just had to let Martina have her way, there was nothing else we could do. We had to take a wheelchair-accessible van and while Martina issued orders to Drago and Luca, who had great difficulty loading Patrick, I sat in one of the plastic chairs by the swimming pool watching dusk slowly fall and the Slovene struggle to push Patrick's wheelchair up the ramp.

Just then Ahmad, the Arab from the computer room, stopped by and asked if I was Slovak, *'t'es slovaque, c'est ça?'*, I nodded and he spoke again, this time in Slovak, *'a-hoj-a-ko-sa-maš?'* hello-how-are-you, he said it slowly, but he did say it. I sat there staring at him, my jaw must have dropped in surprise, so he did understand me in the computer room! He knew what I was writing in the email to my mum!

But it turned out that '*a-hoj-a-ko-sa-maš*' and '*do-bre*', I'm fine, was the full extent of Ahmad's knowledge of Slovak, I questioned him and it turned out that he had a Slovak friend, a girl also from Bratislava who worked here as a nurse last year and still sent him postcards with pictures of the Castle and wrote him letters that sometimes ran to several pages.

Ahmad smiled, he was chuffed to see me impressed, and I told myself that he was actually quite nice, he might be all right really, and so to please him, I heaped praise on him, 'Oh, I see, you speak Slovak, but that's wonderful, who would have thought!' Now Ahmad was beaming with delight and immediately offered to show me the postcards, we could also watch a film in his room, he had a DVD player and a decent collection of DVDs, how about *Matrix*, but by then Drago and Luca had jointly managed to manoeuvre Patrick into the van so I said good-bye, 'Sorry, got to go now, we'll definitely watch *Matrix* together, some other time.'

We were sitting in a café on La Canebière sipping cocktails, shouting and throwing cocktail sticks at one another, Luca told us about Naples, he said it's the only place in the world where passers-by will rush to the aid of the thief, not his victim, everyone laughed, Martina was helping Patrick with his drink, he also roared with laughter and took active part in the conversation just like everyone else, I was the only one who kept quiet, what could I say about Bratislava that might sound funny? I was thinking about the email I'd written the day before to Cédric, my friend from last year's camp, and wondered: will he come? won't he?

If he said he was coming, I could put him up in my room in our little house, the two of us would easily fit onto my mattress and we could wander around Marseille together, just the two of us, if Cédric came to see me I would no longer be jealous of Martina because of Luca and Drago.

At breakfast we discussed where we would go, this was the first time we all had a day off together, I drank my coffee in silence listening to their squabbling but took no part in it, what would have been the point, but Martina did, quite forcefully, she insisted that we went to the beach and took Patrick with us, we might as well take Laurence and Françoise while we're at it, let them enjoy the summer, surely they can't be happy being stuck at the Centre all the time staring at the white walls, but at that point Ingeborg the Swede chipped in: 'I'm sorry, Martina, but I certainly don't want to sacrifice any of my time off just because of your... your... enthusiasm, or whatever that is, it's very commendable of course but... last night with Patrick was quite enough, OK?', the Algerian women nodded eagerly, Luca and Drago lowered their eyes and kept meaningfully silent.

As I was leaving the dining room, Ahmad stopped me and asked me to help him use the toilet, *'pistolet, pistolet,'* he repeated and kept turning his head back until I noticed a kind of container with a wide neck hanging from his wheelchair, it did look a bit like a pistol. I locked myself in the toilet with Ahmad, took the container from the wheelchair, placed his penis inside and took a step back, but as soon as I let go, it dropped to the floor and I realised I had to hold it there throughout the operation. As he peed, Ahmad looked me up and down, amused by my effort to look natural, when he was done I asked if I should go and bring some loo paper and he said with a smile, 'you just need to shake it down.'

I blushed, put it back without shaking it down, zipped him up and ran out of the toilet.

We piled into a red van, everyone except Elena who excused herself for some family reasons, she was expecting an important phone call from Romania or something like that, or something completely different, we left her behind without asking pointless questions, it was none of our business. In the van we lay on the floor on top of one another, giggling and bumping each other every time the van bounced, Luca drove like a lunatic, only just managing to negotiate the turns, he kept turning to us from his raised seat, *'tranquilli, ragazzi, tranquilli!,'* Ingeborg sat next to him with a map in her lap, 'turn right now, then straight ahead, left after the junction, I guess' and Luca, indignant, 'what do you mean, I guess, where the fuck do you want me to go?' Martina and Drago chuckled and so did I, although I felt like puking, I get nauseous if I can't see the road.

We had lunch near the Monument aux Morts de l'Armée d'Orient, a white sculpture by the sea, with the disabled sticker on the van it was easy to find a parking space, we found some benches by the monument, sat down and unpacked our food, fingers greasy with chicken, and paper napkins that kept flying away, sliced peppers and flaky baguettes, the sun blinded us and there was a strong wind, the sea below us churned, almost azure. Suddenly Drago said he'd like to go fishing, I raised my head, looked at the sea and the islands, tossed a gnawed bone into the bin and remarked: 'How about we visit the Chateau d'If on Monte Cristo's island?' at which Luca leapt up from the bench and yelled in mock surprise, 'You can talk! Blanka! My goodness, you can talk!' he repeated, clutching at his heart, and everyone around burst out laughing.

In Pharo Park we settled down on the grass, Drago and Luca ran over to the playing field to kick a ball with the locals, while we girls talked about suicide, for some reason, and this time I chipped in as well. Yasmin, the younger Algerian and I tried to convince Martina that one simply doesn't have the right to commit suicide, it's unfair to one's nearest and dearest, family and friends, committing suicide is like spitting in the face of all the bereaved, suicide as a fuck you, but Martina insisted that a person has the right to do whatever they deem appropriate with their body; everyone should have the choice to put an early stop to all this madness; and to cap it all, of course, nobody asked me if I wanted to be born; all these opinions sounded so familiar, so routine to me, they used to be *my* opinions, too, until one rainy morning Svetlana had given me a proper dressing down on our way from the swimming pool.

We didn't manage to change Martina's mind, but I wasn't worried about her, not in the least, the girl positively radiated joie de vivre, energy, a thirst for savouring every moment to the full, Martina was a born hedonist and certainly didn't look like someone who would ever contemplate suicide. When Drago and Luca came back, out of breath, she leapt to her feet, threw clumps of grass at them and started running down the hill, 'whoever catches me gets an ice cream!' and of course the two of them immediately ran after her like little puppies. I watched them from afar, their somersaults, cartwheels, handstands, laughing, jumping and jabbing each other playfully in the ribs,

I would have liked to join them but how could I, I found it hard enough just to stay upright as I walked down the street.

I dashed off a quick reply to my mum's email, *I've no time for anything… yes, I do use my French here, sometimes even with the Czech girl, Martina… sometimes I can't remember the Slovak word for something and it annoys me… the residents are very smart, some even know where Slovakia is, unlike most ordinary French people, I think… I'm on the afternoon shift tomorrow and have the morning off, we might go into town, I hope Luca's driving won't be as crazy as today… Serge is quite a character, he keeps asking for Nutella even though he's on a diet…* and just as I was about to log out, an email arrived from my friend Cédric.

I rushed to the annexe, really excited, I have to tell someone, this is fantastic news, almost too good to be true! And when Luca opened the door, heavy-eyed, I hugged him and started shouting, 'He's coming, do you hear me, Cédric is coming! He just emailed to say so, do you think I can put him up in our little house? I'm so happy, you can't imagine how happy I am!'

Luca freed himself from my grip, put his hand on my forehead, 'Calm down, please, have you got a temperature? This isn't like you at all, come on, I was having my siesta, lie down over there,' he pointed to a bed and lay down next to me, 'and now tell me what's happened.' We lay on our sides facing each other, Luca very close, with his blond wavy hair and still slightly sleepy eyes, I started to talk, about Cédric, about last year's camp, that he's my best friend, he's on the same wavelength as me, 'there's plenty of room on my mattress for both of us, do you think Michel will be OK with that?' Luca started gently tracing lines on my face with his finger and said pensively, 'Didn't you say you had a boyfriend in Bratislava, you're sure he wouldn't mind if this… friend of yours… came here?'

O my gosh, Peter! I felt dizzy for a moment, yes, there's Peter, I'd totally forgotten about him, it never even occurred to me that Peter… but I tried to sound as convincing as I could and insisted 'I'll be faithful to my boyfriend till the day I die,' and to add gravity to my words, I propped myself up on the bed. Luca gave me a doubtful look: 'You really think so?'

'Yes, I do', I got up uneasily, and just then Drago and Martina came in, stopping in the doorway perplexed, question marks in their eyes, then Martina turned to me, 'I've been looking for you everywhere, Blanka. Elena wants to talk to you, I think she managed to find something for those ants.'

Martina and Drago had a day off, they joined Luca and me and we spent the whole morning shopping, Drago wanted to buy trainers, I was looking for a beach towel (anything but palm trees and sunset!), Martina and Luca traipsed behind us obediently from one shop to the next, we took turns carrying our big shared bottle of mineral water.

Drago picked up a tiny pair of trainers from a rack and showed it to me, 'If I had a son, I'd definitely get him Pumas like this,' then sighed and ordered us to leave, 'haven't found anything, let's go'.

As we walked up La Canebière from the port towards the church of St Vincent de Paul we came to a bookshop, Martina and I rushed in joyfully, Drago went to sit down on a low wall, 'I'll wait outside', and Luca wandered around the shop, commenting on everything, 'Isabel Allende, pfff, what kind of writer is she, she has a new novel out every year, how does she manage that?!' or 'Primo Levi, *Se questo è un uomo*, finally something decent, have you read it, *ragazze*?' but then Martina glanced at her watch and panicked, 'hurry up, Patrick is leaving at one o'clock! We might just make it,' and she rushed out of the shop. Drago jumped up as she ran past him, Luca just shook his head but all three of us followed her, pushing our way through crowds of dawdling tourists, slow-moving cars and olive-skinned locals, I didn't understand what was happening and ran after Martina clutching a copy of Camus' *L'étranger*.

Once we were in the van Martina explained, 'today… Patrick's relatives are coming to get him today… they're taking him…to Tenerife by plane… for a holiday!' so of course, she wanted to say good-bye to him. 'Please, Luca,' she shouted to the front seat, 'step on it, I'll kill myself if I miss him!'

Luca didn't need to be told twice, he hurtled up the hill even more frenziedly than the day before, jumping the lights, sometimes even driving on the pavement. As he drove, he swore loudly in Italian and gesticulated with one hand, there was hooting all around, finally Martina and I couldn't take it anymore and burst out laughing, Drago just said, 'you might not need to kill yourself, Martina, I think Luca will soon kill us all.'

But he didn't kill us and we even made it on time, just as Patrick was being loaded up outside the main building, an elderly gentleman in a suit and a young girl with a pony tail, Martina jumped out of the van and ran towards them but when she got there she didn't dare to kiss or hug Patrick good-bye, she just put her hand on his shoulder with a smile, *'amuse-toi bien, Patrick, et bon voyage.'* Drago, Luca and I watched the scene from afar.

The afternoon shift was much quieter than the morning one, no washing, brushing of teeth or attaching prosthetics, only the TV playing in the lounge, fruit on the tables, boredom, and every now and then a resident needing the toilet. For the past few days Laurence would ask only for Martina or me, it was understandable, we were young women like her, plus we're her *copines*, she would come right up to me in her wheelchair, put the brake on, contort her face, wave towards the corridor and there was nothing I could do but follow her to her room where she would take out her photo albums and show me photos of her extended family, I pretended to admire them while she peed, and when I carried the bedpan to the toilet I would sometimes spill some urine while pouring it out, clumsy me, warm pee on my forearm.

The Thorn Birds was on the TV, I'd never seen the whole series, but I recognised it instantly, one fleeting look at Richard Chamberlain in a cassock and his windswept hair on the beach was enough, I bent down to a resident who was half asleep, he said the French title was *Les oiseaux se cachent pour mourir*. I was blown over by that, *Birds Hide Themselves to Die*, I repeated to myself, and in the computer room there was Ahmad with his idiotic games, his jelly-like body spilling out of the wheelchair, I sat down at a computer next to him and said, without thinking, 'hello Ahmad, you OK?' and only when he gave me a surprised look did I realise that I'd addressed him in English.

For the past few days I'd been switching between languages, speaking Slovak to Martina, English to Drago, French to the others, admittedly I often got muddled up, mixing words from different languages, on a few occasions I even caught myself talking to myself in French, *d'accord, maintenant, je vais dire à Thomas...* surely that must mean that I'm beginning to think in

French, I tried to convince myself, but there was also confusion, the inability to find the right word to express myself, moments when I felt stuck and helpless, trying to remember what it was that I wanted to say and failing.

My mum seemed rather worried, *I wonder if you're getting my emails, you haven't answered my questions… We'll probably go to Čausa for Klára's birthday… I want you to write every day… what do you mean when you say that Luca drives like crazy?… be careful, you know that Marseille is a dangerous place… make sure you don't get into harm's way…* and so on and so on. I sighed and started to write, *hi mum, I'm not sure I can write to you every day, I've lost all sense of time and might not remember in the evening if I've written to you that day or not… and besides I'm trying to keep in touch with at least ten different people and have no idea what I've written to whom… yes, I did get your emails but I don't feel like answering every question… I've totally forgotten that you're going to Čausa, when exactly is that?… Luca is a good driver, except he sometimes jumps the lights or drives on the pavement, but it's a real hoot, Martina and I laugh our heads off, you should see us, don't worry, I'm being careful…*

When I opened the blinds, Serge gave me a worried look, mumbling *bonjour* but I was sure he was really thinking something like: 'oh no, not her again'. I ignored his grumbling and got to work, undressed him, changed his nappy, washed him, dragged in the hoist from the corridor, everything went like clockwork, without a hitch, smooth sailing all the way, until I started to dress him, and he announced that he needed a pee and pointed to the *pistolet* leaning against the wall.

I put his penis into the container and left the room for a while to grant him at least a semblance of privacy, leaned against the door and counted down the seconds, how long could it take? but when I came back in I found him drenched, I clutched my head, how could you be so stupid, the urine had spilled out, of course, you left the poor wretch lying in a horizontal position!

I tried to sort things out as fast as I could, hastily wiped him down and washed him while talking to him in French, 'never mind, it'll be all right, *c'est pas grave, c'est pas grave, monsieur Serge,*' trying to convince myself rather than him. Then he said something I didn't catch, 'excuse me, would you mind saying it again? I didn't get it,' so he repeated it, he'd said I should just call him Serge, drop the monsieur, he felt uncomfortable about the whole thing and he'd rather I said *tu* to him. I tried not to show how uncomfortable it made me, 'of course, if you wish, Mon… I mean, Serge,' and from then on nothing worked anymore, it was disaster after disaster, as I hoisted him onto the wheelchair I accidentally made him sit on the armrest and once he was seated properly I realised I'd forgotten to put his trousers on so I lifted him up and dressed him while he was suspended in the air; I started brushing his teeth but couldn't get the hot water to run, the water from both taps was ice cold; I splattered toothpaste on his T-shirt and had to change him, I kept repeating *c'est pas grave, c'est pas grave* like a mantra but it didn't help at all, I saw he was staring at me with mounting horror.

When I put a clean T-shirt on him, back to front of course, he couldn't take it anymore and said, *'tu fais des bêtises,'* you're messing up, I didn't know what to say but just then the door opened, Isabelle came in, 'What, not finished with him yet? Serge's brother is coming to visit him today! Let me do it,' and she took the shaver out of my hand. I collapsed in a heap, leaned against the wall and watched her, hoping the earth would open up and swallow me at last.

When I suggested timidly that I could manage breakfast on my own, Isabelle just gave a loud sigh and pushed the wheelchair out past me, I went to the staircase to get out of sight and sat there quietly with my head in my hands digesting the disgrace, the humiliation, feeling a bit queasy, that's how Drago found me as he came bounding down the stairs, three steps at a time. He stopped and sat down next to me, 'You all right?' I told him the whole story of the morning wash, he listened intently and said stoically, 'So he pissed all over himself, a big deal,' I looked up at him in surprise and he smiled, 'Just wait till I tell you how I tipped Thomas out of his wheelchair today, you'll feel better straight away.'

It was Martina's idea, she dragged me to the consulting room, stepped on the scales and said, 'Didn't I tell you? Wonderful, five kilos lost!', and she waited for me to weigh myself. 'Four kilos less,' I announced, the nurse gave us a worried look and said, 'Haven't you been eating, girls? How can you lose so much weight in a week?' Martina just shrugged, I stood there with a half-witted smile thinking of Prague, because in Prague just an apple for lunch and zero result and here, with no effort at all, four kilos lost in a week.

I was so buoyed I nearly told the nurse that sharing a table with people who constantly spit into your plate doesn't exactly improve your appetite but I bit my lip, after we left the nurses' room I jumped up and down for joy and in the corridor, on my way out of the building, I hugged Laurence, who shouted something incomprehensible after me but I didn't hear and just waved to her, not caring if I looked silly.

I ran out of the building and sat down on a chair outside, said hello to Serge who was parked under a tree, *'Bonjour, monsieur*

Serge,' he looked at me warily but eventually replied, *'Bonjour, mademoiselle,'* then I smiled broadly at Drago and Luca who were discussing something by the side of the swimming pool, their feet dangling in the water, 'So did you come up with any plans for tonight?'

We expected it to be quite straightforward, we'd get there in the nick of time, the basilica up on the hill was visible all the way from the port, we thought we just had to drive to the top of the hill, straight up, but it took us over half an hour to find our way out of the winding little streets of the old quarter, Ingeborg at the wheel, the sensible Ingeborg who, unlike Luca, never lost her nerve even when it seemed that the basilica was trying to hide from us but every time we were about to give up it suddenly appeared in a gap between houses.

We got out of the van just before sunset, from the top of the hill there was a wonderful view of the whole city, the sea and the islands, Martina and Yasmin the Algerian started taking pictures, I looked up at the Black Madonna, exactly like the one I'd seen last year in Le Puy-en-Velay with Cédric, who now really didn't need to come, now that Martina, Drago and Luca had accepted me as one of the gang. That's what was going around my head as I climbed the steps to the church, but inside it was just as boring as any other, a brief stop to look at the sculpture of Jesus on the cross, a Madonna and child, the paintings, the altar, just keep quiet, walk on tiptoe, don't disturb the worshippers.

Outside I headed for the souvenir shop, Drago turned up moments later, we exchanged slightly embarrassed looks, you too? and then agreed that churches weren't really our thing. To kill time until the others came, we browsed the postcards, found one that almost scared me out of my wits, a blood-red sunset above the Notre-Dame de la Garde, a black sky, a red sun, quite apocalyptic. I took the postcard from the stand and stared at it, fascinated, 'should I buy it, do you think?' Drago thought it was silly, what was the point of buying a photo of a church (however scary it might be) and since I couldn't make up my mind, he took it out of my hand, hid it behind his back, 'left or right?'

So that's how it was decided that I should buy it although I didn't want it anymore, 'you have to buy it now, that's how it works,' said Drago, laughing, and kept teasing me all the way back to the Centre, he said we were all cursed and something would happen to us now that we have this Satanist photo, he sounded almost enthusiastic as he kept saying, 'we're cursed! we're cursed!'

I couldn't fall asleep that night, I kept tossing and turning, my head filled with dark thoughts, Drago's words that had made me laugh in the van now came echoing back in the dark sounding much more ominous, like something inevitable, predestined, I'll have an accident, end up paralysed in a wheelchair, lifeless legs scrunching the gravel by the swimming pool, arms dangling loosely by my side while someone feeds me, porridge dribbling down my chin, between my legs a sodden nappy they'd forgotten to change; a lifetime spent in this place, measured out in daily rituals, washing, breakfast, lunch, siesta, dinner and an occasional visit from my relatives who comfort each other on their way home with hypocritical talk, she's better off here than she would be at home, professional care, appropriate social activities, up-to-date facilities, and all the rest of it, take care, darling, we'll be back again soon.

Eventually I got up, found the postcard of the basilica in my handbag, tiptoed to the kitchenette, tore it into tiny pieces and threw it in the bin, though I knew it was just a silly, superstitious gesture. I was about to climb back into my sleeping bag when my eyes suddenly alighted on the kitchen knife lying among the dishes, my heart started to pound, blood rushed to my head, I got the shakes; just one, a single little cut, I told myself, just to ease the pain, a bit of relief.

I was woken first thing by a text from Peter, *finally managed to kill two mosquitoes that sucked my blood for a week, only three weeks left, my darling and we'll be together, miss you.* I read the message about ten times and couldn't understand a word, groggy as I was after my sleepless night, I couldn't wrap my head around it, Košice and Peter, three weeks and all this will be over, life before and after Marseille, it can't be real, I thought, only the here and now is true, the wheelchairs, hospital odours, *pistolets* filled with urine and feeble people hanging from hoists.

That morning I was assigned to Joëlle and Frédéric, an obese couple, both in wheelchairs, I was told that they met and fell in love right here at Bellevue and were allocated the biggest room in the building after they got married ten years ago. As soon as I opened the door something bit my ankle, I couldn't identify it in the semi-darkness but when I opened the blinds, I saw a chihuahua clinging to my trousers. I gave it a sidelong kick to make it let go, which must have outraged the dog because it didn't stop running around me in circles, growling and yapping furiously while I was washing them. But that was nothing compared to the barking of Joëlle, comfortably sprawled out in her king size bed, four pillows under her head, 'I said the second drawer, not the third, aren't you listening?'. 'These sponges belong on the wash-basin, will you kindly pick them up off the floor?!'. 'My slippers must be under the bed, you just have to bend down and look for them, or do you expect me to do that?' This went on for about an hour, nothing but commands, complaints, needling, bile. By the end I was on the verge of tears, but managed to control myself, I bit my lip, I wasn't going to give her the satisfaction of seeing me humiliated, I submitted in silence, inwardly cursing her.

I remember meeting someone like that once, in a doctor's waiting room, a boy who shoved his fingerless hand in my face, right up to my eyeballs as he flailed about and pushed ahead of me even though he had arrived later, as if his stumps entitled him to everything; the arrogance of some physically handicapped people who want to punish everyone for their infirm body, their missing limbs, their handicap which entitles them to always have priority.

Frédéric watched this abuse without a word, he didn't stick up for me, but when I washed him, he gave me a timid smile, almost as if he wanted to apologise, ask for my patience, I couldn't understand how he could live with this unbearable harpy, an hour in her presence was enough for me, I felt like killing her.

Fortunately, they didn't need help with breakfast, so I joined Drago and Ingeborg in the dining room, buttered my baguette and said, my boyfriend wouldn't mind subsisting entirely on bread and butter with jam all year long, 'morning, afternoon, evening, he just puts butter and jam on a slice of bread, it saves time and money, too.' I said, laughing, 'he's quite thrifty, is my Peter,' and just then Ingeborg suddenly asked what had happened to my arm.

I looked at my forearm, at the thin red line running all the way down to my wrist, as if I couldn't remember, and said the first thing that came into my head, 'oh, it's nothing, I fell down the stairs,' but as soon as I uttered the words I realised how stupid it must sound, down the stairs, it must have been some sharp stairs to leave such a big cut, I might as well have said I'd fallen off a bike or off the Empire State Building, but Ingeborg nodded, 'I see,' and didn't dwell on it any longer, but Drago raised his eyebrows and looked me up and down with something of a sneer.

Elena came up with another excuse, this time she had a headache, needed a rest, something like that, oh well, who cares, let her stay at Bellevue, let her choke on her photos of Bucharest, her modern city, what do we care, we're going to the seaside.

Around four o'clock we gathered outside the main building and waited for a van; sunglasses, swimming costumes visible under T-shirts, beach bags and towels in our hands, 'oh no, it's Luca driving again?' Martina laughed as we piled into the van and I said I'd prefer to sit in the front, next to the driver, because bends, speed, manoeuvres, in a word, with Luca at the wheel, I'd rather not be sick over anyone.

La Plage du Prophète was bang in the centre of town, below the promenade, you just had to go down some steep steps, past the showers and a short walk in the sand, it took us a while to find a free spot to put down our stuff, right opposite the metre-high seawall. 'It's a barrier to break the surf,' explained Luca, he was the first to strip and headed for the water straight away, while Martina and I were still putting sunscreen on. I asked her to put some on my back, but she objected, 'ask Drago, it's much nicer if a guy does that'.

We set out for the sea together, walking on the hot sand, entered the water treading gingerly, slippery stones covered in seaweed close to the shore, I took a deep breath and buried my head in the blue, and when I emerged, suddenly Luca was by my side, he grabbed me by the neck and put all his weight on me, 'should I drown you, what do you say?' I smiled, shook my head and got away from him with a few powerful strokes, swam around the rocks and was out in the open sea, the water was transparent, a fish here and there, hills in the distance, a tanned swimmer I met on the way shouted at me, 'give my regards to Algeria!', I really was quite far out by then. But it wasn't enough, I needed more, I wanted to swim until my fingers crinkled up and my lips went purple, like when I was little and spent entire summer holidays immersed in lakes.

I swam back to the shore and splashed about in the shallows for a while, scouring the sea bottom, saw seashells, sea urchins, even a tiny crab in a cleft between two rocks but when I came out, Yasmin said she wasn't letting me back in the water, 'just look at yourself, you're so pale, it's a disgrace, you'll stay here and not move until you get a bit of a tan.' I shrugged, lay down on a towel and pretended to sunbathe, I didn't want to be a spoilsport, but I knew full well that I would never get a tan, I was completely smothered in sensitive skin cream, factor 50, I've always had a dread of sunstroke, blisters, cancer.

Martina and Luca sat a little to one side, sharing a towel, their faces turned towards the sun, hands buried in the sand, each of them seemingly on their own, but at one point I saw Luca put his arm around Martina's waist and stick his tongue right down her throat. It seemed quite natural at that moment, not at all surprising, logical in the situation, my senses were dulled by the sun, I felt lethargic, slowed down, no one else seemed surprised either. I looked around, no one looked grossed out, there were no derisive comments, almost as if nobody cared; Yasmin and Ingeborg were talking, the older Algerian lay there fully clothed, complete with a headscarf, she must have been sweating like a pig, only Drago was nowhere to be seen.

I went to look for him and started pushing my way through the beach umbrellas and towels spread out on the sand, stepping over arms, legs and sometimes entire bodies, but there was no trace of Drago, though eventually I found him on the seawall, sitting on a rock, gazing out at the sea. When I touched his shoulder, he looked up and said he was definitely coming back here to do some fishing, 'look over there, there are fish in droves, just metres from the beach.'

Ingeborg drove us back, Luca sat in the corner of the van with Martina in his lap, there was something proprietorial about the way he kissed her, as if marking his territory, Drago was asleep, or pretended to be, lying on his side, his face covered by a straw hat, I sat next to him staring at the floor, discomfited by their display of intimacy in the enclosed space of the van, wishing I could close my eyes but I couldn't, as I would feel sick straight away, the road was bumpy and I'd forgotten to make a bid for the seat in front.

Martina was beside herself, her blood boiling, she gesticulated wildly as she marched up and down the room, eyes blazing and cursing Drago, I helped her move from our little house to the annexe behind the kitchen which she and Luca picked for their love nest, but she kept interrupting the packing and turning to me, 'he said it was supposed to be his turn, that's what he said, can you believe that… what a moron, unbelievable! Like there's some sort of waiting list, he'd invested so much time, all those hours he spent with me when I was with Patrick and now that Patrick's gone, it was meant to be his turn, not Luca's! He's lost his marbles, now tell me, is that normal?!'

Once she calmed down a little she confided in me that she was in love and really happy, I shouldn't think anything bad about her, this sort of summer romance really wasn't her thing, it had never happened to her before, but earlier today on the beach one thing led to another, she was sitting on a towel next to Luca, he hugged her, thrust his tongue into her mouth and that was that.

The two of them spent the rest of the evening glued to each other, and instead of holing up in the annexe behind the kitchen they made an exhibition of themselves by the swimming pool, in full sight of everyone, by the plastic chairs where we all sat after dusk in little groups, chatting; Yasmin with Ingeborg, the older Algerian woman with Elena and me with Drago. He was watching Luca's triumphal parade with obvious displeasure, 'I told him on the very first night that I fancied Martina and that I'd like to go out with her… and now, just look at him snogging her, I bet you anything that he's doing it just to spite me.'

I was poking the gravel by the swimming pool with the heel of my shoe, it seemed unfair that both of them wanted her and neither of them wanted me, I didn't feel like comforting him and he must have sensed that because he suddenly snarled at me, 'And what was that supposed to be this morning, your falling down the stairs?! Huh? Do you take us for complete idiots? You think you'll solve anything by cutting yourself? You're like a child.'

I was taken aback by his sudden change of tone and his words, I looked away and shrugged, I was in no mood to discuss the issue, but Drago gave me a shake and forced me to look him in the face, 'What's your problem, Blanka? Tell me what your problem is.'

I wasn't sure if it was a good idea, if I could trust him, but after some hesitation I told him that I felt it coming on again, I could feel it in my bones, the first symptoms and unmistakeable signs, last night I finally realised what had been going on, the anxiety of the past few days; the sudden swings of mood, the inability to concentrate, the urge to cry for no reason, it all fitted a pattern and it was just a question of time before it became full-blown, before it engulfed me, another bout of depression, my third, and dammit, it had to happen just when I was away from home, no medication at hand, no Serlift, Deprex, Seropram, not even any bloody Xanax to suppress anxiety. Perhaps the best thing would be to find an excuse and leave this place, to stop the whole process in its tracks before it's too late.

Drago looked pensive, saying nothing for a long time, maybe I shouldn't have come clean, maybe it was a mistake, but then he said he understood, he just wasn't sure if leaving was the answer. He paused, then said I seemed to be running away from something, as if I was scared of facing up to my own fears, of facing myself so to speak, and if I went on like this, I would never climb out of it, I would never solve the problem. I might be able to suppress it for a while, with drugs and therapy, but it would keep coming back. It would be better to do the opposite, go all the way, let myself be taken over by it, sink all the way to the bottom so that I could bounce back properly at last instead of resorting to medication that only suppresses the symptoms without ever treating the underlying cause. It was about time I found out what the real issue was, what was behind it all, why my depression kept coming back. Sure, it was dangerous, drastic, nobody could tell what might happen, he couldn't guarantee anything, but it was a road to go down and he was prepared to help me, I shouldn't imagine he'd leave me to deal with it on my own, no, he'd stand by me, support me, I just had to trust him.

I said nothing for a while, staring at the ground, poking the gravel with my foot, then I raised my head, looked at him and nodded with sudden resolve. Drago smiled, put his arm around my shoulder, gave me another shake, 'There's a good girl,' then exclaimed, 'I have an idea! Let's go into town, I know this place with a fabulous view of your favourite church on the hill, it's bound to be lit up at night, we can talk on the way,' adding, 'you can sleep in my room tonight so you don't disturb Elena when we come back, I have two free beds now that Luca has moved out.'

As the two of us carried my stuff and sleeping bag over to the annexe I noticed Elena looking at me with a strange smile, it confused me at first, what's got into her, why is she making faces like that and watching us from the door, but then I realised she must have thought I wanted to sleep with him, she must have thought, first Martina got off with Luca, and now me with Drago, as if we had to sleep together just because we'd be in the same room. It struck me as funny, I had to bite my tongue not to laugh, how pathetic of her! Should I put her right? Was it worth it? But in the end I said nothing, she could think whatever she liked if she was so crass, I even wished her good night as I left the little house, 'Good night to you too, Blanka,' she called out, in a taunting voice.

The main gate had already been locked but I remembered the code they'd given us at the first meeting along with the maps and the rota, Drago whistled with admiration when he saw me punch in the six digits from memory and I swelled with pride that my head was still working, things can't be that bad, I haven't gone completely round the bend. We walked down Impasse de Marronnier, leaving Bellevue's park on our right, a housing estate on the left, crossed a bridge above a railway line, some high wire mesh on both sides, and then downhill all the way to Belle de Mai, across a small sycamore park, towards the Boulevard National.

As we walked I told him about my previous depressions, those dreary autumn days when everything seems set in stone, irreversible, of obsessive thoughts of death and how to achieve it painlessly, as soon as possible, the unbearable theatricality and banality of the whole situation – I'm unhappy and I want to die – the mornings usually being the worst, I wake up before five o'clock, roused from sleep by sheer anxiety, I lie in bed paralysed and can't imagine how I will survive another day, the thought of having to function normally again terrifies me so much that I climb under the bed in terror, squeeze my body into the confined space, close my eyes in the irrational hope that no one will find me there, that somehow I will be forgotten, but then I hear the door open, my mother walking in and shouting, what are you doing under the bed again? Why are you doing this to me? And the despair in her voice is so great that in the end I crawl out, get up and start getting dressed, very slowly, my body refuses to obey, it's totally shattered, I can't even raise my arms, I need help to wash, like a baby, my mother goes to work and I'm left on my own, I sit in the kitchen gazing out at the grey courtyard, the radio is on and suddenly it says on the news that some man has suffered mild nutmeg poisoning, fifty grams is enough for a lethal dose, I get up and start rummaging in the spice cupboard, I find a bag of ground nutmeg, empty it into a glass, top up the glass with water, try to stir it but I can't do it, nutmeg is no sherbet powder, tiny lumps float in the water but I try to drink it anyway, it's disgusting, I can't get it down, finally I give up, if nutmeg isn't mentioned again on the radio I'll think of another way, for example, I dig up a hammer from the pantry, place my left hand on the kitchen counter and raise my right with the hammer in it, close my eyes and… nothing, my hand flops, I don't have the courage, I'm a coward, I put the hammer away but the thought stays with me, it won't leave me for a second, the same thought for months and months now, how to put an end to it quickly and painlessly. Later in the morning I go to the university, my sense of responsibility prevails in the end, I sit on the floor, that's where I feel best, in the dust and grime, the dark corridor of the language department, other students around me discussing films, flipping through an Avon catalogue, revising vocab for a test, they laugh, I don't, an hour later Svet-lana and I go out to the bank of the Danube, we sit on the low wall, Svetlana lights up and says – I feel like shit, too, but things will get better one day, I don't know when but I'm sure they will, you'll see, they will at some point, then another lecture, I don't take anything in, I can't hear, I don't take notes, I couldn't even if I wanted to, the medication is making my hands tremble, I sit there and feel like screaming and letting everyone know that I'm dying to make them take me seriously at last, but it's not necessary, most of them have already guessed, this semester I've taken to running out of class for no reason, like today, Svetlana catches up with me on the stairs, I just can't go on, I tell her, I really can't, sorry, Svetlana's hand on my shoulder, she's telling me something, we go back to the classroom together and when it's over one of the other students, the one who always sits in the front row, away from everyone else, tells me she feels a bit sorry for me but is also a bit scared of me, what if I lose it completely and hurt someone, I'm crazy, you're crazy, she repeats with a smile, I run away, lock myself in the toilet, start bawling, afterwards, when I tell Svetlana, she swears she'll smash that bitch's face, but I say no, forget it, I'm back at home by four o'clock, alone, outside nothing but the autumn, greyness, rain, I phone my sister, she's a psychiatrist in Prague, I declare resolutely that I don't want to take the meds anymore because those meds, that's not me, the meds have turned me into some kind of an imitation of who I used to be, a bad copy, and I add, without rhyme or reason – maybe it would be best if they locked me up in a loony bin, maybe that's where I belong, my sister breaks in, you don't know what you're talking about, they wouldn't help you in the loony bin, all that would happen is that a fellow patient would scribble above your head, in shit, 'Welcome Home,' would you like that? Huh? Is that what you want? You've no idea of the kind of people that are in those places, plus, if you ever end up in a loony bin, you'll be marked for life, people will point their fingers at you and say, she's not right in the head, she's been to the funny farm, my sister is insistent, and I can see she's right, in the end I even promise to never stop taking my meds, I put the phone down, it has helped, I feel much better, my mum comes back from work, unloads the shopping in the kitchen and says – you just have to manage somehow until the antidepressants kick in, it can take weeks, months, I believe her at that moment, evenings are always much better, I'm sure I can do it, suddenly this inexplicable optimism, I almost can't understand why I drank that nutmeg in the morning, why I took a hammer from the pantry, it seems absurd, ridiculous and pathetic, but then the morning comes again, anxiety rouses me from my sleep, I lie in bed paralysed and can't imagine how I will survive another day.

We walked down the Boulevard National, past billboards and illuminated bus stops, along Victor Hugo Square and up to the railway station, across a little park full of dog excrement and past a few homeless people in hoodies and dreadlocks in a variety of colours, we sat down on the steps, Drago took off his flip-flops and handed them to me, 'You shouldn't sit on a cold surface, you might catch cold and that wouldn't be good.' I accepted gratefully, no one has ever been so considerate to me, we watched Notre-Dame de la Garde in silence, the view was really perfect, the only interruption a boy with a rucksack who asked about the way to the hostel, 'it's supposed to be somewhere around here,' we just shrugged, 'no idea, we're not from here', and we watched him walk down the stairs to la Canebière. Drago said he felt bad, we could have told him to come with us, so he wouldn't have to sleep on a bench, but I thought to myself, nah, that wouldn't be good, I want Drago all to myself tonight.

We might have spent a couple of hours sitting on those steps, Drago listened to me intently the whole time, he said very little about himself, and at one point he asked about my father because I hadn't mentioned him so far. 'My father, that's a closed chapter,' I said shaking my head, 'I don't want to go there, he's dead and buried, that's all there is to it.' He was slightly taken aback but I changed the subject, told him about my secret crush on Rachel, how I follow her around Bratislava in despair, my plans change the moment I see her, I climb over railings, get on buses, go into buildings where strangers live just so I can be near her for as long as I can, look at her, her raven hair, her death-like pallor, the choker around her neck, the bangles on her wrists, when I see her I'm tempted to change orientation, and who knows, maybe I do like women, maybe I'm a lesbian. Drago smiled and said he didn't believe that, he said I didn't give that impression and suddenly, I don't know why, we found ourselves talking about that wretched semen that always ends up in a gob of spit below the window of the housing estate in Košice. Drago guffawed, putting a hand in front of his mouth, then said he'd never heard anything so weird in his life, I really was *weird*, 'spitting semen out of the window, well, I'd never have thought you were capable of something like that.'

After a moment's silence I nod, yes, he's right, I'm always really tense with people, I don't know what to do with my body, it's like it's not mine, just some appendage, a burden I have to lug around, P.E. has always been absolute hell for me, the P.E. teachers' typical comments – is that meant to be a forward lunge, what you're doing is more like a sideways lumber, I can't even manage a handstand, not even when leaning against the wall bars, I just can't do it, I'm terrified that my body will break. I can't stand people looking at me, whenever a teacher asked me a question at school I'd cover my face with my hands so they couldn't see me, I tried to hide as best I could, even now in fact, on my way home from university, I prefer taking the narrow side streets so that I don't bump into anyone, don't have to smile and say – hi, how are you, how is it going? I would walk along sewers if I could, I find every kind of human interaction difficult, literally exhausting, the same goes for activities where people can watch me, I've never gone to a disco, never been prepared to jump up and down in an aerobics class, I can't stand the fact that I have a body, I feel ridiculous with these two arms, legs, trunk, I know it's absurd, everyone has a body after all and mine is no worse than any other, but still, I can't help it, I'm intensely repulsed by the fact that it performs all the same functions as every other body, organs pulsating, heart pumping, stomach digesting, blood circulating, spots sprouting on the skin, hair getting greasy, breasts bouncing, not to mention the other stuff, in a word, my body gets in my way... in the way of my life. But when I'm with someone I trust, I am totally transformed, you can't imagine, I stop watching myself and obsessing about how I look, the bits I'm made up of, and when that happens, I can undress, make love, even spit the wretched semen out of the window. No problem, I smile.

A couple of hours later we got up and headed back to Bellevue, but on the Boulevard National we realised we didn't know the way, couldn't find the billboard where we had to turn off, we walked up and down the street twice and Drago kept shaking his head, he said he didn't recognise anything, someone must have changed the ads at the bus stops while we were sitting on the steps, there was no other explanation, 'they've changed the ad,' he kept repeating, turning the map round and round in his hands. I followed him dutifully even though it was getting increasingly obvious that we were headed in the wrong direction, we should have been climbing towards Belle de Mai, what on earth are we doing in these desolate, sinister neighbourhoods, the warehouses and derelict buildings with shattered windows? We walked arm in arm, in silence now, exhausted, there was something dreamlike about wandering around the streets of

Marseille at three in the morning, at one point some feral cats joined us, following us at a safe distance, and when we walked into some kind of a tunnel, their meowing was amplified by the echo from every direction. The whole thing was so unreal I suddenly felt like a character in Sabato's book *On Heroes and Tombs*, we're in Buenos Aires and I'm Alejandra Vidal walking alongside Martin, I nearly said this to Drago but was afraid he might not have read the book and wouldn't know what I was talking about. He was quite distressed by now, looking in turn at the map and the houses he didn't recognise, every time we met someone out and about at this hour, he said I should ask the way, 'be brave, Blanka,' he encouraged me and I asked as best I could, explaining with my arms and legs but everyone just shook their heads – they didn't know, they were in a hurry.

Drago kept saying that I would hate him the next day, that I would never speak to him again, but he really was lost, he had no idea where we were going, how we got there and what we were even doing there. I laughed at his confusion and assured him he needn't worry, I would definitely not hold it against him tomorrow, or ever, because I was actually having quite a good time. Soon after three in the morning we caught a glimpse of the sea, somehow made it to the port, found ourselves surrounded by cranes and all kinds of strange machinery, the water glittering like steel in the moonlight and in the light of the street lamps.

I sat down on the ground, leaning against the door of some warehouse, and declared I wasn't going one step further, I would just sleep there, I really couldn't go on, but tired as I was, I couldn't help thinking what fun it was to make a theatrical gesture like this and see how Drago would respond. He looked at me wide-eyed and tried to pick me up, 'don't be silly, come on, please,' he swore he would get us out of there, 'what's got into you, we can't sleep in this dangerous neighbourhood,' he stared at the map helplessly again, so I finally took pity on him, grabbed the map, 'let me try,' and half an hour later we were on the Boulevard National and in another half-hour at the gates of Bellevue. Drago pretended to be cross and told me off, why couldn't I have offered earlier and let him suffer so long, but I just laughed, despite the tiredness I felt better than I had in a long time, I enjoyed wandering through Marseille at night while everyone else was asleep, in the early hours, just the two of us, arm in arm.

Shortly before we got to the Centre he said something strange, that he might keep me at arm's length over the next few days and not acknowledge me, he was like that, scared of being rejected and hurt if he let anyone get too close to him, so it was possible that he might be scared of having got too close to me and that some kind of defence mechanism might kick in and make him suspect that I'm just pretending to like him when in actual fact I'm making fun of him and laughing at him behind his back. Yes, he knew it was nonsense, he knew I wasn't like that, but he wanted to tell me now, to warn me, so to speak, prepare me, 'just in case', because he didn't want to lose me. It was quite hard to explain but he had to tell me – no matter how he might behave, no matter what he might say, I should stick with him, shouldn't let him go, I should wait until he began to trust me again, until he came back to me, 'it's very important, do you understand?' I nodded and assured him he mustn't imagine he could get rid of me so easily, but I was slightly concerned by the prospect of him turning hostile and having to fight for him, against himself, even.

Back in his room we collapsed on the beds and covered ourselves with our sleeping bags, Drago fell asleep straight away, snoring gently but I couldn't sleep and just lay there, eyes wide open, too agitated.

Less than three hours later we were woken by banging on the door, Martina barged in, she seemed quite irritated and immediately blasted away, 'it's long past breakfast time, how come you're still in bed? hello, can you hear me? Blanka, Drago, get up! it's Sunday, we're going for an outing, the van is at the gate, we're only waiting for the two of you!' Drago rolled over, I propped myself up on the bed and fell back again, my eyes glued together, a dull pain in my head.

Ingeborg was at the wheel, Martina sat in Luca's lap and Drago and I tried to catch up on our sleep, sprawled on the floor in the back of the van, everything around seemed to reach me through a screen, Yasmin with her uproarious laughter, Luca's sneering remarks directed at the two of us, look at those cute little turtledoves, he commented on my sudden change of residence. Martina shot me a conspiratorial smile, she seemed almost relieved that I'd got together with Drago because he would leave her alone now, she sent me looks full of gratitude and I was too tired to set her straight, to do anything. Drago took cover under his hat, it was impossible to tell if he was asleep or not, I looked at him every now and then as if to make sure that he was real and that last night wasn't just a dream. On the Boulevard National I gave him a dig in the ribs, look where we are, he smiled drowsily and muttered 'they've changed the ad', then closed his eyes again.

Just before we reached the port Yasmin and Luca invented a new game, *mimic your favourite resident*, and immediately started to come up with tics, twitches, dazed faces and appalling grunts. Martina laughed so hard that tears ran down her cheeks – especially when Luca imitated Adam and his furious banging on the alphabet board, Ingeborg, Yasmin, Luca, the older Algerian woman, everyone was having fun, Drago took off his hat and grinned maliciously, I watched this display of human misery in horror, and in my head linked it to all the palsy and muscular dystrophy I'd seen that week. When it was my turn to imitate someone I couldn't manage anything, the thought of contorting my body into some unnatural position made me freeze, I just sat on the van floor as everyone looked at me expectantly, I didn't know what to do, and finally turned to Drago, who shook his head firmly, 'no, Blanka is not going to mimic anyone.'

We were planning to visit the Chateau d'If where the Count of Monte Cristo was imprisoned, there was an underground dungeon that had been dug for tourists, a boat trip and then a walk to the beach along the promenade, where we would spend the afternoon. I kept myself to myself as we walked along the shore, Drago seemed lost in thought, I told myself, here we go, he's drawing away from me already, just as he said he would, but as we stood on the pier waiting while Ingeborg enquired about the cost of tickets, he came up to me, 'Blanka, why have you been avoiding me?', I was taken aback, 'it's not what you think … it's not me … I just thought you didn't want to … didn't you say…', 'I want to be with you,' he said and looked away. Then he asked what we were doing there and only then did I remember that Drago didn't speak French, and nobody had bothered to tell him what the plan for today was. But Ingeborg came back from the ticket office with bad news, the crossings to the chateau were sold out until Monday, we had to decide quickly where to go, OK, let's go to Cassis, look at the azure bay and the sailing boats, and as we climbed the hill to the van parked near the Palais du Pharo, I put my arm through Drago's and couldn't have cared less what the others would think.

On the way to Cassis I texted Peter, *I'm depressed but don't worry and please don't tell anyone. A Slovene guy is helping me, I think I'll manage without medication this time. Blanka.* It felt a bit weird writing that, depression, what depression? I felt absolutely fine, almost too happy, but in that case what was the crisis after our visit to the basilica all about, the confusion and anxiety of the past few days? was this just a temporary truce? would the switch flip back on as soon as I got back to Bellevue and had to look after the disabled again? why was I the only one who couldn't get used to misshapen people, hospital smells and urine-filled bedpans? I wondered as we stopped in Cassis and spilled out of the van, blinded by the sun and disoriented.

After a walk around the village we sat down to have lunch on a long seawall, Luca had broken off a branch of blossoming oleander somewhere and was now offering it to Martina ceremoniously, down on his knees, and I whispered to Drago that Peter never brought me flowers because he had this theory that it wasn't worth investing in me anymore now that we were in a long-term relationship. Drago shrugged and asked me quietly, 'does it really matter, do you want a man to play the clown for you, like that fool Luca?' I smiled, stretched out on the wall and rested my head in his lap, 'it doesn't matter because you're here now!' Drago grinned vaguely, picked up a stick and started poking me in the cheek, I closed my eyes and listened to the children shouting on the beach, felt the sun weigh heavily on my eyelids, I was happy that this was happening, I'd always wanted to have a friend I could touch, pull by his curly hair and nuzzle, I'd always wanted friendship to have a physical side to it as well. 'I rather like this, this stick, it hurts nicely,' Drago smiled, 'I know you like it, you masochist, you.'

We tucked into our lunch, I found something called Babybel in the insulated bag, a weird little red thing, I shoved it into Drago's face and asked, 'Drago darling, do you think this is edible?' Drago took the Babybel, sniffed it, bit into the red material, spat it out in disgust, turned it around in his hand for a while until he figured out how to open it and discovered that it was ordinary cheese, 'you just have to try it,' he said, and also, 'you have a new life now.'

When we walked back to the van after lunch Drago bent down to me and whispered, 'take a discreet look at the girl coming opposite, her left shoulder.' I couldn't see anything at first, but eventually I managed to focus and as we were passing her I saw some cut wounds, already healed, white scars glistening in the sun. Drago gave me a meaningful smile, then started jumping up and down around me, 'you are not alone! open your eyes, girl!', he sounded almost elated, there are so many people in the world who cut themselves, so many people with problems, he said, if I could just manage to break free of that rich inner world of mine, I would see straight away that we're all deep in the shit.

We drove to the *presqu'île*, stood on the hill taking pictures of sailing boats in the azure *calanques* and pine groves, little stones scrunched under our feet, cicadas chirped in the bushes like there was no tomorrow, afterwards we walked down to the beach, Drago and I were last, gawping at the millionaires' villas we passed on our way, commenting on everything, 'wow,

I wouldn't say no to this one,' 'I absolutely must buy this one,' 'this one is a bit too… for my taste', every front garden boasted a manicured lawn, palm trees and a furiously yapping dog. Drago liked the ceramic house numbers on the walls, with painted flowers, he said he would buy one of those if he could find it in a shop, so that when he was back home he would feel he was still in the south of France. I looked in every shop trying to find a decent *serviette de plage* without palms, sunset, galloping stallions and absolutely no Britney Spears, but I was out of luck, I envied Drago his beautiful black-and-white beach towel, he said it was a present from his sister, she had impeccable taste, and he promised to share it with me on the beach, he wouldn't let me sit on the rocks, that's what friends were for.

I couldn't go swimming as I got my period that morning, so I lay on Drago's towel for an hour or so, soaking in the sun and quietly envying the others who were jumping off the rocks and frolicking in the water, returning to their towels refreshed and wet, dripping water onto my hot skin. I admired Drago's curly black hair, ran my fingers through it and laughed that he must have some black ancestors, he should grow it and wear it in a pony tail, long hair would make him incredibly sexy, all the chicks would go crazy about him, in the discos of Ljubljana or Maribor, wherever he wanted. He listened with his eyes closed, his head resting in my lap, smiling.

La Ciotat seemed quite scary at first sight, all cranes and other spine-chilling structures rising from the sea visible from afar, monsters blocking the sky and swaying perilously in the wind, I watched them from the van window and asked myself, what on earth is this, Jesus Christ, what sort of place is this? But I was pleasantly surprised in the end, the city had a picturesque centre, a nice promenade by the sea, with stalls, little shops, cafés. Finally a chance to buy some presents for my relatives, I had it all done in a jiffy, a T-shirt that said Cassis for three-year-old Klára, tiny bottles filled with sand and seashells for everyone else. Drago was haggling over the price of ceramic house numbers but ended up not buying anything, just waved his hand, it would look ridiculous on their shabby house anyway, he said after he came out of the shop, and as we returned to the promenade we found the others sitting under the awning of a bar ordering cold drinks, ice cream sundaes, banana splits.

We stopped at a souvenir stall, its three-dimensional mobile stickers with animals caught my eye, almost transparent, you could stick them directly onto the screen, making phone calls would be more fun straight away, except that I couldn't decide between a butterfly and a shark, I mooched about until Drago took the decision for me, 'get a butterfly, that's more you.' Before we joined the others, I asked him to keep an eye on my shopping because it was the first sign that something was happening to me, the first symptom so to speak, buying crap, squandering money, mindless shopping sprees, loss of control, compulsive purchases, I want that! this is it! one piece of junk worse than the next. Drago nodded that he understood and promised to keep an eye on me, no more butterflies or souvenirs, 'just a *serviette de plage*', he laughed, 'because you really need one.'

In the bar I told him about a film I'd seen a few weeks before I arrived, Christopher Nolan's *Memento*, the film is split into five-minute segments that unwind backwards, in reverse time sequence, so that the viewer can get into the skin of the protagonist who's lost his short-term memory and from a certain point can no longer form new memories, so he basically lives in the present, he has some important information he mustn't forget (YOUR WIFE HAS BEEN KILLED) tattooed onto his body, he jots everything down on slips of paper and most of the time has no idea what he's doing, where he is, why he's there, what he was planning to do and who the people around him are.

As I tried to explain all this to Drago, I suddenly felt I was in exactly the same place, that I was just like Guy Pearce in the film, because I, too, hadn't been able to concentrate on anything for several days now, couldn't hold on to a single thought and give it as much time as it required, couldn't keep it in my head even for a moment, no, instead this total mess, thoughts racing in a frenzy, chasing one another, yet I can't capture them, get hold of them, they just fly through my head without leaving a trace, and, what's even worse, I'm finding it more and more difficult to keep some continuity, memories of the most recent events are disappearing, everything is getting mixed up and I am often so confused and thrown off kilter that I grind to a halt, suddenly, in the middle of the dining room, in the doorway of the consulting room, pushing a wheelchair down a corridor, for no reason at all, and looking so genuinely frightened that the others put a hand on my shoulder and ask me, alarmed, 'are you all right, has something happened?'

Drago wanted me to write down the film's title for him, he would definitely go and see it, although he was also surprised that a girl like me would watch a film like that because, as I didn't look like someone who might do that. I chose not to ask him what sort of films I looked like I might watch, in the van I talked to Martina, she told me what it was like with Luca, the van windows were open and I said in Slovak, '*fúka strašný vietor,*' it's terribly windy, when Drago heard that he laughed like crazy, repeating, *'fuka veter, fuka veter,'* and when Martina and I asked what was so funny about that, it turned out that *fukati* meant *to fuck* in Slovene.

That night I stayed with Drago again, we both took it for granted, the thought of going back to the little house by the bamboo grove and listening to the old Romanian woman snoring all night never even crossed my mind, when we got back to Bellevue I just assumed that I would head for the annexe with everyone else and crash out on Luca's old bed.

We went to bed quite early, just after ten, but kept talking for a long time in the dark, recalling the worst dreams and night-mares we'd ever had, Drago told me about his mother who died of cancer when he was eight, how for nights on end she used to visit him in his dreams and how he had suffered because even while dreaming he knew it was just a dream, and while Svetlana, as she once told me, adored the kind of dreams where she knew she was just dreaming because she could do anything she wanted without suffering the consequences, these dreams made Drago anxious because he knew that his mum would no longer be there when he woke up, and of course the fear of waking up woke him up every time. And I told him how Norman Bates used to visit me regularly in my sleep when I was around fifteen or sixteen, each time he tried to kill someone dear to me, a relative or friend, that grotesque dressing gown, wig and a kitchen knife as he ran past me, I would wake up drenched in sweat and screaming, and to overcome the fear I would watch *Psycho* during the day over and over again, replaying all the scenes with Anthony Perkins until I knew them by heart, repeating them like a mantra, *I think that we're all in our private cages. Trapped in them. And none of us can ever get out…* I believed in fighting fire with fire, but it took almost two years for Norman Bates to stop visiting me, for me to find an even keel and stop being scared to fall asleep at night.

I took a deep breath, 'but more recently I've been having nightmares of a different kind, the circumstances vary but the essence is always the same, I can't speak, I'm suffocating, sometimes because a gigantic piece of chewing gum has grown inside my mouth, I struggle all night to try and pull it out but it's no use, the more I try to get rid of it, the more it sticks to my gums, teeth, throat, or there's something else in my mouth, a kind of blockage that stops me breathing and talking, like bluebottles, huge dead flies, a whole tangled mass of them explodes from my mouth when I cough, I'm standing in the middle of a narrow room with white walls, no exit in sight, not a single door or a window, and I just keep coughing, can't draw breath, I've coughed up so many flies that a black heap starts to form by my feet and I still can't draw breath…'

Drago chipped in, 'now that you've brought up disgusting stuff like that, let me tell you about this dreadful dream I had the other night. I was going somewhere on a bus, holding on to a handrail and looking out of the window. We were about to enter the tunnel under Ljubljana Castle when I noticed something on my arm, I took a closer look and saw worms teeming on my forearm. They drilled into my flesh and emerged just as easily, you know the kind of worms, the white ones, with rolls of fat. They were feeding on my flesh as if it was quite normal, and that's when I realised what it all meant, it meant that I was rotting away, I was dead! I can't describe the horror that came over me. Of course, no one on the bus noticed anything, they were all looking out of the window, they weren't the least bit concerned…'

'Yuck,' I shuddered in disgust, 'I wish you hadn't told me that.' Drago chuckled, 'sweet dreams, honey', but I mumbled, 'no dreams for me tonight, thank you very much,' and rolled over towards the wall, I always fall asleep facing the wall, with my back to the light, as if I needed privacy, to be just with myself.

I opened my eyes wide convinced that someone somewhere had screamed out in pain, a kind of animal groan, mortal agony, terrified, I gazed at the ceiling trying to locate the origin of this terror, to find my bearings, and suddenly I realised it was me who had screamed with pain, I was still screaming although I was mute and my mouth stayed closed, dry and cracked. My heart was thumping wildly but when I looked around everything seemed fine, in its place so to speak, Drago was asleep, he'd kicked his sleeping bag onto the floor, his right hand was behind his head and leaning against the wall, bright light outside the windows, Marseille in the morning, only I was trembling and sweating horror-struck, gasping, confused, and that's when the thought came back, hitting me with such force that it winded me and an even greater wave of anxiety swept over me because at that moment I grasped the fundamental truth about life, though grasp is not the right word, because deep inside I had always known it, sensed it, but now I could suddenly give it a name, was able to articulate it, the words now pounded right in my chest, *we all hate each other*, suddenly nothing but this truth, this knowledge, or rather the realisation that there's nothing but hatred in this world, that to grow up means to understand and accept all the world's hatred directed at every single person, and therefore also at me. And the other thing I realised at that moment was that I was all alone in the world, naked and helpless, like one of the handicapped people during their morning wash, not even certain that I could hold in my urine and faeces, and with a clear understanding that in this new place there was nothing I could hold on to, no certainty, that my body was totally vulnerable, out of control, like that of a new-born baby, that after nineteen years I'd awoken from childhood and into this reality, the ultimate, the only reality that was impossible to escape, not by means of medication or drugs, there's only this naked awareness and the rest is nothing but a void.

Just then I heard a mumbling, Drago rolled over onto his back in his sleep and said something like, *'jaz nočem… poslušaš me?… govorim, da ne grem s tabo… nikakor…'*, there were some other words, sentences that sounded eerily familiar, and the feeling that Drago was telling me something fundamental but I couldn't decipher it, the despair at not being able to grasp what he was trying to tell me in that language of his, which I so wanted to understand at that moment. I jumped out of bed and ran over to the Slovene, shook him and shouted, 'Drago, I worked it out now, we all hate each other, don't we? We all hate each other, you must have known for a long time!' Drago sat up in his bed, suddenly fully awake and he frowned as I repeated: 'Drago, is it true, that we all hate one another?' And without a moment's hesitation he said: 'yes, that's right, we all hate one another.'

And I ask, is everything, everything gone
In a flash, you say, in an insane
* instant it went down, down*
it vanished
Dane Zajc [1]

---

1 A poem by Dane Zajc, "Dol dol", Translation © Dane Zajc, Sonja Kravanja, 2000. In: *Scorpions*, Slovenian Writers Association.

For minutes on end I stare at the three-dimensional butterfly on the screen. I turn the mobile in my hand so that all its transformations, shades of colour and nuances come to the fore. It's fluttered its wings! And now it's wiggling its antennae! I gaze at it as if it were a spiral in which I am losing myself, a vortex that runs deep, sweeping me off my feet and dragging me along, I spin around and fall down,

What day, month, year is this? when's my shift? morning or afternoon? am I lying in bed while somewhere in the main building they're looking for me, cursing me, badmouthing me for being irresponsible? is a resident waiting for me somewhere, incapable of turning over, having lain motionless on his bed for hours now, his eyes wide open in distress, have they forgotten about me? is that possible?

I ask Drago but he just rolls over, I don't know anything, let me sleep, what's got into you today?

What's got into you today?

I'm throwing up, bent over a bowl. I feel the gastric juices in my mouth, a sour taste, I vomit up a sticky liquid, it comes out with great effort, I haven't been eating, my stomach is empty, yet I keep retching. I hear someone brushing their teeth next door, suddenly Yasmin puts her head round the door, are you all right,

Blanka? should I tell them in the office that you're not feeling well? would you like to take the day off?

I look at her in horror, I even forget to wipe my mouth and think: just go away, you're one of them too, get the hell out of here, you hate me too, stop putting on this show, you Algerian bitch, you who're always laughing,

All morning there are moments when everything goes black, everything starts to spin, if it weren't for Drago, I would collapse in a heap on the floor of our room, but Drago is always here, Drago always catches me, pats me on the cheek, sprinkles water over me from a bottle to bring me round, you'll be fine, it's just an attack of nausea, everything is all right, I'm here, I'm with you, don't worry Blanka, you'll climb out of it,

In my head a parade of faces, one after the other, my childhood friends, classmates, acquaintances, they fill the room to bursting, soon there won't be enough place for them between these four walls; everyone who has ever hated me and mocked me behind my back, laughed at my naiveté and childishness; all the people who grew up before me and learned how to play the game, how to deal and receive blows,

My classmates who used to sit together giggling all the time, the hours I spent trying to figure out what was so funny, but now I know: it was me, it's always been me; or the girl from next door who used to unnerve me with her incredible stories, I swear it's all true, it was my dad who damaged the swans in the fairground and made them tip over, he'd sneaked in at night, she would tell me on our way from Horský park with a deadpan face; and I believed her, of course I believed her,

How could I have been so blinkered for over nineteen years, totally blind and so self-satisfied at the same time,

But in fact, I had nearly done it a few times, I nearly managed to cross over to the other side, surely depression is nothing but a clear mind, an understanding of the real state of affairs, each time I got closer to this knowledge, to the boundary between childhood and adulthood, I would start to thrash about, scream at the top of my voice, no, I don't want to, I can't do it, I'd rather kill myself, anything but this, and so each time they calmed me down with medication, numbed me, swallow this, wash it down with some water, all those antidepressants, anxiolytics, suppress, suppress, back to childhood if there's no other way because my entire body, every cell rebelled against adulthood,

I'm convinced that my family back home know what's happening to me, that's why they sent me here, to make me face up to it at last, with no way out, without medication that would just take me back to square one, to make me finally break out of this vicious cycle, undergo a baptism of fire like everyone else, this is my last chance of going through depression all the way to recovery, to adulthood,

Because that's bound to happen if I stand firm, if I don't give up too early, a rebirth, a perfect transformation, a new lease of life, and this body that's temporarily out of my control can become a real weapon if I learn to take charge of it; I'm sure it will be capable of things I can't even begin to imagine now,

The way I used to bump into a wall with my eyes closed when I was little, longing to be like the ghost of the fabled white lady, to be able to pass through walls, all you have to do is concentrate, all you have to do is believe that it's possible, but in fact I'd never really believed it, only now I know that it really can be done, that my body is capable of it, a body controlled by the mind, a body tamed,

My cousin, sitting in the kitchen in our flat in Jančová Street near Horský park saying, this is a flower, I touch it and my fingers feel that it's a flower, I smell it and know it's a flower, but what are my senses, who's given them to me, how can I be sure they're not deceiving me?

I can't yet control my body though, it's all too new, I rummage through the meds my sister has packed for me, there's something for diarrhoea, I swallow three tablets at once, I'm quite scared of my body, I don't know what tricks it might play on me now that it's broken free of all the laws of physics, that's why three tablets at once, to be on the safe side, I don't want to end up like the residents, I'm terrified at the thought of losing control over my bowels,

Because it's their own fault, of course, no one else's, I see it clearly now, their bodies are just a reflection of their soul, of their shackled mind, you only become misshapen, feeble and incontinent when you lose control over your brain,

I stare at a photo Svetlana has sent in an email, it shows her with her boyfriend, some kind of artist's studio in the background, in the bottom right-hand corner it says *regards from our new sublet*, it reassures me, I know that Svetlana wouldn't…, this is one of the very few certainties I can rely on, she won't team up with them, Svetlana loves me, she's not like the others, she's always stood by me, she has always got me out of the deepest shit, listened to my depressive outbursts on the stairs, dragged me into the classroom by force when necessary, she was the one who read me the riot act about suicide not being a solution, she was the one who pulled me back from the balcony when one of my legs was almost dangling over the railing,

Drago peers over my shoulder, who is this? some artists? your girlfriend? I don't want you to have girlfriends, I want to be your only friend, your best friend, he's jealous of Svetlana, tries to push her out, supplant her, take her place as if this was some sort of sparring match that can have only one winner, but you have to understand, Drago, I can't just erase Svetlana from my life, Svetlana is like family, I try to explain, reassure him, but Drago won't listen, he slams the door behind him,

There's an email from Cédric, *so when do you want me to come, are you still there? why haven't you written for four days?* How could I have forgotten about Cédric, forgotten that he's coming! I bash out a quick reply, *you mustn't come, I'm really sorry, I can't go into the details now, but I beg you, don't come to Marseille,*

I keep coming back to it, Drago, is it really true that we all hate one another? and he nods every time, yes, we all hate one another, but that's terrible, I object, I can't live with that knowledge, why not, Drago says, that's what it's all about, oh look, here's Elena, he jumps up from the mattress, we're in the little house by the bamboo grove, Elena walks in and Drago goes, Hiya, Romania! It's a modern country, right? How are you, Elena from Romania? He's laughing like a drain and Elena raises her hand to him, you rude brat, I'll show you,

So, what did you think, that everyone loves you? Drago shakes his head, I resolve to adapt, to learn to play the game like everyone else, to repay hatred with hatred, and isn't the Bellevue Centre just the place to try it, nowhere else is hatred so concentrated as it is here, all these cripples who suffer daily humiliation when they're being washed, with each intimate movement, who have no choice but to watch the nurses openly making fun of them, mock them with their rude health, firm calves and resolute steps, where else could I find so much despair and frustration in one place, served up on a platter, here you are, help yourself, just reach out with your hand, this almost tangible misery, the walls steeped in hostility, false smiles and fake cheer. Yes, this is the place that will transform me into someone new.

A woman sits in a wheelchair in the dining room and screeches, nobody talks to her, nobody strokes her, nobody gives her tranquillisers, let her screech, it's none of our business, what's it to do with us. I've always avoided her, run away from her screams but not today, today I stand before her, look into her half-open mouth from which the screaming emanates and smile,

I listen to her with satisfaction because she's the one who's screeching, she's the one in a wheelchair, she's the one with the feeble body, not me, I'm on the other side of the barricade, I have control over my brain, I'm home and dry. I smile at her, savour the groaning of dying prey, and then suddenly notice that Marie is watching me from a nearby table, a young woman with whom I've not exchanged a single word yet, but I know that she's OK in the head, it's just her legs, paralysed, an accident, apparently. She looks at me, I can't read her face. I stop smiling straight away, anxiety gnaws at my stomach, I beat a retreat,

During the day I feel confident, but I'm terrified before going to sleep because at night I lose control over myself, sleep can't be controlled, I have difficulty breathing in the evenings, I cry into my pillow, what if I'm not strong enough? what if I'm not up to this transition? I burst into tears, Drago just gives a loud sigh, what is it, Blanka, what's the problem now, why are you doing this to me? I want to sleep. But Drago, I'm so scared that I might piss myself or shit myself at night, that my body will stop obeying me, I'm so terribly scared. Jesus, Blanka! Drago exclaims, his nerves frayed, can't you just think of something else, like… oh, anything, a meadow in bloom, could you try that? imagine flowers, colours, bumblebees, you're running through this blossoming meadow, clouds above your head, your feet sink into the moist soil and you…

'Drago?'

'Yes?'

'Would it be very bad if I started wearing a nappy at night?'

How many days have gone by since I lost all sense of time? Sometimes I catch myself in the middle of doing something, like wiping Laurence's bum, and suddenly become aware that I'm in her room, wiping her bum and laughing at some stupid joke on the radio: how did I get there? what were the steps leading to this? I can't recall anything, although she must have talked to me in the corridor, approached me in her wheelchair, mumbled her request and I had to get into the lift, walk all the way to her room, turn the radio on and take the bedpan out of the wardrobe. And yet, an empty head, a blank,

I spend hours lying on the bed half asleep, I open my eyes every now and then, glance at the alarm clock on the fridge and find that it's only four-thirty, a restlessness that doesn't let me sleep in the mornings, anxiety rouses me from sleep, my eyeballs stir under my eyelids, I register every sound that reaches me, sometimes I scream, eyes bulging, Drago jumps out of bed and shakes me to wake me up, 'stop it! stop it!' he puts his hand over my mouth, the main thing is they don't hear us in the room next door, they mustn't find out about us,

I'm trying to be helpful, I see that he's exhausted, he's fed up with me, he seems to be avoiding me, as if he, too, was on the brink of a nervous breakdown, so I bring him fruit, stroke his hair and hand him cloths to fling at a hole in the wall, I've no idea why he enjoys that, tossing dirty tea towels at a hole in the wall after lunch, I keep begging him not be cross with me, to forgive me, I know I'm being impossible, I know how difficult I make things for him, but it's just for the time being, I'm sure everything will be all right again soon, just bear with me for a little longer, I don't have anyone else here, everyone else hates me, please, Drago,

And Drago doesn't have anyone else here either, just me, his French interpreter, he can't go anywhere without me but ever since the truth about the world has been revealed to me, we have both stopped going to staff meetings with Michel, we just lounge about in bed instead, we have no clue what the other volunteers are up to, what the plan is for the day off, we just about manage to glance at the rota on the board but we often skip our shifts, or work when it's our time off,

He often touches me, it gives him pleasure and I let him, he says that a lovely feeling washes over him when he's running his fingers down my back, your skin is so soft, did you know that? lots of women have great skin but yours is something special, you're as smooth as velvet. I object, how can I be smooth, I've lost eight kilos since coming to Marseille, so be careful what you say, young man! He laughs, you're smooth whatever you may say, just take a look, have a feel, compare. And I do, I also touch Drago, his sinewy body, he's tall, over six foot, sometimes I hop up and down in front of him as a joke, hey you up there, let me look you in the eye, and he says, anything for you, I'll come down to your level,

We're alone in the room, I sit cross-legged on my bed watching as he works out on the floor by the fridge, abs, crunches and other exercises with names I don't even know. I love watching him, encouraging him, go, Drago, one more time, give it your all, no slouching at the back there! he always ends up laughing and has to stop, chases me around the room, pushes me into a corner, grabs my forearms, 'stop making me laugh, you naughty girl, how am I supposed to concentrate?' and we both collapse on the bed in a heap of laughter,

But then comes the morning and along with it anxiety, my sister's diarrhoea tablets that I wash down with some disgusting sugary drink from the fridge, sometimes there's retching in sync with the sunrise, but otherwise just intermittent dozing, eyes fixed on the white ceiling until the others wake up, just the ceiling, Svetlana always says that depression is when you've memorised the ceiling down to the last crack, when you know the ceiling better than you know yourself, and I'm certain Svetlana is right, because every morning…

If at least I could crawl under the bed, cover myself with the balls of dust that gather down there, rest my body on the cold linoleum and tell myself, yes, it's all right now, nothing can get to me anymore, I'm safe now, but there are drawers underneath these stupid beds, stuffed full of old blankets and old clothes, too narrow to squeeze my body into,

During the morning wash I stop in the doorway of Marie's second-floor room to reassure myself that it was just my imagination, that nasty look she shot me the other day in the dining room, I want to present myself in a positive light, admire her tastefully furnished room, the pictures on the wall and especially the view of the sea, the Chateau d'If and the Frioul Islands, how wonderful, I gush, a view of the sea straight from your bed, aren't you lucky, Marie, I wish I could change places with you,

Marie scowls,

Only then, horror-struck, do I realise what I've just said,

Sometimes I have this incredibly intense and spine-chilling feeling, it can be triggered by a sideways glance or a gob of spit on a plate or a wheelchair going over my feet, *oh, excusez-moi, mademoiselle,* but I know full well that he's not apologising, on the contrary, he's happy to have hurt me, 'ah, mademoiselle has two legs? good, at least she'll really feel them now'.

I can't stand the presence of people in wheelchairs for more than an hour, then I run out of their room, lock myself in the toilets, withdraw behind the safety barrier in the stairwell, Drago sometimes finds me there, he doesn't use the lift if he doesn't have to. He sits down next to me, I rest my head in his lap and repeat, I can't stand them any longer, everyone is against me, they keep doing things to spite me and pretend it was an accident so that I can't point my finger at them, I'm sure Michel would laugh at me and say I'm paranoid. Open confrontation or revenge is always best, Drago says with a smile,

I walk down the hill towards the bamboo grove, I've just come off my shift and I am almost congratulating myself, it all went without a hitch this time, I managed something resembling a normal conversation with Laurence and had no problem hoisting Serge out of his bed, when suddenly there's a stamping of feet, Drago, he seems to be in high spirits, he stops, leans against my shoulder to catch his breath but I see that he's about to burst out laughing, haven't you forgotten something, Blanka?

I shake my head, no, what could I have forgotten,

'A red light is on above one of the toilet doors!'

Oh my God, Thomas!

I cover my mouth, I've totally forgotten about him! I start running up the hill, past the swimming pool, across the dining room and then down the corridor, and indeed, the light above a door is on, of course it is, I left him there a good hour ago,

Thomas, I'm so sorry, please forgive me, but Thomas just shakes his head, *c'est rien, c'est rien,* no big deal, he's just had a longer sit, never mind, he wasn't in a rush anyway,

I wipe him off and keep apologising, I'm not listening to him, I ask his forgiveness so many times that he also ends up looking worried and later in the afternoon, as I sit with Drago by the swimming pool, Thomas buzzes up to me in his automatic wheelchair and starts to apologise, he didn't want to give me extra problems, he's sorry about what's happened, he really shouldn't have turned the red light on, it was selfish of him, he should have waited patiently for someone to notice,

I shake my head, no, oh no, for goodness' sake, what are you saying,

I'm awfully embarrassed, Drago is laughing his head off next to me, his eyes fill with tears, you got him, Blanka!

As we wait at the bus stop, he tells me that he lives in a house similar to the one across the street, it's a detached house but two motorways have been built around it, there's noise, constant roar of cars, but you can get used to everything, including hatred, he smiles. Why didn't you move, I ask, why have you stayed in a house between two motorways? And he goes: my father put his foot down, everyone else moved away, to the village up the hill, but my dad, being a true Serb, said that nothing, not even a four-lane motorway to Istria, would make him leave. I laugh and I can see him in my mind's eye, the stubborn Serb and the house, I picture it with an advertisement on the side wall, a huge billboard showing a lascivious young woman wiggling her rear and selling stockings, beautiful nylons, guaranteed no ladders, the advert must have gone all black, covered in motorway dust churned up by all those cars. Drago says I shouldn't be surprised that they agreed to put an advert on their house, they did it for the money, everything for money, darling, so you can imagine how comical a beautiful ceramic house number would look on the gate, you know one of those we saw in Cassis,

But then, somewhere between Belle de Mai and the port, I suddenly feel violently dizzy, I slump down on the dirty floor of the bus, black out for a second, but I've come to now, Drago is picking me up, Yasmin shouts at the driver to stop, damn it, stop the bus, she's unwell! the older Algerian woman clutches at her heart, her black headscarf makes her look a bit like a cockroach with twisted legs. I scramble to my feet, I need to get out, we all stream out, curious faces on the other side of the glass but the bus is leaving, it's turned the corner. I stagger to the park where there's a drinking fountain, and Drago being Drago, he sticks my head under the stream of water, it's ice-cold, I shiver, but I feel better straight away, the Algerian woman strokes my back and keeps saying, '*qu'est-ce que tu as, ma fille, mais qu'est-ce que tu as?*' although it doesn't sound like a question, more like a statement that something's not right with me, that something inside me is broken, wrecked beyond repair. On the way to the market Drago tells me that he can't stand it, that it really gets on his nerves, the Algerian's constant *ma fille* and *mon fils*, he's no son of hers and I'm not her daughter and if she says it one more time, he won't be able to control himself and,

And I interrupt him, yeah, he's right, the old Algerian is not our mother but he shouldn't be cross with her, it's just a kind of linguistic tic, we all have one, but the two of us, we're almost like siblings, don't you think, I feel that I'm starting to be aware of my roots, it's partly thanks to you, I'm proud to be a Slav, that's another reason why we're so close, almost like a brother and a sister, aren't we, Drago, you feel that way too, don't you,

We part ways in the market place, the Algerian women go one way, we another, Drago has stopped at a shoe stall, he's still looking for trainers, we've divided up the tasks right from start, I keep looking for a *serviette de plage*, he for trainers, I walk around the market, register the hubbub, the shouting, rushing about, swearing, a genuine Arab market but then, all of a sudden, my vision goes all granular, everything starts to splinter, crumble, I grind to a halt, fascinated by the scene unveiling before my eyes, Drago, I don't know what's happening to me, Drago, I can't see! and indeed, the granularity fades into darkness, everything goes black again, Drago is in position, ready to catch me, he's holding me and when I come round he helps me out into the fresh air, sits me down on the kerb and asks, feeling better now? has it passed? and puts his hand on my shoulder,

I nod but as soon as we're back among the crowd I start to concentrate, I try to bring it on myself and very soon I succeed, suddenly everything goes red, then blue, I grab Drago's hand, squeeze it, things change shape before my eyes, I can't see, I can't see anything! I shout but this time I don't collapse, with some effort I manage to stay on my feet,

Drago throws confused glances at me, he's afraid to let me out of his sight, he keeps checking on where I am, what I am doing, makes sure I don't go too far away, like an older brother,

I don't quite understand what's going on, but it seems wonderful that I'm able to change my vision by sheer force of will, to induce hallucinations, I do it on purpose, revel in it, change the colours before my eyes, the flashing, shining, darkness, I fall again but without any fear because I know that Drago will always come to the rescue although,

We're sitting on the kerb again, Drago is giving me an earful, he tells me, explains, insists that I mustn't do that, he knows very well what's happening to me, it's great that I've started to discover new dimensions of existence and test the limits of my body, but I can't FUCKING keep on doing this to him, I'm being like a child and if I don't stop it right away, he'll be so pissed off that he won't catch me anymore, he'll let me fall, let me be trampled to death by hundreds of dirty Arab feet,

I listen to him perfunctorily, everything goes in one ear, out the other, I'm not taking it seriously, I'm convinced that he wouldn't let me fall, wouldn't let me get trampled to death, I don't care that he's cross with me, I'm too enthralled by my discovery, but nevertheless, I keep repeating mournfully, sorry, I'm so sorry, because I think that's what he expects me to say,

'But Drago, tell me how I should stop it, I'm not doing it on purpose,' I lie, and he knows, because,

'JUST STOP DOING IT!' he screams and then says he's really fed up with me and clutches at his head as if he were in incredible pain,

You know shit about life, Blanka, if you were fighting for survival, if you were penniless, had nothing to eat, but not this, I don't know how to get it across to you, you just can't keep doing this to other people, not everyone has the patience of Job like he does, not everyone *understands*, but I mustn't think that he hates me because that's the only certainty he can give me, the certainty that he's not like all the others,

We go back to the market, the Algerian women are haggling furiously, Drago is mildly disgusted, no decent trainers, I buy a hairnet, a horrible red one, it costs one euro, it's got some

kind of metal stud or whatever it's called at the back, it's
covered in wax, the kind of net Arab women wear, their hair
all combed back, I know it's horrible but Yasmin and the older
Algerian praise it, *'c'est joli, non?'* Drago disagrees, he hates it,
on the way back he mutters through his teeth, why did you
buy that? just because it's cheap? and then, I'd better start
watching you, make sure you don't buy junk, you said it was
a tell-tale sign,

I'm sitting on a mattress in the little house toying with the red
hairnet, pulling it over my knee and relishing the sight, Drago
appears in the doorway, sits down next to me, looks at me for a
while and then says he's just talked to Luca, Luca stopped him
in the main building and asked what I'm like,

I look up at him flabbergasted, what am I supposed to be like
in WHAT way?

And then I get it, I see, I say and smile, lower my eyes and bite
my lip to stop myself from laughing, everything is making me
laugh today, the hairnet has definitely lifted my spirits, so what
did you tell him, what am I like?

'I told him I'd never experienced anything like that before,'

'You didn't say that! silly, now he'll think that…'

'Let him think whatever he likes, and besides, it's not a lie, I've
really never experienced anything like this,'

I think of us wandering around the streets of Marseille all
night, then, slightly ashamed, of the last few evenings and me
moaning how I was sure I'd piss myself or shit myself at night,

I'm sure it would be humiliating for a man to admit that he's
not screwing his roommate, that he's just helping her dispel her
fear of incontinence rather than,

To give Drago some satisfaction, I nod, oh yeah, we've been at it like rabbits, day and night, you said the right thing, and if Martina asks me anything, I will tell her something similar, I smile, I like the idea that everyone thinks we're shagging,

Drago seems lost in thought, suddenly he jumps up from the mattress and starts mumbling something about other levels of consciousness, the dervishes, for instance, they believe they can achieve a higher state of consciousness by spinning round,

He starts to spin round,

I shout at him from the mattress, stop it, that's enough, you must have reached a higher state of consciousness by now, stop it, please! but he won't stop, he laughs and spins faster and faster,

Now it's up to me to catch him,

We collapse onto the mattress and just then the automatic door starts to open,

Seeing Elena, Drago shouts at her, laughing, viva Romania!

And then he whispers to me with a malicious grin, we all hate one another, that's what makes the world interesting,

We all hate one another,

It sounded funny and playful at that moment, I laughed with Drago at Elena's furious face but when night comes and I start trembling with anxiety, and can't fall asleep while Drago is happily snoring away, I'm weighed down by the hatred of the world and not even a text message from Peter can lift it, it arrived at around ten o'clock and I'm reading it now, horrified,

It's as if Peter has sensed that something has been going on between me and Drago, the words flicker grotesquely in the darkness, *I love you, petal,* the words march up and down my head, making a terrible din, trumpeting, drumming, blasting away, *I love you, petal,* he can't be serious, me and petal! my sister always laughs at me, says I walk like a bulldozer and when I run down the stairs it sounds like a herd of elephants.

Me and petal?

And the insistent thought, what if Peter is also on their side? what if he's also one of them? the doubts and the gripping fear,

Early in the morning I make a checklist which I can take out of my pocket at any time during the day and make sure I haven't forgotten anything crucial:

> *You're depressed*
> *It's Friday*
> *It's your day off*
> *Cédric is not coming, you told him not to*
> *Drago is your friend*
> *The others don't know you're depressed*
> *Watch your words*
> *Try to change*
> *Don't hurt people around you*
> *Always think before you speak*
> *Never tell anyone about Drago*

> *DON'T BE A SELFISH PIG!*

I can almost feel the warmth of the piece of paper in my pocket, but by early afternoon I'm no longer sure if all the points on the checklist are true, even though Drago keeps repeating that he's the only one who knows what state I'm in, but can I really believe that … those sideways glances, and sometimes the feeling that I'm being observed, scrutinized, at times the ominous certainty that they know, that they will take action against me,

Like Luca, the look he gave me when I wasn't able to help him lift the hundred-kilo Louise who fell out of her wheelchair,

I'm walking past her door and he calls out to me, hey, Blanka, can you give me a hand please, someone's taken the hoist away, I stand in the doorway staring at that limp obese woman rolling about on the floor, I must have stared at her too long, looked too puzzled because Luca is suddenly standing right next to me (how did he get here, when?), puts his hand on my shoulder and asks: are you all right?

Are you all right?

Why did he ask that, why? He must have sensed something, he wouldn't have asked if he had no idea,

The question may be only seemingly banal, that piercing gaze of his, like he could see through me, like he could read my mind,

I grind to a halt in the middle of the dining room. But what if he does know?!

The thought hits me with revelatory force, a naked truth that's always been there only I never saw it, not because it's been kept secret from me but because I couldn't be bothered to look it in the face,

Being in control of your body can't be everything, surely it can't, another part of being adult must be reading other people's thoughts, a level I have yet to reach,

Everyone around me knows what I'm going through, they've been watching me closely, laughing behind my back,

Like that little girl in one of Hitchcock's horror stories who could read other people's thoughts, it gave her incredible power over everyone else so the people in her village learned not to think about anything, instead they would just go: one two three four five, it's a lovely day today, six times six is thirty-six,

Maybe lots of people function in this way, to prevent others from getting inside their head,

Maybe reading people's minds is the highest goal, to be attained by only a few individuals, a handful of the chosen,

But maybe it's not like that at all, I wish I could ask Drago, I'm sure he knows, but Drago is on his shift right now, grappling with nappies in somebody's room, and besides, he seemed rather annoyed this morning,

It must be me, it must something I did, I must have made him cross again,

Laurence, or rather, the wheelchair with Laurence in it, stops before me. She shoves a booklet into my hand, a notebook in hard covers, I give it back to her, what does she want from me, why won't she leave me alone, this woman who can't even control her own body, but she insists, she forces it on me shouting: *'peeen! peeen le! ouououououvr!'* I open the notebook and see it's an address book, with phone numbers,

'You'd like to make a call, Laurence?'

She nods fiercely and points to the corridor where the phones are,

I dial a number but I'm not sure I got it right, the notebook is covered in scribbles, many numbers have been crossed out, some are hard to read (I wonder if Laurence wrote them down herself) and on top of that I can't work out who it is Laurence wants to call, Madame Dupin? Mr Médeuf? so which one is it? no? not on this page? why are you grabbing it back, Laurence, I don't understand you,

'I don't understand you,'

Eventually I dial a number, listen to it ring out, and when someone picks up and a woman's voice says, *âllo?* I put the receiver to Laurence's ear and step back, sort of, your privacy is sacred, Laurence is trying hard, she mutters something incomprehensible into the phone, fidgeting all the time but in a kind of furious way, she's getting more and more agitated, she flings the receiver at the wall, I watch aghast, she starts to scream and howl,

What's happened, calm down, hello? anybody there?

And there is someone at the other end, someone shouting, what's this supposed to mean, *putain!* you can't call a number and then just start babbling down the phone like this! I listen to the indignant female voice, I'm confused and stutter, but it was Laurence, Laurence would like to speak to you,

'Laurence who? I don't know any Laurence, listen, stop taking the mickey, don't think you can get away with it,'

I put the receiver down,

Laurence, I think to myself, some strange friends you have if they say things like that on the phone, but I keep quiet, I don't want to infuriate her even more, just then I notice that she's started drooling, I am suddenly overcome by tiredness, I give her back the address book, leave her there, I walk down the corridor, it's my day off today (at least that's what it says on my checklist: it's your day off), I stop by the lift,

And suddenly I get it, I must have dialled the wrong number! this can't have been anyone who knows Laurence,

I'm so stupid! I clutch my head, I'd like to go back and apologise but I don't have the strength, my will isn't strong enough, I slide down to the floor and don't care that people are staring at me from their wheelchairs, some even smile, like they're happy to see that I no longer act superior, that I've sunk to their level at last or, better still: I'm closer to the ground than they are, hitting the bottom, seeing that I have problems must fill them with happiness, they wish it on me, they hate me, it's this hatred that's crippled them, that's what has moulded them, deformed them, the enormous power of hatred,

As I head for my quiet spot at the foot of the stairs, to my surprise, I find Drago sitting there already, his eyes are closed, he's gnawing the knuckles on his right hand, I join him,

'Shift over?'

He nods, and I tell him the whole story of the wretched phone call, my own stupidity, Laurence's fit of rage, how people stared at me from their wheelchairs when I was down on the floor,

He just shrugs, screw them, forget about Laurence, please Blanka, screw them all, just two more weeks and we're out of here… I can't wait, I've really had it up to here, the nappy changing and trimming of nose hairs… what I'd like now is to be at home, sit on a bench in the garden under the trees… I feel totally empty, you understand, here inside, he looks at me,

'Are you even listening to me?!'

I'm startled by his sudden change of tone, of course I'm listening, Drago,

'So, what was I saying? What? Repeat it!'

'You were saying… you were saying… something about a bench under the trees,'

'I was saying that I feel totally empty, do you understand that, do you have any idea?'

I nod,

'You don't know shit!' he shakes his head, 'I'm wasting my time with you… I mean it,'

'Come on, Drago, please, I've tried…'

'Ah, so you've tried… Well, you haven't tried hard enough, that's what I think. You see, it doesn't really seem fair that you expect me to be here for you all the time, to be by your side, at your beck and call, listening to you, comforting you, looking out for you, catching you when you pass out, singing you sweet lullabies, but you're never here for me, you never hear me out, you don't give a toss about what I feel, what I think, you see only yourself, your own problems and everyone else can go to hell, isn't that right?'

'No, Drago, it's not true,'

'Oh yes, Blanka, it is.'

He pauses, 'You know, one of these days I might have had it with this one-way relationship… Fuck, why does it always have to be me?'

I say nothing, my eyes stare at the ground, I dig the tip of my shoe into a step on the stairs,

'… I thought I was going to die when he asked me, can you imagine what it would be like, with Adam?! you know Adam, the one with the huge head and matchstick arms, but that idiot Luca just laughed, said he didn't mind, he was happy to let me go out with him, said he wouldn't be jealous, but when I imagine how the people in the restaurant would gawp…'

Martina and I are in the little house, I'm sitting on what used to be her bed, she's changing for the night, we haven't talked for a long time and it looks like she wants to make up for neglecting me but at one point she raises her finger, ah, but I know you haven't missed me that much, I've heard from Luca, he told me about you and Drago, she giggles,

I laugh with her, I even blush, quite genuinely, although I've been avoiding Drago all day, wary of a confrontation, I'm scared of what he might say when we're back in our room in the evening, how he will come down on me, and it will be quite justified, no I can't afford to lose Drago, I'd be adrift without him,

But in the evening, when we all gather in the dining room, he doesn't seem angry at all, he's wearing his Bermuda shorts and a blue T-shirt, gives me a wink from the far end of the room, I say good-bye to Jean-Claude, the night porter, with whom I was chatting about Czechs and Slovaks, how they always manage to worm their way into everything, here at Bellevue we have a Czech or Slovak every year, Jean-Claude laughed, it's almost a tradition now,

Drago and I are in the port, walking arm in arm, *fúka vietor, fúka vietor,* I say, I'd do anything to make him laugh, to put him in a good mood and make him forgive me for being so damned selfish, for not listening to him today on the stairs, I let him do all the talking, he says that since our engagement is now official and everyone knows about us we might as well take care of the practical side of things, so should we go for golden wedding rings or silver ones?

Definitely silver, that goes without question, sweetheart, we goof around for a while, straggling behind the others who are already on their way to a café, 'I'm dying for a banana split', I hear Yasmin say,

We sit outside on the terrace lit by green paper lanterns, stirring our spritzers with cocktail sticks and tossing ice cubes into the ornamental shrub pots, Drago roars with laughter, the ice cubes are flying all over the place, how embarrassing,

We watch a stocky man staring dreamily at motor bikes, Drago points him out to me because, unlike me, he registers what's going on around him, just look at that fatso by the Harley, I guess he's a latent Hell's Angel, Drago guffaws, just like you're a latent Satanist, I fling a green cocktail stick at him, watch your tongue; waiter?

We pick up some free postcards from a stand in the bar, Yasmin gives us an astonished look, did you nick those? she actually thinks we've stolen them, so Drago whispers to her, we could steal some for you as well, would you like some? and Yasmin claps her hands in joy, yes please, then she whispers: but be careful, make sure you don't get caught, we go back and pretend we're casting furtive glances around to make sure no one sees us taking the free postcards,

In the evening, we sit on our beds and I tell him about Svetlana, how she spent a whole summer in some Latvian squat and sent me unstamped postcards, on which she wrote just a big letter T, and in spite of that all her postcards arrived. Drago says a friend of his does the same, except he writes 2FA-BE on his cards instead of a stamp, so we decide to try both tricks and see which cards are delivered,

I croon, *je ne t'aime plus, mon amour, je ne t'aime plus, tous les jours,* and Drago looks at me through his green cocktail stick, wow, this is magic, you're green!

Let me see, give it to me, I reach for the cocktail stick, but he pretends he wants to stick it up his nose, I encourage him, go on, do it, just one quick shove and there'll be peace and quiet at last!

He frowns, you really want me to punch a hole in my brain? do you hate me so much, Blanka?

I'm startled,

But Drago is in stitches, you should've seen your face, incredible, you fell for it,

I'm seeing black again, nausea, something's happened to my vision again, I'm throwing up in a toilet at a McDonald's, everything is spinning, I stagger out of the bog bumping into people as I walk,

Drago grabs me by the hand, leads me out and to the park, to L'Arc de Triomphe, we lie in the grass, my head resting in his lap, he's chewing a blade of grass, my eyes are closed, neither of us speaks, we're waiting for it to pass, this time he can see I didn't do it on purpose, he says my face has taken on an attractive greenish hue,

I'm lying on the bed in the little house, I ask Martina to beg the nurse for some sleeping pills, I haven't slept for days, I'm tired but feel incredibly energized at the same time, my brain is active around the clock, yet I can't concentrate on anything,

Martina brings me a glass of water, sits down by my side, hands me a sleeping pill to swallow, I raise myself on the bed, pick up the glass and spill it straight away, my hands are shaking uncontrollably, 'wait, let me hold it for you,'

Martina wipes me down, holds a towel to my chin and helps me wash the pills down with the same caring movements she uses with the residents, I apologise, infirm, desperate, horrified that I'm not even capable of taking a drink of water on my own, but Martina reassures me in the professional manner she's picked up over the two weeks of working with the handicapped, 'don't worry, Blanka, it's all right, everything's fine,'

But she seems to blame it mostly on Drago and our life together, the nights we've spent carousing and probably screwing like there's no tomorrow, she shakes her head with a hint of a smile, 'what have you and your loverboy Drago been up to?'

Luca insists, you know what I'm trying to say, I've got to do something when I'm alone with a woman, you know what I mean, and then, with slight agitation, please stop laughing like an idiot and say something, come clean, what's Drago like in bed?! but I just keep laughing, hand in front of my mouth, I wipe tears from my eyes, leave me alone, Luca, just leave me alone,

Today the weather is not right for swimming, it's too windy, says Ingeborg who's behind the wheel of the van and sure enough, as we drive past the beaches we see black flags fluttering in the wind, not a soul in the water,

So it has to be the park, where else can we go, how else can we spend the afternoon, the Parc Borély, with merry-go-rounds and a pond, on the way there Drago and I buy some incredibly sweet and sticky pastries that make us all grubby, calorie bombs, never mind, ten kilos down since I arrived, I am delighted with my flat stomach and breasts that stand out at last, all my trousers are falling off and my T-shirts sag limply on me, like on a hanger, finally I feel good in my own body, finally I feel in control of it, it's so simple, it's all just a question of willpower, I wish it hadn't taken me nineteen years to figure this out,

Martina says she feels like doing something crazy, and as we enter the park, Drago hires a bumper car, a kind of dodgem, we can ride it around the park for an hour, he gets in and steps on it straight away, his six-foot frame squeezed into the small vehicle, he waves to us and drives off down a tarmac path, the rest of us find a place in the grass under a tree and spread out our blankets,

Martina asks if I want to go for a little stroll and as we walk she starts to interrogate me, she's been wondering what's going on, she and Luca have been worried about me, I've been so pale, almost green lately, I've fainted and often don't notice when they're speaking to me, they are both very concerned and would like to know what's happening with me and if there's something they can do to help,

I thank her like a grown-up and responsible person, there's really no need to worry about me,

'Come on, Blanka, you're as green as this pond!'

I pause for a moment, that might well be true, but everyone is responsible for dealing with their own problems,

And that's it, I refuse to discuss it further and Martina gives up, starts to talk about herself and Luca, they get on so well that she's been wondering if she should drop out of school and follow him to Italy, to Taranto, and start a family,

'Good grief, Martina, you're only seventeen,' I interrupt,

But Martina won't let up, she just knows Luca is the one, yes, she's aware that to someone else this may seem like a rash decision, they've only been together for two weeks, 'but if only you knew, Blanka, how we understand each other in every way,'

Then she sighs, she wishes this holiday would never end and we could stay in Marseille forever, she doesn't want to go back to her tedious Czech life, 'college, homework, the halls of residence, I wish I was as carefree as we all were that first week, in Pharo Park,'

But by now we've come back to our blankets, Martina races ahead, pounces on Luca from behind, gotcha! Terrified, he leaps to his feet and starts chasing Martina around the meadow, just then Drago calls out to me, 'wanna come for a ride? it's really fun,'

So, we fool around on the bumper car for an hour, I'm an even crazier driver than Luca, people jump out of our way as we shout, *'bonjour, madame! bonjour, monsieur!'* Some smile at us with understanding, others shake their heads and Drago points out some especially interesting specimens, a bare-chested bodybuilder in particular makes us laugh as he stands in the sun with his dumb-bells, all puffed up, casting furtive glances around to see if everyone has taken notice of those pathetic muscles of his, Drago says he loves fooling around when he's away from Slovenia, someplace no one knows him, where he can do whatever he likes and not worry about anything,

At one point I burst into a men's toilet, two young men raise their eyes from the urinals in surprise, I find that funny too, I roar with laughter in the doorway before making myself scarce,

We give back the bumper car and lie down on a blanket facing each other, Drago amuses himself by sticking bits of grass under my T-shirt and mocking me, 'tits, show me your tits, girl,'

To get back at him I try to poke his eye out with a twig,

Back in the van we check if I would make a good junkie, Drago ties his T-shirt around my arm to see how well my veins stand out, but no luck, it's hopeless, you'll never make a junkie, Drago sighs, a bit disappointed, and when we spot the Virgin logo outside, we both have the same idea, we could buy a DVD of *Pulp Fiction* and watch it in Ahmad's room! Luca, stop! We jump out of the van before it's even screeched to a halt,

Drago and his usual 'be brave' because I'm too shy to speak French, especially to complete strangers, eventually I pluck up courage and ask an assistant at the Virgin store about the DVD, but he just shakes his head, not available, come back early next month when new stock comes in,

We push our way through the crowded streets of Marseille, using our knees and elbows trying to find a bus to take us somewhere near Belle de Mai, I buy a couple of T-shirts at a cheapo Vietnamese shop, two euros a piece, one red, one azure blue, this size has always been too small for me, I spin around in front of the mirror admiring myself quite uncritically, ten kilos down, I keep telling myself, how do I look, I ask Drago, but honestly, does it suit me?

Drago says, come on, you're beautiful but that's enough now, he pretends to be bored but I saw him staring at my breasts, they really stand out in the clingy red T-shirt, I can't help smiling as I pay, I've got a firm grip on this boy, this time I'm the one who's in charge of the situation,

The last few days I've been feeling like a different person, like I'm turning into someone more powerful, more beautiful, more aware of being alive. I feel blood pulsating through my veins, every molecule getting stronger, at times I'm aware of my entire body, and I know that this is not the end yet, it's not yet over, this growth, this transformation, this is just the first phase,

I've also been feeling less and less compassion for the people in the wheelchairs, they're nothing but worms, wimps who have holed up in this institution to hide from the world, they can't be bothered to stand up on their own two feet and face life like the rest of us, they are so scared of confrontation that even their bodies have adapted to this fear by twisting, each in its own way, with tics, atrophy, epilepsy, unnatural deformations, but they're basically all the same, layabouts! cowards! losers!

On the bus I try to explain to Drago that you have to be strong, not afraid of life, able to stand up for yourself, overcome obstacles, no matter how hard, but you have to manage on your own, with your own resources, with a little help from a good friend if absolutely necessary, but you mustn't resort to crying, weakness, nausea, depression, to medication that suppresses fear the way I used to until recently, for years, in fact ever since I realised how frightening and horrible this world was, but the time has now come for me to prove that I'm strong enough, that I'm up to it, that I won't let a few cripples break me, humiliate me, that I can dig my way out of it, fight tooth and claw if need be, but on my own, without doctors,

The bus is noisy, the driver has put on the radio full blast, we're holding on to the bars and have to shout to make ourselves heard but Drago catches most of what I'm saying, nods, he even smiles at me, albeit in a slightly patronising way like an older, wiser brother,

Plastic chairs by the swimming pool, dusk falling, it's quite chilly, the two of us, legs outstretched, on the edge of the pool, Martina and Luca talking softly, Serge parked under a tree (*bonjour, monsieur Serge*), the siesta almost over, peace and quiet,

'Luca, where's your mobile?' Drago asks, 'I thought I heard it ringing somewhere,'

'What, my mobile? Don't know, must be in my room somewhere,'

Drago bends down to me and whispers, now watch, I'll teach Luca a lesson, the wimp, I won't be humiliated by a bloody Italian! he gives me a wink, leaps out of the chair and flings himself on Luca with a yell,

Both of them tumble into the pool, Luca emerges, shouting, '*coglione! che cazzo!*, my mobile is in my pocket,' he pulls a drenched Nokia out,

'But I did ask you where it was,' Drago scratches his head,

He spends the next hour drying the mobile using a hand dryer, brings me a chair from someone's room so I can sit with him in the bathroom, eventually he manages to revive it, he's relieved, at least I don't have to buy him a new one, that would blow my budget,

We decide to celebrate on the roof of the main building, Drago grabs a wheelchair parked in the corridor and invites me to take the other one, let's have a race,

I shake my head, no, not that, Drago, this is definitely not my thing, I'd only break it,

I make excuses because the real reason is that once I sit down in a wheelchair it will be a final capitulation, an admission of defeat, surrendering to fate. What if I can't get back up, my legs, suddenly limp, shuffling along the linoleum, sudden loss of bowel control, and the all-knowing smiles of the residents to boot, we knew it, welcome to the club, welcome among us, you're finally one of us,

The only thing missing is a nappy between my legs,

Drago objects but Martina couldn't care less, she's not a child she says, and why should we get lost anyway, Jesus, Drago, don't be like my dad. She just waves and heads for the books section, soon disappearing among the bookshelves,

Nouvelles Galeries Lafayette, FNAC, music section on the third floor, I wander among the CD racks trying to recall the names of my favourite bands, why can't I recall a single name, how is that possible,

I walk up and down, pick up CDs at random and put them back, I tug at my ponytail absent-mindedly, I can't understand how my memory could have deteriorated so much in such a short time, what's his name again, shit, that androgynous-looking guy, short black hair, it starts with an m... m... something like milk... Molko! Of course, Brian Molko! wait a minute, how can I be so stupid, I've been carrying his picture in my wallet for over a year now, all I had to do was take it out and look,

I dash over to the CDs starting with M,

Nothing, I stop, confused,

Ah, of course, that's the name of the singer, the band has a different name,

I'm getting annoyed with my own incompetence, the lapses of memory, I glare at a guy who's been watching me for a while, he's leaning on the rack with the new Madonna, I've noticed him, of course I have,

But he reads my frown as an order to attack, comes up to me, *'vous êtes charmante, mademoiselle'*,

A sleazy type, one of those who induce nausea on the spot, well, in me, at least,

Although he's tall, slim, almost muscular,

I shake his hand, *'enchantée*, Blanka' – 'Cyril,' I pay no more attention to him, because I have other things to worry about, my brain is seizing up, that's more important than some slea-zebag, I laugh to myself that someone finds my confusion charming,

But he keeps following me, asks what I'm looking for, offers to help,

I'm angry that he forces me to speak French, so I head for the first pile of CDs that I see, found it! I wave a Ziggy Stardust triumphantly, the *30th anniversary 2-CD* edition and Cyril smiles, great taste, we'll get on well,

He hangs around while I queue up at the checkout, follows me to the DVD section, says he also loves Truffaut, and *Les quatre cents coups*, and Godard and *À bout de souffle*, all the New Wave in fact, just like me, we have so much in common, seen any Éric Rohmer?

I'm at a loss how to get rid of him, the way he touches me from time to time as if accidentally, the fact that he crouches down with me each time, the way he tries to catch my eye,

I spot Drago, he's standing by a wall listening to Jamiroquai, I head towards him, Cyril at my heels,

Drago takes the headphones off, he knows what I want, I just smile, you guys should meet, this is Drago, this is Cyril, and then, I'm off now, you two talk, I say,

Drago bursts out laughing: even if you hadn't told me that you are studying English at university I would have guessed as much from that polished sentence,

I poke him in the ribs, don't be cheeky, boy,

Again, this feeling of power over both of them, I know I look great, I know they're attracted to my strength, my trans-formation, my new body, new confidence, arrogance almost,

I find Martina, she's sitting on the stairs reading Marguerite Duras, she raises her head from the book and smiles at me, *'ukaž, co sis koupila za cédéčko, Blanko'*, let's see what CD you bought,

I show her the CD, we leave FNAC and wander around the corridors of the department store, Drago and Martina walk ahead of me, the traitors! I give evasive answers as Cyril nudges me to come to the beach or have an ice cream, how would I like a walk along the promenade, I pretend I can't understand, when that doesn't work, I explain that we're not allowed to walk around the city on our own, the Bellevue Centre is responsible for us, do you understand, Cyril,

We're in another shop now and I shoot Martina a desperate glance, help me, tell me how to get rid of him, what does he want from me anyway? Martina is rummaging through T-shirts, I think he'd like to pull you but he's not doing too well, just tell him to cool it,

We leave the shop, I take a deep breath, it was a pleasure, Cyril, but we've got to go now, please understand. I watch him leave, he doesn't look back once, maybe he's hurt, maybe he didn't understand,

I talk it over with Drago, what did he want from me, that moron, that sleazebag... Drago looks at me mockingly, you're a big girl, Blanka, surely you know what a man wants from a woman, don't you? I blush, but why me? Because of your pretty face, he smiles, and I don't know if he really meant it or if he was being sarcastic,

We fool around a cheap clothes shop for another hour or so, trying on the tackiest items and hooting with laughter, the shop assistants look daggers at us because we make a mess and don't buy anything, but nobody says a word,

Martina says, time to head back now, it's getting late and she's on the evening shift, I freeze in horror, so am I! I've totally forgotten,

Luca grabs my hand in the dining room, come over here, I'd like you to meet someone, she's just started today, her name's Amélie, she's about fourteen or fifteen, she's terribly shy, she's been sitting on that chair for an hour now and hasn't dared to look at anyone or speak to anyone, I'm sure you'll get on with her,

Before I have time to object, we're standing in front of her,

The TV is playing in the background, several wheelchairs are parked in front of it, every face upturned, Thomas drooling down onto his T-shirt, Joëlle devouring Richard Chamberlain open-eyed, her husband regularly clenching and unclenching his right fist with a resigned face, Laurence is also there, as soon as she sees me she waves and swivels her wheelchair towards us, she'd love to join us, I can't stand the sight of that face of hers, all tense, in a spasm,

I signal that this is not a good time, turn my back on her and look at Amélie,

The way she gives me her hand, the way she lowers her eyes, the way she looks at the floor,

Her hand is soft, with no will, no strength,

She sits back down, quickly draws her legs together and places her hands on her knees,

'I'll leave you to it, girls,' Luca says, 'I've got things to do,'

He leaves, we're alone,

Amélie is evidently embarrassed by my presence, she sits on the chair frozen, slouching grotesquely, a caricature of herself,

I can see she wishes she were somewhere else, in denial about all the suffering around,

I can see she doesn't know how to handle it, everything is still too new, too horrible,

I can see that she's terribly embarrassed to be alive, with two legs and two arms, sinews, bones, muscles, everything in place, saliva in her mouth and not on her T-shirt, a well-proportioned body, a huge sense of embarrassment about being healthy, just like me,

I see myself two weeks ago,

I see a child,

The silence between us turns heavy so I start to ask her questions,

Amélie answers, her eyes drill into the floor, her father is a taxi driver, I think to myself: a taxi driver in Marseille, *belle blague!* she's just finished primary school and is here on a placement, she has two weeks to decide if she wants to train as a nurse working with the physically disabled,

If she wants to spend the rest of her life wiping bottoms,

If she wants to cuddle them and comfort them, while secretly hating them,

If she wants to ask *'ça va?'* as they writhe in front of her in convulsions,

If she wants to watch bodies gradually deforming, sinews shortening, muscles atrophying, bones turning brittle, speech deteriorating,

If she wants to wake up in the middle of the night drenched in sweat wondering if she's wet her bed,

I smile, well, this is hard work but it's very rewarding, it has to be said,

She raises her eyes and looks at me for the first time, hopefully, you think so?

My mum has written, five emails already, how long since I was last online? she's worried, or rather: she sounds frantic, her emails are full of typos: *Blanka, for godsakes, get in tuoch, whats going on, you've not wirtten for a week, is something wrong? has something happnd? We're off to Čausa with Klára for a fes days, we won't be online, get in touch pleas… "*

I've completely forgotten they're going to our cottage in Central Slovakia, ah, my happy summers in the bosom of nature, playing table tennis with my cousins, plastic animals on the carpet, hiking in the mountains and a courtyard shared with thieving neighbours who've been helping themselves to tools from our shed for years, who regularly ask to use our shower to save them the cost of hot water, because we posh people from the capital can afford it,

I log out, the mere thought of replying exhausts me, and what could I say anyway, they must have sensed what's going on with me a long time ago, the diarrhoea tablets I've been taking for a week now, why else would my sister have packed them, I'll soon wean myself off them, in fact, I only take them as a precaution now, I'm not so scared anymore that,

What's the point of writing, they've long realised that their little Blanka is growing up, finally turning into a woman, learning to gain control of her mind and body, she doesn't always manage it, but everything needs time, at least that's what people say, right? so what's the point of writing before this process is complete?

I get up from the computer, Ahmad bars my way, grinning as he always does when he sees me,

This Arab guy won't leave me alone, he constantly seeks me out, bars my way with his wheelchair, says *'a-hoj, Blan-ka,'* wants me to help him have a pee, invites me to his room to watch *Matrix* and every now and then makes a comment about my tight azure blue T-shirt, how it suits me, how pretty I am, how white,

And he's always beaming, speaking slowly, spluttering, I can hardly understand what he says, sometimes I have to bend down to hear him and every time he uses the opportunity to touch me, to have a squeeze of my shoulder or hip,

Drago sees this sometimes and then whispers, he's coming on to you, be careful, he's is really trying to chat you up, then he bursts out laughing, the wicked Drago,

But he's in a foul mood today, I must have done something to upset him again, he says, why are you being so selfish, but Blanka why, why don't you oblige him, what would it cost you to watch bloody *Matrix* with him just once?

He turns to Ahmad, *'écoute, mon ami',* we'll come to your room tonight and we'll watch a film together, 'd'accord?' And mademoiselle here will also be there, you have my word for it, we just have to go to the laundry room now, put some clothes in the wash, but we'll be there after dinner, agreed? a deal!

A *pistolet* is hanging from the back of the wheelchair, filled to the brim, it stinks, the whole room is steeped in the stench, it makes me queasy but I don't dare say anything, or go and empty it in the toilet, what if Ahmad feels hurt, what if it makes him feel that I find his urine unpleasant,

Drago is standing by the window choosing DVDs from a shelf and commenting on them, I say, Ahmad, I'd never have thought you'd have Britney Spears, wow,

I jump to my feet and plant my hands on my hips: *She's so lucky, she's a star, but she cry, cry, cries in her lonely heart, thinking, if there's nothing missing in my life, then why...* can't remember the rest,

Drago grins, then whispers, nice singing, but I think Ahmad uses the cassette for other purposes...

I don't understand,

I mean, Ahmad uses it, you know what I mean, maybe it helps him, when he wants to... hm,

I whisper: you think Ahmad masturbates to a Britney Spears cassette?

Drago winks: you got it in one!

I wince, glance at Ahmad who's lying in bed but Drago has already picked up another DVD, what do we have here, *A.I.*, I've heard about this one, it's supposed to be quite good, it's a Spielberg movie,

We sit on the floor with our backs to the door, I don't even notice the smell of urine anymore, my eyes are fixed on the screen, but the dialogue eludes me, I don't understand a word, yet as I sit there, I'm getting more and more scared, as if I knew what was going on, in a kind of intuitive way,

I'm beginning to understand why Drago picked this film, what he was trying to tell me, the robot-boy who hurts everyone around him, who can't understand human relationships, connections, who always takes and never gives,

That boy is me,

I close my eyes, I don't want to watch this. I wish I could turn it off, but I don't dare suggest it. There's an appalling rumbling in my belly, my anxiety is growing, there's a knot in my stomach, I don't want to be like this, I don't want to bulldoze everyone, I don't want to be a robot,

Drago remains silent, glances at me from time to time, watches me, saying nothing,

I jump up, mumbling, I'll be right back,

Out in the corridor I lean against the wall, take deep breaths, I have to get a grip on this, the film, the truth about myself, I have to face up to it, change myself,

Drago comes running out of the room soon afterwards, I'm sure it's because of me,

He can't stand it with me any longer, he's at the end of his tether, the film was a last-ditch attempt to change me, to make me think about myself,

I'm scared of losing him,

After the film, as we unload the washing machine, he can't control himself anymore and explodes, Blanka, will you please tell me why you sat through most of this film although you clearly didn't want to?

I say nothing,

'Stop lying to me, OK? Stop playing games, I'm really getting fed up!'

'But Drago, I don't know what to do, I don't know what you want me to do,'

He clasps my face in his hands, just stop lying, to yourself and to others, am I making myself clear? can you manage that? are you even capable of that?

Back in our room I undress in the dark, suddenly Drago beckons to me to come to the window, look at those two, in the house across the road,

I left my glasses on the fridge, I can't see anything at first, it's just a blur, some light in one of the windows,

But slowly my eyes focus, as if of their own accord, the outlines become clearer,

I see it now, it's a couple making love, on the floor, on yellow tiles, their bodies intertwined,

I see him thrusting, grabbing her hair, his face distorted in arousal,

Is it possible that I can control my vision? That I can improve it by my own willpower?

I give a laugh, slightly embarrassed, turn away,

Drago is grumpy, just don't tell anyone, especially not the women next door, I don't want everyone to watch this like some spectacle, it's made me totally depressed,

And after a pause: I've been alone for two years now,

The next morning, I wake up feeling that I have to start working on myself, that's the reason why I say yes to an invitation from

Sylvester, a toothless, legless old man,

I walk around his room admiring his pictures, he's painted them himself, in tempera, huge canvases covered in a tangle of lines, from left to right, from top to bottom, everything is splattered,

I don't understand anything,

I walk from one painting to the next nodding with admiration,

I smile at the old man parked in the middle of the room, every now and then I say

'mais c'est magnifique!' and also *'quelles couleurs!'*

I don't know what else I can say about it,

Suddenly I notice that not only is Sylvester missing his legs from the knee down and most of his teeth, but also his fingers, he has just stumps covered in skin,

Sylvester notices my gaze, smiles triumphantly,

"In my mouth, I hold the paintbrush in my mouth,"

I even manage to reply to mum's text, like a good girl, *everything's fine, don't worry, I'm run off my feet, on my way to wipe Laurence's bum, have a good time in Causa,*

We serve lunch, each table gets a bowl of salad, a carafe of water and wine, napkins and trays with beef, and that's when I spot her, as in a flash of revelation, it's little Amélie, she is tottering around the room, her head down on her chest, bent double, hunched up, eyes nailed to the floor,

She's ashamed, it's blindingly obvious, she's ashamed of her body, of her budding breasts,

But something… For a moment I see her like that, quite normally,

For a moment she seems upright, then again, she's all twisted,

My head spins, what's happening to my vision?

I go up to Drago, whisper to him, do you see that girl over there, next to Olivier?

'Yeah, what about her?'

'See how hunched up she is? it's horrible, ruining her spine like that, even though she's quite pretty, her name is Amélie, I talked to her yesterday but, Jesus, why is she so dreadfully hunched up?'

Drago smiles at me, suddenly he hugs me tight, 'Blanka, do you know what's just happened? Do you know what you just did?'

I'm almost frightened, what did I do?

'You've actually started taking notice of other people! you're on the mend,' he adds cheerfully,

Early in the evening we hug each other again, spontaneously, like two friends who haven't seen each other in years,

We meet halfway between the main building and the annexe, by the flower beds, Drago opens his arms, I throw my arms around him, cling to his huge six-foot frame,

'My darling Drago,'

'Blanka, my dear girl',

Hold your hands like this, he shows me, while I giggle like an idiot, are you serious?

We're standing in front of the mirror, Drago has decided we would brush each other's teeth, I his, he mine, we'll try doing it at the same time, to make it more of a challenge,

The girls next door have gone to bed already, we're the only ones still up, our voices echo in the bathroom, green tiles, piercing light, our arms intertwined,

Spit out, rinse,

Drago encourages me, don't worry, press harder, brush properly,

'I don't want to make your gums bleed,'

'So what, bleeding gums won't kill me,'

Done!

He bares his teeth, well, clean now?

I nod happily,

Drago frowns, 'bollocks, they're totally yellow, bloody hell, Blanka, can't you be honest for once, you can't always say to people what they want to hear,'

And on the way from the bathroom he adds, 'the more you try, the less you see,'

'Have you seen *Papillon*, with Dustin Hoffman?'

We're in our room, each in our own bed, I'm by the wall, Drago by the window, I was just dropping off when he asked, I roll over to look at him but see only a faint outline in the dark,

'No, why, is it any good?'

'It's not really about whether it's good or not, it's more about the plot, it's a story of these two convicts, they've spent years and years exiled on this island and they eventually manage to escape… I don't think I could last so many years in prison, I'm sure I'd go around the bend or kill myself…'

He speaks very softly, then sighs, oh, never mind, good night, Blanka,

A minute later he's fast asleep, I hear his peaceful, regular breathing,

I replay the exchange in my head, what was he trying to tell me? why mention prison, people suffering injustice, death and madness? What's it got to do with me?

And then it dawns on me: maybe it was a warning? That something like that could happen to me if I don't start behaving normally, don't stop being a pain in the neck? That they've been thinking of the best way to get rid of me?

Suddenly a chill runs down my spine: there are two Arab women in our group, how come I haven't figured it out sooner! Peter did warn me before I left but I laughed it off, silly me, he knew perfectly well why he said that at the station in Košice, maybe he already had an inkling,

I jump out of bed, run over to Drago, shake him, Drago, Drago, wake up please, I've got to ask you something, and Drago, drowsily, what is it? what's it this time, Blanka? just let me sleep,

'Drago, promise you won't sell me to a harem? tell me you won't sell me to a harem, to some Arab guy,'

'What… what harem? What are you on about now?'

His surprise looks genuine, maybe they haven't been planning it after all, I say: oh, I was just wondering if perhaps you might want to sell me to a harem, like, to get rid of me,

'Blanka, I will keep you in my own harem, OK? please go to sleep now,'

I go back to my bed, repeating: in the Slovene guy's harem, in the Slovene guy's harem…

The idea sounds quite appealing,

'You don't have to follow me everywhere, Blanka, can't you find something better to do, all right, come along if you really want to, but I have to warn you, you'll be bored,'

Earlier this morning Drago borrowed a fishing rod from the deaf-and-dumb internet room manager, asked Ingeborg to give him a lift and is now packing up his gear in our room, while I sit on the bed, giving him imploring looks even though it's obvious that he'd rather go on his own,

In the end he gives in, what am I to do with you,

I take my yellow notebook, the one in which I used to write down Peter's text messages back at home, when they still seemed important, and also my camera, the one dad brought me from America,

Ingeborg takes the van, drives us all the way to the promenade and promises to pick us up in two hours,

We climb over the fence and we're on the rocks, facing the islands d'If and Frioul, the beaches and white cliffs on the left,

Drago prepares his rod, I put some of his suntan lotion on my face and lie down on the rocks,

I squint into the sun watching Drago as he takes a few steps, he's now stopped right on the edge, the rod is in the water, I'm convinced he won't catch anything, I'm convinced the fish are not that daft,

I doodle in my notebook and watch Drago, he barely moves from the same spot for the two hours, only once coming back for some mineral water,

Not biting? I give him a smile him and show him a picture I've drawn, it's me jumping out of a pram saying: please forgive me, I'm sorry that I exist,

I translate the writing for Drago, I say that it means, roughly, *I'm sorry that my existence is bothering you,* he smiles and says, so this is Blanka as a baby that's constantly crying and apologising, spot on, now you should draw Blanka as a bulldozer that crushes everyone to make it perfectly clear that,

We're sitting on a bench, if you can call it that, it's a kind of stone structure that runs the length of the promenade, the fishing rod has been stowed away, as superfluous as it's been throughout this entire fishing expedition, Drago's arm is around my shoulders, he doesn't seem too disappointed,

Every now and then a man in a tracksuit runs past, whenever it happens, I turn my head in sync with him and tell myself how lucky I am to be sitting here, lucky that I don't have to run,

Drago talks about his sister who expends too much energy on other people, she's capable of sacrifice and many people take advantage, her name is Špela and the two of them are like day and night, they're totally, but totally, unlike each other,

For a second I wish we were friends, me and Špela, I wish she would sacrifice herself for me, too, but I don't say it out loud of course, I just say I hadn't noticed the colour of his eyes so I lean close to take a look and I see myself reflected in his pupils, a discovery on which I comment effusively,

Drago isn't cross with me, he lets me jabber on, we're both happy, relaxed, maybe it's to do with the time we've wasted so successfully, maybe it's the sun being so serene in the early evening,

A big garden spider runs down the bench, next to Drago, I jump up and start yelling hysterically, a spider, a spider! I cover my mouth with my hand in horror, but Drago doesn't even move, he just rolls his eyes, so what, a spider, and when he sees I'm still frozen, he asks: so you're going to gawp at it now to make yourself even more scared? and gives the spider a flick, sending it flying down to the ground and it disappears in a crack between the rocks, maybe dead, or perhaps just with a leg torn off,

Ingeborg arrives, she hasn't brought the van but an ordinary car, she's pissed off, she gets started straight away, tells us that everything that could possibly have gone tits up at the Centre today did go tits up, I'm in the back seat with my left arm sticking out of the window, listening to Bob Marley on the radio, I don't really follow Ingeborg's account, she's mostly talking to Drago anyway but I do catch the bit about Luca burning the celebratory meal, there's a party at the Centre tonight, he's burned the seafood risotto and then ran riot in the kitchen, giving the elderly cooks a fright,

'You didn't catch something by any chance, did you, it would come in handy now,'

We turn right at Pharo Park, away from the sea, Drago shakes his head, oh well, Luca ought to control himself a little, why does he always have to act like a bloody stereotypical Italian, he's totally fed up with him, and then he says,

'Some people are so fucking living their own lives,'

And he looks at me when he says that, he even turns to me in his seat so there's no doubt that he also means me, he means especially me,

The dining room is festooned with streamers, balloons, candles, the tables have been pushed together and arranged in a semicircle, at least two carafes of wine on each, a radio on the floor in a corner blasting out awful *Nostalgie* station tunes, nurses tottering about the place, residents buzzing around in wheelchairs, Jean-Claude the night guard running around with a water pistol squirting everyone who bumps into him, Martina sitting on the edge of the swimming pool, laughing, Luca trying to make himself heard over the racket and get everyone organised,

Drago and I stop in the doorway, mildly annoyed that the day should end miserably like this, we grab some nuts, crisps and dried fruit from the table and sneak away to sit on chairs by the pool and observe the goings-on impassively from there,

Before dinner Jean-Claude throws a squealing Martina into the water, she climbs out and runs after him, the squelching of trainers, water streaming off her, her blue T-shirt now see-through it's so wet,

Drago says it's bad for her, Luca should fetch her something to put on, a jumper or something, so she doesn't catch her death, he's being irresponsible, but it's not really Drago's problem,

And later, after dinner, free entertainment on the dance floor, tables pushed to the walls to make more room, nurses dancing with wheelchairs, spinning them around the room, the residents laugh, stammer, splutter with joy, gratitude, exhilaration,

After dusk the deaf-and-dumb internet manager comes up to us, asking for his fishing rod back, he raises his right hand and turns it palm up, nods and points to the rod, then to the empty bucket, Drago gives a shrug to say no, he didn't catch anything, the two of them share a laugh,

Jean-Claude again, by now he's got me, too, completely drenched, he'd like to throw me into the pool as well, like Martina, but Drago gives him such a death stare that he changes his mind and takes himself off with this water pistol,

All this has given me a headache, I'm tired and just then I notice Olivier, he's stood up, leaning on his wheelchair but standing on his own two feet, standing up and singing, belting out the Marseillaise, with everyone applauding, cheering him on, I stare at him and the meaning of it doesn't sink in at first, Olivier is standing although he's paralysed, all he needed was a few drinks and he's forgotten about his disability, all it took was a little willpower, a bit of an effort, but nobody seems to be surprised, nobody shouts, it's a miracle, they all know that any one of them could walk, straighten up and start to live like a normal human being, without a wheelchair, without the Belle-vue Centre, any one of them could stand on their own feet, they just don't want to, they're scared of the world out there, of the hatred, they want to remain children until the day they die, they want someone to look after them, change their nappies, wash them, they don't want to take their place among the adults, be responsible for their own lives,

And then Olivier plops back into his wheelchair with all his weight, some thirty seconds have passed, I guess he's realised that he'd overdone it, given himself away, maybe he's scared that he might be thrown out, but no, everyone smiles at him, pats him on the shoulder, how could they be angry with him, they're all just children, incapacitated, frightened, simple-minded, and it's our job to look after them, comfort them, keep them at this larval stage,

I'm on the afternoon shift, Drago says he has to go into town and get some money out of the bank but later, when I return to our room, I find him on the bed, he's lying there staring at the ceiling and when he sees me he sits up and says he doesn't feel like going anywhere, maybe we could go for a swim, what do you think, you can't be too busy, it's only the afternoon shift,

This is actually the first time I use the Bellevue swimming pool, until now I've only been swimming in the sea, at first it feels like we're behaving indecently somehow, in full view of the residents sitting in the communal lounge watching TV, and we're splashing about in the chlorinated water outside their window, fooling around, but soon I forget about them, all that's left is Drago and the swimming pool hoist that we cling to, holding our breath, strokes under water, diving, headstands, somersaults, laughter,

I'm leaning against the swimming pool wall with Drago facing me, so close it's almost alarming, he grabs my forearms but lets go of them immediately, water drips down his cheeks and nose, water streams onto us from the wall and Drago says the stream of water is like a vibrator, it feels nice, try putting your hand under it,

I slap him on the head, gently, playfully, I'm not listening to this kind of banter, understood? I pretend to be angry but in fact I'm not really angry, I put my arms around his neck and he says I've surprised him again, he didn't expect this, this delight in water, in fact I'm rather good, I told a lie the other night about the handstands, I'm actually rather good at it!

Suddenly he grabs me around the waist, lifts me up and deposits me on the side of the pool with one powerful swing of the arms, although I'm really heavy with all the water streaming off me, I sit there splashing him with my feet but he gets out as well, hoists himself up on his arms and I notice he has a hard-on, I look away quickly so he doesn't see me smile but he must have noticed because he quickly lies down on his stomach, resting his head on his folded arms,

I sit on his buttocks and start massaging suntan lotion into his back, he likes it, says I would make a good *masseuse* and just then Ahmad stops next to us in his wheelchair and says the yellow swimsuit makes me look like a canary, just like a canary, smiling as he says that, but it's a sinister kind of smile, that grinning face in the sun, the rigidity, the rictus,

All of a sudden I feel it's gone dark and cold, I get goose pimples on my arms, the cheerful mood of a few minutes ago is gone, I get up, hurriedly wrap myself in a towel and move away without a word, I want to go back to my room and get changed as soon as possible, I want to lie down on the bed, close my eyes and forget Drago's erection and Ahmad's gaze, but as I walk down the lounge, Marie suddenly stops in front of me, bars my way with her wheelchair, I try to walk around her, push the wheelchair aside, I smile apologetically, but she grabs hold of my hand, squeezes it with all her might and asks, when do you bugger off, when will you finally get the hell out of here if you despise us so much, if we make you so sick?! and as she says this she stares at me with so much hatred in her eyes that I only manage a few words, I just stutter, I-I-I don't know... I am leaving... I might, and I start running, into the depth of Bellevue,

Drago finds me cowering in the stairwell, he's put some clothes back on, he's wearing blue shorts and a white T-shirt, his curly hair is dry, he sees me there, crying, sits down next to me with a resigned sigh, what is it now, Blanka, he asks, why are you crying, tell me please, and I start muttering, incoherent sentences, 'she said I hate them... she really did... she wants me to leave... asked when I was leaving... she asked me out of the blue... what makes her think... what have I done to her...

I don't know what I've done to her... what should I do, Drago... everyone hates me here... do you hear me, they all hate me!'

Drago hugs me, holding me in his arms for a long time, tells me to calm down, caresses my head, 'everything's going to be all right, just calm down please,' he keeps repeating, but I know that nothing is going to be all right, he's only saying it to stop me crying, because of course I know, we've been through this so many times before, the hatred and how to live with it, the omnipresent hatred, the hatred of the whole world, and yet, this is the first irrefutable proof that it's true, Marie didn't mince her words, she articulated her hatred for me and I know she really meant it, even though Drago insists it's not true, even though he lies that everything is going to be all right, 'it's a misunderstanding, we'll sort it out, come on, let's go and see her together, you'll tell her that she's wrong, that she's misunderstood, just stop crying please, you don't want to give her the satisfaction,'

As I get up, my head is spinning, for a moment I can't see anything, but Drago holds me tight, I've stopped crying now, I splash some water on my eyes in the toilet, they're still a bit red but she might not notice, I can see her now, her wheelchair is parked in a corner, our eyes meet, I walk up to her and say she got it all wrong, it isn't at all the way she thinks it is,

She listens to me with a smile, I'm smiling too, we smile at each other and we both know that in reality we hate each other, that all this is just a show for the benefit of the others, we're like two tragic actresses who would scratch each other's eyes out backstage if they could,

And suddenly I feel superior again, it's the superiority of the healthy over the sick, my smile broadens, it's almost genuine now, I am sincerely pleased that I'm standing here in front of her and she's sitting in front of me, and I tell myself, I'll be out of this place in two weeks' time but you, dear Marie, you're going to rot here for the rest of your life,

Xavier shrugs, it's no big deal, we should just tick the box that seems most appropriate, these forms are only for information, internal stuff, and it's all anonymous, for Concordia, the French equivalent of Inex, they just want to know what we think of the camp, if we like it here, if we're happy with the Bellevue Centre,

We're sitting on the plastic chairs by the swimming pool, it's almost midnight and Drago is calmly ticking boxes, working his way systematically from one question to the next, every now and then he gives a yawn and never manages to cover his mouth with his hand in time, he's lazy, bored, like he couldn't care less, like the answers don't really matter,

I give him a baffled look, doesn't he get it or is he just pretending? I pore over the questionnaire in a frenzied state, dozens of pernicious questions, do you like the food: very much – not very much, how do you find the work: very difficult – very easy, would you come again: most probably yes – most probably not, lots of other questions,

I'm seized by panic, it keeps growing, surely this is a trap, a ploy to expose me, to prove my guilt, I need Drago's advice, I need him to tell me which box to tick, I chew at the fingernails on my right hand furiously, I don't know what to do, bloody hell, how am I supposed to work out which questions really matter and which ones are just there to pull the wool over my eyes,

I look up, Martina has just handed in her questionnaire while I haven't answered a single question yet, I notice that Xavier is looking at me, when our eyes meet he smiles and says it's nothing to worry about and winks, don't worry, we're not going to tell the cooks if you say you don't like the food,

I chat to Xavier for a while, he says he remembers me from the first day, how I barged into the room with that enormous rucksack on my back and stood there bewildered, he laughs and says I look just as bewildered now as I did two weeks ago,

'If not more,' he pokes my side,

I manage to force a laugh,

It's two in the morning, I'm standing in the shower, I've only just managed to soap myself down, I'm leaning against the wall, letting the water stream down my body, but my hand holding the showerhead keeps flapping limply by my side, I wonder if it would look very stupid if I called Drago and asked him to give me a hand, like the other day when we brushed each other's teeth, to wrap me in a towel and carry me to bed, tuck me in and wish me good night, but I don't have the strength to shout to him through the wall,

I crouch down and stare into the drain, at the water disappearing into the ground in a whirl, any remaining strength I might have has being washed away with the dirt, I close my eyes, I want to dissolve and drain away too, to bring this entire machinery to a halt, to alight from myself like you get off a train, pretend that all this has nothing to with me, that it's just passing me by, I wish I could just watch like a dispassionate observer,

I'm suddenly frightened by the recent physical transformations that have made me so happy, what am I turning into, what kind of monster, capable of regulating her own vision, twisting anyone around my little finger, I don't want to live in this world that's filled with hatred, insecurity, loneliness, I don't want to adapt to it totally, be one of them, if I could I would lapse back into carefree childhood, into ignorance,

Except that it's impossible, it's obvious to me, I've reached the point of no return, the turning point was the moment when Marie openly declared war on me and the only thing I can do now is respond in kind,

Martina says: let's go Pharo Park, it'll be fun, we can turn somersaults like last time, Ingeborg says: absolutely not, we're going to the seaside, I suggest Plage du prophète, we had such a good time there the other day and it's not that far either, Elena says, 'count me out, ladies and gentleman, I'm staying here at the Centre and will finally get a proper manicure, I'm not wasting my day off on some… what was it? somersaults?' Luca gives a spiteful laugh, Martina glares at him, a few days ago she confided in me that things hadn't been going so well lately, she's no longer thinking of ditching college for a life of bliss in the south of Italy, although I don't give a toss what Martina does, what she thinks, what she lives for, Drago keeps quiet, sipping his coffee and I keep telling myself: we'll go to Cassis, I want us to go to Cassis, you will do as I say, but I don't say it out loud because I'm convinced it's not necessary, they will succumb to my will one way or another, they'll all bend to my will,

I get up from the table leaving a pile of breadcrumbs and sticky splodges of honey, let others wipe it off, clean it, lick it, I will never demean myself before other people again, I am on my way out of the dining room, and suddenly see something familiar out of the corner of my eye, something that reminds me of home, I squint to get a better view of the TV that's permanently playing in the corner, I come closer, can't believe my eyes but it's true, there's Armageddon in Prague, the Lesser Town is under water, Werich's house flooded up to the first floor, the

Vltava churning its way down city streets, I see people swept along by the current, people on top of wardrobes, people on roofs waving to airplanes,

unperturbed I tell myself, my sister and her family live in Prague, who knows if they're safe, if they managed to escape, it looks terrifying, like the beginning of the end, and yet I'm not shocked at all by the possibility that my sister is now floating down the Vltava clinging to some driftwood, a kitchen door for example, Prague is so far away and what separates me from it is much more than just kilometres, Prague simply doesn't concern me anymore, this morning I realised that my transformation is complete,

Yasim comes up to me and asks if the city on the telly is anywhere near my part of the world, yes, I say, this is Prague, I correct myself, this was Prague, a city that used to be important to me, Yasmin laughs, wow, you seem to be in a fatalistic mood today, she gives me a cheeky pat on the back and I wonder for a moment if I should kill her on the spot, swat her down with one mighty swing of the arm until she bursts like some annoying insect, but Drago stops me with an imperceptible movement of his head, a gentle nod that means no, he stares at me hard, he also understands, who else should understand if not he, my companion, I can see in his eyes that he's proud of me, although he may not be able to gauge the full extent of my power, its range, or rather, the way it has expanded, the power that suffuses me, he is proud like a teacher who's been outshone by his own pupil, I give him a conspiratorial smile which encompasses everything, understanding and reassurance, don't worry, even if I decide to kill everyone, I will spare you, you are important to me,

I walk down the corridor, past wheelchairs, cripples with a sense of self-preservation that is sufficiently developed to realise that they mustn't ask me for anything today, or ever, the gulf between us is too vast, they're worms and I'm God, although I don't actually need people in wheelchairs to realise that I am God, it's so obvious, so self-evident that I want to laugh and I do, I roar with laughter, I don't even notice that someone is following me, I'm not aware of the sound of wheels gliding down the linoleum, of the inarticulate yelling, only once outside do I realise it's Laurence, she's shouting at me, shoving something into my hand, I pick it up and see that it's photos, a page ripped from a photo album,

the first photo shows Laurence lying in the grass, in dark glasses, a white hoodie, her wasted legs tucked into a sleeping bag, bending over her an older woman with grey hair, maybe her mother, and all around, parked wheelchairs, disabled people in the grass, it looks like a camp for the disabled, an outing of some sort,

the other picture is also of Laurence, this time in close-up, checked orange trousers, pink jumper, she's lying by the side of a forest path, her legs strangely gnarled sideways, her face stares out at the photographer, slightly twisted in a rictus smile, white teeth bared, next to her lies a girl in black, curled up, legs close to her body, hands pillowing her head, maybe her sister,

I look at the two photos and don't understand what it's all about, I try to hand them back to her but she shakes her head, waves her hand, no, they're both for me, she's ripped them out for me, she wants to give them to me, I stand there for a moment, taken aback, why did she do that, why did she ruin her photo album just because of me, why is it so important to her that I have these two banal photos, why did she insist on ripping them out instead of asking a nurse to gently unpeel them from the photo album,

I feel I ought to give her something in exchange, I remember the postcards of Bratislava in my backpack, without a word I dash over to the little house by the bamboo grove, only Elena is staying there now but it's where I've left my seventy-litre backpack, at the bottom of which should be those picturesque postcards and a pop-up book,

I rummage through the rucksack, suddenly a phone rings, since when has there been a phone in the little house? I trace the sound to the other room, pick it up, someone is asking for Elena in French, is she there, do I know where she might be, can I tell her to call back as soon as possible, it's important?

I run back up the hill telling myself this could have been a trap, who knows, maybe Laurence isn't for real either, they've realised how powerful I am and now they're doing everything they can to distract me so that I can't focus on my destructive plans, they must be worried that I'll set fire to the Bellevue Centre, to Marseille, the whole world, I feel that just by focusing my gaze I could set a tree on fire, tear down a building, they sense it but in spite of that I look for Elena, I'm not quite sure if I want this, all the destruction, the killing, the deluge, the dead, I hate them, I know that it's the only certainty in my life, but is that reason enough to kill?

I run across the car park in front of the main building, among the vans, Laurence, too, is sitting there in her wheelchair, she shouts at me but I'm in a hurry, I have to find Elena now, she's in the computer room, she's been trying to set up an email account for three days now, she's not quite up to it but none of us has offered to help her, I stop in the doorway and say, Elena, I'm so glad I've found you, there was a phone call for you in the little house, something urgent, you should call them back as soon as possible, and Elena goes, but who was the call from? I look at her, puzzled, it was them, of course, of course, but who is them? Well, you ought to know that! I snap and run back,

I pass the laundry room, Drago calls out to me, he's in there ironing a shirt, he tells me something but I don't take it in, I say yes, of course, and keep running down the corridor, Martina stops me in the lounge, have a look at this cake, isn't it wonderful?! it's for Joëlle and Frédéric's wedding anniversary, they've been together for ten years, oh, I'd love a slice! I look at the cake and it starts to transform before my eyes in a strange way, at first it seems to be near and in focus, then it moves away, becomes blurred, but never mind, that doesn't bother me now, now I know for sure that they're doing everything they can to distract me, they want to save their skins, I don't blame them, if I were in their shoes I'd also be fighting for my life, I wouldn't accept a cruel fate either,

we're in the van, bouncing around, Luca is at the wheel, Drago lying next to me, face covered by his straw hat, he removes it every now and then and stares at me, sort of reproachfully, sometimes it seems he's about to tell me something, to open his mouth but then he changes his mind, my eyes are fixed on him, full of hatred, I don't really know why I suddenly hate him so much, what is it that I have against him, I just hate him and make my feelings clear until he can't stand it anymore and throws his hat at me, stop it, Blanka, will you? he laughs and I turn my back on him, offended, although all the hatred is gone in a flash,

I turn to listen to what Xavier is saying, he's with us in the van, sitting in the front, leaning against the door, deep in conversation with Martina but I can see him casting furtive glances towards me, he's registering what's going on between me and

Drago, he sees everything while telling Martina that there are dozens of pyromaniacs around here, in the south of France, so many crazy people who start fires in the summer months, in August, when there's no rain, the grass is tinder-dry, he shakes his head, isn't that awful,

anxiety grips my throat, panic seizes me, has he been reading my thoughts? I quickly look away from the window, I don't want to see those flammable trees, I could set them on fire merely by looking at them, I could make them go up in flames in an instant, it terrifies me as much as Xavier's presence, now I understand why he's come with us, he's been sent by the high-ups to keep an eye on me, they've read my answers to the questionnaire and now they know, everything is clear to them now, Xavier is here to make sure I don't destroy the whole world, to prevent me from committing the horrendous things I'm capable of, they know I'm out of control, the Slovene hasn't managed to carry out his assignment so they've sent someone else, Xavier, he must be very strong, perhaps he's a God too and wants to pit his strength against another God.

Luca brakes abruptly, we get out of the van, we're in Cassis, the white cliffs on the left, the village on the right, of course, another confirmation of my omnipotence, earlier today I expressed a wish that we should go to Cassis, no one else suggested it, and yet here we are now, here of all places, walking down a tarmac road towards the rocky beach,

we find a place near the cliffs, I change into my swimming costume, run into the sea, literally run, sharp stones cut into my feet, I trip and graze my knees on the rocks, they start to bleed, I don't care, I hurl myself into the water, almost hoping that some undercurrent will overpower my legs and drag me away, a kilometre from the beach, somewhere far away from Xavier,

I sit on a rock, ask Drago for his suntan lotion again, I forgot to bring mine, like so often before, Drago laughs, he says I'm a fetishist, I love my body too much, I take pathological pride in it, it's not healthy, he says, as if he didn't see all the wounds I am bleeding from, how bruised and battered I am all over,

Xavier starts to take pictures of me, without saying a word, close-ups, he concentrates, he's capturing my likeness for eternity, it must be their documentation, to have my pictures on file in case I kill someone, he takes photos of me as if I were a dangerous criminal, which is what I am, in fact, I don't smile, you're not supposed to smile in police mug shots, I even cooperate, turn sideways so he can get a profile shot, as is right and proper, but enough is enough, I want to leave, get away from this sickening beach where I've shed so much blood, and as if on command everyone starts getting up, packing up their things, getting dressed, incredible, they always sense what I want them to do, they always succumb, they must be so scared of me,

we climb up the hill towards the van, I'm the last, I pick up an empty cigarette packet lying in the grass, turn it around in my hand, look at it, Drago catches up with me, we walk in silence for a while, then he says, fuming, why are you so quiet, you seem lost in thought, won't let anyone close, you're actually enjoying it, aren't you, being all alone with your thoughts, with your hatred? he's waiting for my reaction, gazing at me provocatively, I throw the cigarette packet away, yes, I shrug, I'm enjoying it, the last thing I need is to let some Slovene brat provoke me,

we walk through a pine grove, soon we catch up with the others, they've stopped in a clearing, a picnic spot, benches, tables, even some litter bins, we unpack our plentiful supplies and start eating, so much grub, it would be enough for a week, after lunch I take Laurence's photos out of my bag and look at them, I repeat to myself, Laurence loves me, Laurence is a human being, I mustn't hurt Laurence, I mustn't kill her, she's ruined her photo album just for my sake, that means something,

I rest my head in the older Algerian woman's lap, she strokes my hair and repeats, *ma fille, ma pauvre fille,* as if trying to comfort me and indeed, all of a sudden I feel like crying, I'm frightened that I might kill someone, I'm frightened that I will cause an accident, the van bounces up and down again, the bends are too sharp and with Luca at the wheel the Algerian woman must be afraid too, that's why she is treating me so kindly, almost maternally, that's why she is stroking my hair, trying to rekindle the last vestiges of humanity in me, I turn around and catch Drago's disgusted look, but Drago, this really is the best way to save us, by channelling my power which I can't control myself, this old Algerian woman is not as stupid as you might think, I tell him in my head,

we're in a car park, the motorway rumbles high overhead on a viaduct, we pick up our bags and start walking down the tarmac road in the direction we guess the sea might be, I walk in silence alongside Drago, who is kicking at tiny stones, also in silence, it's hot, the road is melting, giving off steam, there are beads of sweat even between my fingers, we stop at a few stands, I want to buy a *serviette de plage* and suntan lotion, we've used up almost all of Drago's but everything is dreadfully expensive, everything costs a packet, thirty euros for a spray, Drago shakes his head every time, forget it, I won't let you waste that sort of money, and when I insist that I can afford it, he reminds me: didn't you ask me to keep an eye on you, make sure you don't buy rubbish, and especially no rash purchases?

we run to catch up with the others, they haven't waited for us, Martina walks arm in arm with Xavier, Luca obviously doesn't care, he's happily chatting to Ingeborg, we walk along the hot sand almost as far as the sea, lay our towels down and I stare wide-eyed as Xavier puts a huge book on his beach towel, is it any good, Martina asks, and he says, it's not bad, a novel about the clash of civilisations,

I strip down to my swimming costume, Drago and I get up at the same time and head for the sea, we elbow our way through the crowds, this beach is very different from the other one, it's sandy, packed, noisy, the water is dark green, murky, I don't like it, I barely dip in and say to Drago, let's go back, no more swimming today,

we share a beach towel, Drago digs out a little seashell from the sand and hands it to me, a little present, just for you, I smile and stow it in my bag, I haven't brought anything to read so I just squint into the sun and gleefully observe all the shapeless bodies sprawling around me or walking along the beach, the others talk, I don't listen, I feel good, languid, I'm dozing off, then suddenly I catch the word harem, I turn around in panic, did someone say harem?

my eyes flit from one person to another, so my foreboding the other night was true, they are planning to sell me to a harem, suddenly everyone bursts out laughing, faces contorted in a grimace of joy, shiny with sun and sweat, teeth bared ominously, they are laughing at me, I've fallen into their trap, there's no escape now, they're talking about me, the life that awaits me in the Slovene's harem,

I will spend the rest of my life as a slave, sharing Drago with other women – who knows how many he keeps in that house between two motorways – I will struggle in vain to break free, will keep trying to escape only to be caught every time, it's quite certain now, I'll spend the rest of my life in the wild Balkans, in Slovenia, the country that has become my destiny,

what will they say at home when they find out, if they ever do? will Drago let me make at least one phone call to my mum to let her know, ask her to send me some clothes, my stuff, and what about Peter, poor chap, we were planning to start a family, have children, that's not going to happen now, we'll never have children, we'll have nothing, but he had sensed it, this is exactly what he warned me about, he predicted it but I wouldn't listen, I laughed at him back in Košice at the station, I wasn't on my guard, I've been winding Drago up, everyone saw it, and now they have all taken his side against me, especially the two Algerian women, the bitch in the headscarf who pretends to be my mother, protector, but in reality,

I jump to my feet, livid, determined not to make it easy for them, I start to pour sand on Drago, I throw it in his face, eyes, mouth, you bastard, I keep repeating in my head, you won't get me so easily, do you hear me? he defends himself, stretches out his arms to stop me, are you off your rocker, Blanka, what's got into you again? everyone stares at me, dumbfounded, suddenly silent,

I start running along the hot sand, towards the car park, away from them, past the stalls with the ridiculously expensive suntan lotions, past stalls with Britney Spears beach towels, I turn back a few times, nobody is chasing me, they've all stayed behind, they must think I have no way of escaping, that I'm trapped, but I'll get away from them, I'll make it to Bratislava somehow, I will hitch a ride, someone is bound to give me a lift, someone will help me if I explain the situation,

I'm walking on the concrete, the soles of my feet are howling with pain, fresh wounds seem to be opening, blisters swelling up, the tarmac is scorching hot, I stop, suddenly unsure, I hop from one foot to the other, there's a motorway bridge ahead, it might lead home, if only I'd brought some money, my passport, but now, how am I going to cross the border, and wearing just my swimming costume at that?

defeated, I let my head sink, all right then, I'll go back to the beach, succumb to the fate I have brought upon myself, I'll accept it, I won't resist, and who knows, maybe I'll come to terms with it one day, blend into the Slovene's harem, maybe even reach an important position within it, if I am a good wife to Drago, obedient, meek, docile, if I fulfil all his wishes and never talk back,

I join him on the beach towel, he pays no attention to me, he's talking to Martina, I remember the little seashell he gave me less than an hour ago, maybe things won't be so bad after all, I'll get used to my new role, I'll learn to love him, but what about Peter? oh well, Peter can spend the rest of his life jerking off, I chuckle at the idea, but I get a little fright, what if I said it out loud? Drago turns to me, well, are you done fuming? I smile modestly, lower my eyes and say: yes, master, then raise my head and look at the others, most of them are smiling at me, knowingly,

and at that moment I realise, they really mean well, what's the point of all the screaming and seething, isn't it evident, so obvious, so natural, that my place is by Drago's side, and it doesn't matter if I have to share him with five, ten or who knows how many other women, it's probably normal in his country after all, harems in Slovenia, I repeat to myself, as if in a dream, harems in Slovenia, my life has suddenly taken off in a new direction, steam has stopped rising from the pavement, I walk alongside my new master, I walk on the pavement, he on the hard shoulder, suddenly a car coming from behind, it's too close, I swiftly pull Drago onto the pavement, watch out, don't get run over! he seems surprised, my gesture catches me by surprise too, what's got into me, he says softly: I thought you hate me, I shake my head, no, I love you, the words come out of my mouth completely naturally, without thinking, and his face broadens into a smile, he picks me up and lifts me up in the air, I laugh, put me down, you silly Slovene! I knew it, I knew it! he repeats, he looks really happy, he hugs me, I'm happy too,

we hold hands as we walk back to the van, far behind the others, he keeps turning to me, squeezing my hand so hard it's almost painful, so this is what the problem has been all along, I've fallen in love, how straightforward, banal, embarrassing, all the fury, confusion, the theories of hatred and growing up, of my divine essence, and there's this stupid explanation, I'm in love,

Ingeborg is driving so it's not as bumpy, I sit by the open window gazing at the scorched countryside, the sun is setting behind the horizon, the wind blowing in my face, I'm thinking, trying to make sense of it all, trying to put my thoughts in some kind of order, find some sense behind everything that's happened today, is still happening now, I'd like to ask Drago what the deal is with the harem, does he have one at home and is he going to disband it now that he's got me, will he throw those sluts out into the street, sell them, give them to someone as a present, who cares,

I want Drago just to myself, I won't tolerate any other women by his side,

I just hope I'll be enough for him, maybe he can get used to a life as a couple, just him and me, in that house between two motorways,

but first I'll have to sort things out in Bratislava, pack my bags, take a year out, change my resident status, move to Slovenia, the idea unnerves me, it won't be easy, how will I break the news to them at home? my mum won't approve, that's for sure, she'll make a scene, I can almost hear her: think again, Blanka, don't throw away your future just like that, finish your studies at least,

and Peter, he'll be furious too, I know him, he'll appeal to my good sense, argue that I'm immature, duplicitous, cowardly, demand an explanation, I can picture him: Blanka, you've got to be responsible, you have obligations to other people, I happen to be one of them, like it or not, and however hard I might try to make him understand that there's no rational explanation, that he just has to accept it, he will insist,

what if I just cut and ran to Slovenia without telling him anything, he'd find out sooner or later anyway, but from someone else, that's what matters, Svetlana, for instance, she'll tell him at registration at the beginning of the term, when he arrives on the night train from Košice, exhausted after a sleepless night,

we're back at Bellevue, it's getting dark, the journey passed so quickly, we get out of the van and head for the dining room, I saunter behind the others, Drago must have noticed that I'm worried, he keeps turning to me, giving me alarmed looks, yes, I do love him, but will I be able to sort things out in Bratislava?

at dinner all of us volunteers sit at the same table, Elena has joined us as well, it's our day off, no one is on shift, I feel that all the others are smiling at us, everyone has guessed what's happened between the two of us, and Drago positively flaunts it, he literally dances attendance on me, bringing me food, passing trays, plates, bottles, he always knows what I want before I even point to it, I give him a bemused smile, I nod, accept what he's giving me but I'm taking in less and less, I'm becoming agitated, a feeling of anxiety courses through my body, when we finish eating, I turn to him with a serious face, Drago, we have to talk,

we are standing in our room facing each other, I am trying to explain my apprehensions about my future in Slovenia, the complexity of the situation, he doesn't let me finish, puts his hands on my shoulders, you know, Blanka, I suspected something like that has been going through your head, come over here. We sit down on the bed side by side, and he says, this is not quite what I had in mind, I wasn't thinking of a permanent relationship, a long-term commitment, rather... the kind, you know, like Martina and Luca, a holiday – I interrupt him abruptly, so you just want to sleep with me? he sighs, yes, if you must put it like that, but I suppose I wasn't making myself... – Fine! I break in, he raises his head, so you're OK with that? I nod, he can't believe his luck, he's so happy, maybe even happier than when I told him I loved him, I can't believe this is happening, I can't believe it – but on one condition, I say, that we do it right now! he's taken aback, what do you mean, now? in the middle of the day? someone might come in, I swallow hard, I've made up my mind, let's do it now!

I hold my knees, rocking on the bed, looking at him, waiting to see how he reacts, he seems alarmed, he's walking up and down the room, come on, Blanka, this is silly, can't you see, we're off to the cinema now, didn't you hear, Xavier announced it at dinner, it would be really awkward if the two of us didn't show up, everyone would know immediately... do you understand,

I shake my head, no I don't, I start to jerk my head furiously! I don't understand! I don't! I don't!

suddenly I start bawling, I go over to my bed and collapse on it, curl up into a ball, I wait for Drago to come, as he always does, to comfort me and say that everything will be all right, but when I look up Drago is gone, instead there's Luca, he's kneeling by my bedside, looking at me intently, Blanka, he strokes my head, Blanka, you can tell me everything, I know what's going on, I know what's wrong with you, my brother has the same thing, I mean it, don't be scared, Blanka, I'll help you, just tell me, you can trust me, I look up, go fuck yourself, Luca, OK? go fuck yourself! I push him, he almost falls over,

I close my eyes, I hear the door slam shut, and then – nothing, I'm lying there, slowly calming down, silence everywhere, it's getting dark, the room is increasingly shrouded in gloom, I dry my eyes, sit up on the bed, put my feet down on the linoleum, how come I don't hear any voices from next door? you can always hear Yasmin there, that horsy laugh of hers, have they gone to the cinema already? have they really gone and forgotten about me? surely not Drago, he wouldn't leave me here in this state, I tiptoe to the hallway, turn on the light, I stop, Drago is on the other side of the door, I know it, he's next door, he's probably crawled under the bed to hide so the others wouldn't see him, he's not gone, he's stayed here with me, I bet he's cross with me because of the scene I made, I don't dare open the door, all is quiet on the other side, but Drago is there, I know it, under the bed, or maybe in a wardrobe, I put my ear to the door, are you there, Drago? I listen (nothing), please don't be cross with me, Drago, pretty-pretty please, come out of there, they've all gone (nothing), I crouch down, Drago, it's me, Blanka, we'll do it your way, I'll go along with it, we'll just sleep together, I won't demand anything else from you (nothing), I won't interfere with your life, I promise (nothing), I start knocking on the door, come on, Drago, come on out, it's only me, they've all gone, they really have (nothing), Drago darling, I know you're cross but please come out now, please, or I'll get worried (nothing), do you want me to pull you out from under the bed by force? (nothing),

I take a deep breath, open the door, the room is dark, I turn on the light, not a soul in sight, he's hiding, as I suspected, I cross the room, look under every bed, Drago, come out, come out wherever you are, Drago, this isn't funny anymore, where are you hiding? I open both wardrobes but he's not in there either, I look around, stunned, I can't believe he's really gone and left me like that, it takes me a while to process the information, I look over the room one more time, turn the light off hesitantly and leave, closing the door behind me,

I'm standing in the hallway, and suddenly – voices! laughter! they're approaching, I run out to the balcony, happy to see them come back, Drago! I shout but – no response, silence everywhere: the voices, the laughter, the steps, everything suddenly stops, I gaze out into the night, towards the main building, but nobody is coming from there, nobody's laughing there, nobody talking loudly, I'm bewildered, how is it possible, I just heard them, the laughter is still echoing in my ears … so where did the laughter come from if there's no one around?

and just then I realise that it's happening, I'm hearing voices, even though I'm here on my own, someone was laughing but only in my head! I panic and rush back in, lock myself in the room, turn the lock twice as if I could shut out the evil lurking on the other side of the door, I stand motionless, not daring to move, it's my father, it's all his doing, my father is here, with me, in this room, I can feel his presence, I feel him inside me, he's me, I'm turning into him, *I'm off my head*, I run my fingers through my hair, I don't want to! I don't want to! my fingers run more and more furiously through my tangled hair, I dig my finger-nails into my skin, pull out whole strands of hair, they're stuck between my fingers, my father also used to tear his hair out, I'd find the blood-covered clumps in the bin in the morning, stop it! right now! I can't, he's the one holding my hands, he's the one tearing my hair out,

calm down, you have to calm down or you're done for, you can do it, do you hear me? you just have to concentrate, *be aware*, stop tearing your hair out, that won't solve anything because, of course, it's you tearing it out, I take a deep breath, lower my hands and let my arms hang loose by my side, I make a fist, unclench it, something's happening to you, yes, you heard voices and there's nobody here, there's no denying that, but if you're careful, if you deal with it in a responsible way nothing bad will happen, you're not Catherine Deneuve in Polanski's *Repulsion*, there are no arms reaching out to you from the walls, you haven't murdered anyone yet, it's just a flare-up, a minor aural halluci-nation, you heard some voices, laughter, steps, it's nothing, you have to nip it in the bud, like the flu,

I go to the fridge, pick up my yellow notebook and write Xanax, Deprex, Seropram, and an arrow pointing to each name, the meds I know, meds I trust, meds that will have to do until I'm back in Bratislava, I know they have them in the consulting room, I saw them when Martina and I went there to weigh ourselves,

I run out of the annexe, along the gravel and into the dark-ened main building, the clock in reception is ticking, it's past eleven, the deserted corridor looks ominous, the consulting room is locked of course, but I find Jean-Claude the night porter in the dining room, he's watching TV, a blue light in the corner of the room, he sees me and smiles, signals for me to sit down next to him, there's a rather good thriller on, he says, it's only just started, I stand still, inhale, I need some medication, I'm not well, he looks at me, doesn't understand, I repeat, medication! in the consulting room! I almost drag him there, he doesn't resist, I poke my finger at the page, Xanax! Deprex! Seropram! you've got to give me at least one of these meds! he doesn't move, I insist: I heard voices and there was no one there, I've been hallucinating, and then, imploringly: I don't want to murder anyone, do you understand, that's why I need medication, you've got to give it to me … Jean-Claude, *aide-moi*,

we stand there face to face, I look him in the eye and suddenly feel his fear, quite physically, his fear has materialised and is now floating in the air between us, Jean-Claude is scared of me, and just then his stomach begins to rumble, horrid harsh sounds that reverberate around the room as if anxiety had knotted his stomach, like before an execution, I gulp, I realise – nobody has ever been this scared of me before, so genuinely, I would like to tell him I'm not dangerous, he should calm down, I'm not going to kill him, but I keep it to myself, I just point to the cupboard, Deprex, that's the medication I need, I reach out, it's only then that he recovers from his stupor, he stops me, no, I can't give you that, I'm not a doctor, I withdraw my hand, that's true, I hadn't thought of that, but, he goes on, I have something to help you sleep, would that help? he takes a small box from a drawer, and then tomorrow all the doctors will be here, including the Centre's psychiatrist, and you'll have a word with him, OK? Jean-Claude has now relaxed somewhat, he gives me the medication, take this with some water now and tomorrow, when you wake up – we both turn to the door, someone is coming down the corridor, Elena appears in the doorway, what's going on here?

as I walk away I hear Jean-Claude trying to explain to her what's happened, I don't want to hear it, I know I've taken a step I can't take back anymore, the machinery has been set in motion, but I don't want to think about that now, all I want to do is sleep, that's the only thing I'm interested in, I dive into the nearest toilet and wash the medication down with water from the tap, disgusting floury taste, I have to swallow a few times to get rid of it, the white van is parked outside in front of the main building, so they're back from the cinema, I slowly head for the annexe, Yasmin, Ingeborg and the older Algerian woman are already there, ambling between the bathroom and the hallway, Yasmin comments on the film gesticulating wildly, Ingeborg is just in a T-shirt and knickers, she's flailing her toothbrush about, I give them a wave and head for our room, lie down on the bed, draw the sleeping bag all the way up to my nose, close my eyes tight,

I give a start – the door has opened, Drago walks in, throws his bag on the floor, grabs a chair and puts it down next to my bed, sits down, folds his arms, takes a deep breath and is about to say something but just then my stomach churns, I jump up, make a dash for the toilet, I only just make it in time, it's the dissolved tablet and all the water, everything goes black again, I stay there for a long time rinsing my mouth then wiping it thoroughly but when I come back to the room Drago hasn't moved, he's still sitting on the chair with his arms folded, I walk past him and climb into bed, I'm about to turn my back to him ostentatiously but then dismiss the idea, we just stare at each other for a good while, finally Drago quietly says that he's heard what I've done, what I've blathered out to Jean-Claude the night guard, how immature was that, you know, Blanka, he sighs, one day you may realise that you've taken the wrong path, you're never going to solve anything this way, I just hope you didn't do it to get my attention, because you know very well that you don't need to fight for that, you already have it,

his eyes drill into me, tell me the truth, did you do it because of me? and I clutch at his question like at a lifebelt, yes, yes, wouldn't it be wonderful if it was true, I didn't hear any voices, any laughter, any steps, I'm absolutely fine, it's all just because of Drago, a histrionic gesture to attract his attention, to show him how much I need him, love him, that he mustn't abandon me, leave me to my own devices,

he watches me in tense anticipation, waiting for my response so in the end I just nod, yes, it was because of you, and before I can absorb it – Drago gives a whoop of joy, leaps off the chair, locks the door, turns the light off and climbs into my bed – it's all happened too fast, and suddenly there's a man lying next to me,

I move over to the wall to make room for him, it's dark here, I can't see, I just feel and hear, because Drago talks to me incessantly, he's talking as if he wasn't sure, is it really true, is this all right, are you OK with this, his hands rove about my body exploring it, discovering it, his questions come tumbling out one after the other without waiting for a reply, may I touch you, here too? will you give me a kiss? can I go lower? is this OK? are you sure this is best for you?

out of the blue, I pipe up, I heard voices, outside, at first I thought it was you lot, that you've come back from the cinema, but when I looked out on the driveway, there was nobody there,

Drago is silent for a moment, then says: but that's what you wanted, wasn't it? you wanted us to come back so that's why you thought you heard us?

y-yes, I guess so, that must be it, I lie, because he obviously doesn't want to know what really happened, he doesn't want to acknowledge the real state of affairs,

it doesn't take long, and when it's all over, he says: you're good, you're really good, but why were you in such a hurry? I'm lying on my back, staring into darkness, my arms and legs attached to my body but my head somewhere else, after a while I come out with: I was thinking of Peter, that I'm only doing it for him, only because of him,

Drago literally freezes, I can feel it, our bodies are still touching, he scrambles out of bed without a word, crosses over to the other side of the room, gets into his bed without saying good night,

I wake up very early, at dawn, get up quietly, put the sleeping bag on the chair he's left there and start shaking out the sheet, more and more vehemently, more and more furiously, out, out, out with all that semen encroaching on my bed, what's it doing there, I don't want it there,

Drago wakes up, I notice he is watching me, he frowns, you're pathetic,

I sit in the dining room drinking coffee, buttering the bread, perhaps I'm on the morning shift today, I ought to go and find out, take a look at the rota on the wall, it's just a few steps away from the table where I'm having breakfast, but what does it matter now, everyone knows already, the word must have gone around Bellevue at lightning speed, everyone loves a bit of juicy gossip, don't they, they're watching me from every side, casting furtive glances so I don't notice, they've surrounded me in their wheelchairs, occupied all the strategic positions, if I tried to get up they would instantly block my way,

Drago pulls a chair over to me noisily, gives me a mighty slap on the back and asks with fake joviality: how is it going, love? having breakfast? his voice sounds unnatural, half-strangulated, what yummy things do we have here today? bread, butter, jam, hmm, I like that, I could eat that, oh… *every day even!* he gives me a meaningful look, smiles, I look at him in horror, he sits there buttering his baguette as if nothing had happened, quietly humming a tune, think, quick, what else have you told him about Peter, apart from the fact that he eats bread and butter with jam every day? what did you tell him about yourself… that night?

oh my God, everything! he knows absolutely everything about you, the bread now refuses to go down, the acute awareness – he can destroy me with a flick of his finger if he chooses to,

I get a coughing fit, reach for the carafe of water, suddenly someone puts a hand on my shoulder, the nurse Isabelle, she bends down, whispers to me, come, Blanka, the doctor will see you now, he's in the consulting room, I get up, look at Drago imploringly, I'd like to say something to him but can't find the words, he has a baguette in his left hand, he's stopped smiling, he stares at me and says through gritted teeth: the honeymoon is over,

Isabelle leads me through the dining room, down the corridor, across the consulting room to the room next door, when we reach the doorway she lets go of my hand, gives me a little push and closes the door behind me, I stop uncertainly at the door, there's a middle-aged man sitting at a desk, emerging bald spot, horn-rimmed glasses, he lifts his head from his papers and gestures to me impatiently to take a seat opposite, and even before I reach the chair he announces that he has a flight to the Maldives to catch in three hours, he should have been on his way home ten minutes ago, and besides he hasn't quite finished packing, so please be clear and concise, tell me what the problem is, in a nutshell,

I launch into my story straight away, my throat stiff with anxiety, my voice panicky: please believe me, I really don't want to kill anyone, you can be sure of that, I'm not dangerous, I just need some medication, last night I asked Jean-Claude to give me some but he refused, said he wasn't a doctor... something's happening to me, I think it's depression, it might have started about a week ago, I know, I should have said something earlier but... I didn't want to cause any problems, I thought I could manage on my own, by sheer will-power... that may sound a bit silly, but you know what I mean, don't you? but then last night, I heard voices when everyone else had gone to the cinema, I was alone in my room and suddenly heard voices outside... or laughter maybe? well, some noises anyway, but when I ran out onto the balcony I couldn't see anyone and so I thought to myself it was, you know... hallucinations,

(he doesn't seem to believe me, I have to convince him), depression runs in my family, my father had it, he was, you know, manic depressive, he had bipolar disorder or whatever it's called these days, I don't have that, fortunately, but I had two episodes of depression, because of school... (the psychiatrist raises his eyebrows),

I haven't been feeling well for the past few days, a kind of anxiety, sometimes it seems to ease off for a while, but most of the time it's there, a kind of fear or how should I put it, I have this fear that I'll end up in a wheelchair, paralysed, that at night I will... well, wet myself, you know, like them, when I look at them I feel awful, I can't look at them, the convulsions, the suffering, a kind of oppressive fear, right here, in the pit of my stomach... that's why I need medication, some antidepressants, if you have any, Xanax would do, that usually helps with the anxiety,

'what is it that causes your anxiety?'

hatred... (I pause), I feel it between these walls, a kind of dense hatred, it scares me, I can literally sense how everyone here hates me, how they wish me harm, all these disabled people, they bear me a grudge because I'm not disabled, they're so envious... because I'm healthy, because I can walk on my own feet while they... sometimes they drive a wheelchair over my foot, they do it on purpose, I know it's deliberate although I can't prove it, or they force me to look at their excrement or inhale their urine, out of spite,

'in what way do they force you?'

well, Ahmad for example, he didn't have his *pistolet* emptied before going to bed and I had to breathe it in while we watched an entire film, I couldn't even go and empty it in the toilet because... because that might have made him think I found the smell unpleasant, I didn't want to hurt him... this is probably not a good example but Marie, you know Marie? she's in a wheelchair, I don't know her surname, she's the one with no legs from knees down, she told me she hates me and that I should leave the Bellevue Centre, she actually said that, and also that I despise them, that they make me sick... I tried to explain to her that it's not true but she didn't believe me, she insisted she was right, and what was I supposed to do? it made me feel really low, I felt like cutting myself after that... in fact, I did cut myself a little, when we went to see Notre-Dame de la Garde, later that evening,

'do you have suicidal thoughts?'

oh no, no, not at all (how I could have forgotten that I must never mention cutting to a psychiatrist!), I don't want to die, really, I believe that one doesn't have the right to take one's own life, it's a terribly selfish thing to do, unfair to one's family, one's nearest and dearest, only sometimes, when the mental pain becomes unbearable, sometimes it helps a little to... well, actually...

(I have a clear sense that the conversation is not going well), I just need some medication, that's all, maybe you could give me something for the depression, some antidepressants, back at home I usually take Deprex, but it doesn't really matter, Seropram would also do, or whatever you have here, I'm not choosy (I give a forced smile),

the doctor gets up, walks over to the door, invites Isabelle to come in, turns to me, listen, I can't prescribe you any medication, I can't do it just like that, do you understand, he turns to Isabelle, keep an eye on her, call an ambulance if need be... there's nothing else we can do at the moment, he looks at his watch agitatedly, shit, is it that late? I really have to dash now, he grabs his briefcase from the chair and says goodbye on his way out,

I sit there, aghast, I look at Isabelle, she smiles at me, come on now, I make no move, my heartbeat seems to have speeded up, I give Isabelle an incredulous look and then realise that she's pleased, I can see it in her face, she's delighted to see me so frightened, because an ambulance can mean only one thing, they want to lock me up in a loony bin,

my God, that would be the end, I mustn't let that happen,

as I walk back to the dining room every head turns to look at me, the residents look up from their baguettes and mugs, some with knowing smiles, others munching pensively, but Martina, Luca and the other volunteers look the other way, they don't want to look me in the eye, it strikes me that this is our joint disgrace, our joint failure, only Drago stares me in the face provocatively, grinning, as if trying to say, well, happy now? you've got what you wanted!

I walk across the dining room without pausing, I need to be alone for a while, to sort out my thoughts, I lock myself in the annexe, sit on the bed: *if need be, call an ambulance* still ringing in my ears... I cup my head in my hands, think hard: if what? hallucinations? but no one can see those, apart from you, no one hears them, all you need to do is keep quiet so that you don't give yourself away, just keep washing the bums of people in wheelchairs, keep your trap shut and not rock the boat, as grandpa used to say, you mustn't give them any excuse because these people hate you so much they wouldn't hesitate for a second, they would call an *emergency ambulance* straight away, happy to be rid of you at last, it's been sanctioned, authorised by the Centre's psychiatrist,

it was a mistake to mention the voices, yes, it's now clear to you, but who could have known that this psychiatrist would turn out to be such a bastard! just don't panic, everything will be fine, yesterday was yesterday, today is today, from now on you have to be on your guard, watching what you do, what you say, how you behave, no twaddle, hysterics, cutting, fainting, you'll be nice, helpful, obliging, when someone asks how-are-you-feeling, just say *ça va très bien, merci*, you won't give them the slightest reason to call the loony bin, keep calm, you can do it,

I take a deep breath, get up, leave the room, Ingeborg says in the hallway: would you like to go to the cinema with me this afternoon, I saw on the rota that we're on the same shift, we could take Ahmad and Oscar, it was Ahmad's idea actually, he'd love to see *Men in Black II*, Michel has given his approval, we'll take the van and go to a shopping centre in the suburbs, what do you think? it will be nice and restful for you, she puts her hand on my shoulder and smiles reassuringly,

I'm sitting in the van between two wheelchairs, Ahmad's and Oscar's, they're discussing something over my head, I sit on the floor wondering if I've strapped them in properly, what if one of their wheelchairs comes loose on a sharp bend, crashes into the door, I see a wheelchair flying past me, I see the door giving way on impact, I see a smashed-up figure on the motorway, a wheelchair wedged under the wheels of a car, entrails, something spilling out of a cracked skull, and blood, lots of blood, blood everywhere, red, magenta, everything around is covered in blood, repellent, slimy, mixed with some other, unidentifiable fluids,

never mind, I've read all about it in my sister's psychiatry books, compulsive thoughts, like when you're itching to tell a pregnant friend that you're going to kick her in the stomach, a passionate lover that he's got a small one, an angry employer that he understands shit, everyone has the odd sick thought from time to time, come on, it means nothing, my sister keeps saying, it's just obsessive-compulsive disorder, show me someone these days who doesn't obsess about books being perfectly lined up in a bookcase or doesn't return to the door ten times to check he's locked up properly, look at it this way, as long as you're not tormented by faecal fantasies…

reluctantly, I raise my eyes to the two *pistolets* bouncing up and down at the back of the wheelchairs,

Ingeborg pulls up at the car park, we push the wheelchairs down the ramp and head for the shopping centre, I don't need to do anything, the Swede takes care of everything, organises everything; she buys the tickets, popcorn, a sickly-sweet drink of some sort, I follow her lead, I have no will of my own, I push Ahmad's wheelchair into the auditorium, we find our seats, the two wheelchairs are in the aisle, one behind the other, the two of us side by side in comfortable, deep seats, we sink into them, I put the popcorn in my lap, we have a few minutes left, I relax a bit, even manage to smile at Ingeborg, everything is just as it should be, I sit in the auditorium looking around, listening to the music from the speakers, waiting for the show to begin, nothing can happen in a cinema,

the lights go out, the ads start to roll, I take my glasses off, I want to check if my vision has deteriorated or improved, I focus, look at the screen, decipher the writing, at times I can see quite well, then everything goes blurry again, misty, but I don't put my glasses back on, I have to be strong, I have to learn to control that bloody eyesight of mine, only weak people need glasses, those who are scared to look the truth in the eye, those who hide, turn their gaze away, look down, but I want to cross from the side of the losers to that of the winners, I want to grow up at last, not be afraid to look at the world around me, face up to who I've become this past month, who I really am,

what if hallucinations are simply a part of growing up, a sign that the mind has freed itself of simplistic rules? maybe that's what it's all about, and I have panicked like a silly girl! I should have taken a more detached view of things to begin with, let it rest, I should have asked Drago, I'm sure he would know the answer, except I can't ask Drago anymore, I can't ask him anything, Drago hates me, the way he looked at me at breakfast today, those words, *the honeymoon is over*, he saw me shake out the bedding this morning, I'm sure he holds it against me, maybe he'll want to take revenge, humiliate me, push me right down to the bottom, into the mud, his hands are free now, he can do whatever he likes to me, because who would believe someone who hallucinates, a crazy person?

and what if he rapes me tonight?!

I jump to my feet, terrified by the thought, I drop the bag of popcorn, indignant shouting from the row behind me, I'm blocking their view, I turn to Ingeborg, I have to pop out to the loo, OK? I'll be right back, I start to push my way out through the seats,

out in the corridor I take deep breaths, everything keeps going black, here it comes again, the nausea, I hope I won't faint now, that wouldn't help at all, I throw the toilet door open, shove my head under a tap, let cold water run, afterwards I straighten up, look at myself in the mirror, I'm very pale, bags under my eyes, hollow cheeks, my heart still pounding, calm down, no, surely he wouldn't do that, he wouldn't dare, and even if he did try something, you'll start to scream, yell, you'll scratch him, kick him, wrench yourself free and escape next door to the girls' room, yes, no need to be scared, you'll get out of it somehow,

I splash more water on my face, a bit calmer now, return to my seat in the auditorium, but I can no longer follow the film, I just sit there pondering effective methods of self-defence, and when we come out into the shopping centre, I don't have the faintest idea what it was all about, *Men in Black II*, I recall some kind of talking pug, I smile in a noncommittal way and listen to Ahmad's comments, and Oscar's and Ingeborg's,

we head for the DVD shop, we split up, me and Ahmad, the Swede and Oscar, I walk behind the buzzing wheelchair but don't take anything in, I don't see the films displayed on the racks, the only one I notice is *The Lord of the Rings*, a whole pyramid of DVDs, Ahmad stops in front of it and considers buying it, he picks it up, puts it back, picks it up again, asks my opinion, I just shrug, it's up to you, it's your money, in the end he doesn't buy anything, they're waiting for us at the door anyway,

Ingeborg glances at her watch, it's seven o'clock, we could have dinner here, in the shopping centre, what do you think, there's a fast food place over there,

we sit down, greasy formica tables, rickety chairs, glass cases with promotional baseball caps and T-shirts on the walls, hamburgers and chips on the trays before us, people shooting us sidelong glances from nearby tables, I don't blame them, I understand the perverse compulsion to gawp at a cripple, this is actually the first time I'm feeding a resident in public, at Bellevue I no longer notice the drooling, the bits of food dribbling out, it's quite normal there, but here, in this dirty fast food joint, they stick out like a sore thumb,

suddenly Ahmad notices that his wallet has disappeared, it was next to him on his wheelchair and now it's gone, Ingeborg and I look at each other, how much money did you have in it? where, when did you last see it? but Ahmad can't remember, he doesn't know, he just jabbers on about having put it there on our way here, in the van, it was still there when we unloaded him outside the cinema, that's the only thing he's sure of, it was still there before we went in,

I jump up, I'll go and look for it! and before anyone can stop me I bolt out of the restaurant, run down the gleaming corridor of the shopping centre, my head throbbing, it's your fault, you were by Ahmad's side the whole time, you should have looked after him, you were in charge, he was your responsibility but instead… what now? what if I don't find it?

what if they suspect that it was me who took it?

I look into every aisle in the DVD shop, walk up and down among the shelves to see if he hasn't accidentally dropped it somewhere, but no, nothing, I rush back to the cinema, the next screening hasn't started yet, the woman in the box office looks at me with suspicion, do you know what the wallet looked like? I throw my arms up helplessly, I don't know, it belongs to Ahmad, the guy in the wheelchair I was looking after, I just want to take a quick look, please let me in, just for a moment, by the time I barge into the auditorium I'm drenched in sweat,

and there it is, it's fallen under my seat, I pick it up, check the contents, fortunately there is still some money in it, his ID too, I hope it will be all right,

Ahmad barely thanks me, doesn't even look inside, just puts it beside him and keeps calmly chewing his food, they've nearly finished eating, they haven't waited for me, Oscar's greasy lips, Ahmad's empty tray, but I can't concentrate on the food, I know they suspect me anyway, I can see it in their eyes, they think I pinched it and came up with this clumsy way of bringing it back after it was discovered,

I try to justify myself, explain where I found the wallet, it was under my seat, who knows how it got there, maybe I bumped into Ahmad's wheelchair as I went to the toilet during the screening, maybe Ahmad dropped it as we were leaving, but I didn't see it, honestly I didn't notice it, I should have been more careful, I know, it's not going to ha…

OK, OK, says Ingeborg with a resigned sigh, can you just get on with your dinner so it's not totally dark by the time we get back,

a knot of anxiety in my stomach, so she doesn't believe me, she thinks I'm lying, she thinks I'm a thief, that I wanted to take the opportunity to run away and take the money,

perhaps I really should run away? with no money, without anything, just get up and go, hitch a ride, right here on the arterial road, instead of going back to Bellevue with them, what if Ingeborg tells everyone, or maybe not even everyone, just the nurse Isabelle, all she would need to do is tell her what happened, that it was me who stole Ahmad's wallet, what if Isabelle will want to have me locked up, what if she calls the police, or even worse, *an ambulance*?

I get up: I just need the toilet, I'll be right back, I walk out of the fast food place without thinking, in the corridor I open the first door to the left of the staircase, lock the door, look around in surprise, the room seems too big somehow, the toilet is raised, what are the bars by the wall for? then it dawns on me, I've picked a disabled toilet by mistake, I didn't look where I was going, the women's toilet must be someplace else, up the stairs probably, what now? I look around in horror, Jesus Christ, what now? I start backing away involuntarily, as far from the door as possible, I hit the wall, hunch up, crouch in the corner, I'm lost, I repeat to myself softly, everything is lost, the only way they can read this is as a provocation, first I steal a wallet and then I lock myself in a disabled toilet?! they'll never believe I didn't do it on purpose, that it's just an unfortunate accident, what will happen to me now? my God, will they lock me up in a loony bin? is that sufficient grounds? I put my head in my hands, start to cry,

someone knocks on the door, waits, then knocks again, I don't respond, battering on the door, banging, kicking, I shout: *occupé*, from the other side I hear, are you all right, Blanka? what are you doing there so long? it's Ingeborg, she's come to get me, she wants to take me to Bellevue, she wants to spill the beans to Isabelle, she wants to help her organise my transfer by *ambulance*. Go away! I shout, leave me alone! a moment's silence, then: open the door please, I shout: you bet, you're just the person I'll open the door for! she starts yanking the door handle again, Blanka, open the bloody door! we have to go back to the Centre! it's late! just go without me, I shout, I'm not going back to Bellevue! I'm going home, right now! on the other side Ingeborg starts to kick the door with all her might, Blanka, open up this minute or I'll get the staff! do you hear me? we'll break the door down! I know she means it, she's determined to do whatever it takes, so I get up, I'm not going to disgrace myself publicly, I splash some water on my red face, slowly turn the key in the lock, Ingeborg is leaning against the doorframe, but she looks more horrified than furious, she grabs me and drags me along the corridor, she says, if Michel knew that I left two residents without supervision in a fast food restaurant he'd bite my head off, I shrug my shoulders, I couldn't care less if both residents were kidnapped by extra-terrestrials,

we come out of the shopping centre, I shuffle behind the others, dejected, I don't give a toss about anything anymore, I'm resigned, reconciled to my fate, we walk to the car park, Ingeborg breaks off a few oleander twigs on the way, when we get to the van she tucks them behind the residents' ears, she wants to give me one too, but I duck, leave me alone! don't you touch me! the Swede looks at me mockingly, flings the flower at my T-shirt, and here's a flower for our little Blanka, she says, I shake it off straight away, the guys in the wheelchairs laugh at me,

I don't say a word on our way back to the centre, I'm sitting on the floor again, between the two of them, Ahmad has fallen asleep, a long stream of saliva dribbling down his shirt, Oscar is looking out of the window, the Swede is whistling at the wheel, sometimes she shoots me a quick glance, as if checking that I'm still there, that I haven't run away, that I'm not about to jump out of the moving van, but I'm tired and I don't care about anything, I don't care what happens to me, what they'll do to me at the Bellevue Centre, but then suddenly I realise that I screwed up again this afternoon, suddenly there's some clarity in my mind, clear judgment, I know that despite all my efforts, despite all my morning resolutions to fit in and behave normally my reactions haven't been normal, and certainly not inconspicuous, natural,

when we reach the Centre and unload the guys with their wheelchairs and I lock myself in our room in the annexe, it occurs to me: in the past twenty four hours you've managed to make not just one but two enemies, first Drago, now Ingeborg, and later on, when I go to the bathroom to brush my teeth, the door to the girls' room is open and I hear the Swede describe my behaviour to the other volunteers, it sounds grim, and she doesn't even have to embellish anything, I quickly rinse out my mouth and go back to the room, a little later the door opens, Drago stands there looking me up and down incredulously, he shakes his head, are you normal? I bury my head in the pillow, tell me, are you normal! he repeats, more loudly this time, I look up, raise myself on my hands, smile at him, a coltish smile, wanna come to me now? I kick the sleeping bag to the wall, just in my T-shirt and knickers, provocative, Drago hesitates for a moment, then crosses the room and slips into my bed,

he's touching me again, passing his hands over my body like the day before, but I suddenly feel the urge to laugh, a terrible compulsion that I can't control, and burst out laughing, push his hand off my thigh and start telling Drago how funny it was when the Swede battered on the toilet door, tears of laughter well up in my eyes, I blurt out disjointed words, I wonder what the people out there made of her begging me, threatening, not sure if she should be pissed off or worried, not sure what to do with me and later on, the way she stood there leaning against the doorframe when I opened the door, she looked as if she'd just finished running the marathon, face flushed, sweaty, her hair glued to her forehead, at the end of her tether, you should have seen her, Drago, you should have seen her, I laugh hysterically, I'm choking, spluttering,

Drago doesn't laugh, he's lying next to me, silent, frozen, suddenly he says, you think it's funny, hey? that people are worried about you? that's just not something you can imagine, is it? that someone might be concerned about someone else? I guess that's never happened to you, has it? I take Drago's hand, come on, I didn't mean that, please don't be like that… but he pulls his arm free, gets up, you're really not worth wasting time on, he goes over to the other bed, climbs into his sleeping bag, I'm quite sure he turns his face to the wall too.

I've got to get out of here, is the first thought in my head when I open my eyes in the morning, I've got to get out, that's the only solution, clear out, get away from this place somehow, or I'm finished, at breakfast I tell Martina that I've made up my mind, I want to go back to Bratislava as soon as possible, there's one more week left till the end of the camp but I don't believe I can last that long, but I don't say that to Martina, all I say is, help me to get out of Marseille, please help me to get home, she furrows her brow, nods earnestly, she too thinks that this might be the best solution, she takes my arm, we leave the main building,

Michel looks at me pensively, tugs at his lower lip, eventually says, *très bien*, he's prepared to meet me halfway, he'll get in touch with my relatives straight away because he can't let me travel on my own in this state, surely I understand that, it would be extremely irresponsible on their part, he will immediately book a Marseille-Vienna flight, but someone will have to come from Bratislava to pick me up, a doctor preferably, is there a doctor in the family by any chance? two psychiatrists even? excellent! Michel is delighted by this coincidence, if that is a coincidence, pushes us out of his office, we should go and bring the phone numbers, my documents, passport, and he'll make the calls, reservations, sort everything out, make all the arrangements,

we go to pick up my things from our little house next to the bamboo grove, Elena takes no notice of us, she's preoccupied with her pedicure, raises her eyes for a moment, pretends I'm not there, since the time she talked to Jean-Claude the night watchman she's been ostentatiously ignoring me, our camp leader has rather lost control over the situation, can't forgive me for this fiasco, her own failure, but I couldn't care less about her, I don't even bother to say hello, just empty the entire contents of my rucksack onto the mattress, rummaging through the piles furiously, we find the documents and go back up the hill to Michel's office, Martina is resolute, marching steadily ahead of me, I'm hesitant, walking ever more slowly, we should give it some thought before we buy those tickets, how much might it cost, a flight from Marseille to Vienna, including one return flight, that'll make a hole in our rather tight family budget, wouldn't it be better to back out of it?

Michel says he could only get through to my uncle, my mother and her family are out of town, in some place called *Vailquay Tchaoushi*? Michel has some difficulty deciphering his notes, raises his eyebrows, Martina gives me a questioning look, I give myself a slap on the head, of course, they've gone to Veľká Čausa, I've totally forgotten, it's a small village in Central Slovakia, in the mountains, but Michel is not interested in picturesque Slovak villages, there's no phone there, he continues, no direct line, my uncle will ring the neighbours, I told him they should get in touch with us as soon as possible, I said it was important, you're not well,

outside the office we bump into Drago, he asks what's going on, seems unpleasantly surprised that I've approached Martina and not him, gives me an angry look, he's just popped out from work, he's on the morning shift, he's got to go back to Ahmad in a minute but wants to know what I'm up to now, what new and original idea I've come up with this time, but when Martina tells him that I've decided to leave Marseille early and that my psychiatrist sister is flying over from Vienna to get me, he nods approvingly and says that's a good solution, I've finally made the right decision, but I'm not so sure anymore, how much can three tickets from Marseille to Vienna cost, the thought keeps bothering me, it niggles away at me, drills a hole in my head, maybe it would be better to take a train or the bus, it would be much cheaper, I can cope with the journey, surely any retard can manage to get on a bus? but I should have thought of that sooner, the machinery has been set in motion, the wheels have started to turn, any minute now my mum will learn that I'm in trouble, but the main thing is: I don't have my passport anymore! I've given all my documents to Michel and he won't let me travel on my own! he said so himself, he said it would be extremely irresponsible, so what now, that's the million-dollar question,

I stop in my tracks, Martina and Drago look at me startled, I've changed my mind, I say, I'm not going anywhere, I'll stay here until the end of the camp, it's only a week, it's not a big deal – one week, I can manage, no problem, don't worry, I smile, I hope I made it sound convincing, thoughtful, sensible, that's the only way I can ensure I get my documents back, I can make them forget this as an inconsequential incident, but Martina and Drago don't look too pleased, I'm staying, I'm all right, I repeat, do you understand? I'm absolutely fine, I turn my back on them, pissed off, start to walk away, down the path toward the annexe, Martina catches up with me, takes me by the hand, Blanka, what's got into you now, you have to go back home, you know you're not well, you mustn't run away from it, this is nothing to be ashamed of, it's not your fault, Drago nods, I stop, slide down to the ground, or rather the lawn, I'm at my wits' end, what now, what should I do, I say it out loud, I really don't know what to do, Drago and Martina sidle up to me, one on either side, like bodyguards, yes, that's it, they're guarding me discreetly, keeping an eye on me in silence, watching my every move, I'm hemmed in,

Martina says, you have to behave responsibly, do you understand, Blanka? surely you don't want your family at home to be concerned, you don't want your mum to be worried, can you imagine how she'll feel today when she hears the news? I look at her in horror, my heart starts pounding, is she being sarcastic? is she trying to needle me because she *knows*? so Drago has already spilled the beans, told her what he and I had talked about last night? does he go around complaining about me behind my back to everyone? does he keep the others posted about what's going on between us? I look at him, try to read his face but can't, he's deadpan, dispassionate as always, mildly annoyed, as if wanting to say: I have nothing to do with what Martina has said, but maybe he's just putting it on, pretending, that's what I hate about him – I never know what's really going on in his head, he just sits there watching me silently, like now. Martina, on the other hand, insists, Martina must have decided to hound me out of this place at all costs, believe me, Blanka, it'll be better if someone comes for you and takes you back home, you'll only get worse if you stay here, and besides, what will Michel think if you change your mind so suddenly, what will he think of all of us, he'll think we're just bullshitting, right, Drago?

just look at Martina, Drago chips in, she's behaving like a responsible adult, although she's only seventeen, if anything happened to her, Michel would go straight to prison, he employed her illegally, officially all the volunteers doing this work have to be of age,

I look daggers at him, he said that on purpose, about Martina behaving like an adult, unlike me, that's what he meant, he just wanted to humiliate me even though he knows how hard I've fought for my adulthood these past weeks, how much I tried, the hell I've been through, I hate him, if I could I would lash out at him, right here and now, pummel his back with my fists, but I control myself, don't let the floodgates of my rage fly open, I have to put all this aside now, all the emotions, I run through all the options in my mind dispassionately, every possible solution one by one, there's a lot at stake, I have to take the right decision now, a mistake could prove fatal, I take a deep breath, all right, I'll do as you say, I'll leave Marseille, I'll go and pack my bag now so that I'm ready when my sister arrives,

I walk past the main building, the parked vans, down the hill to the little house, fortunately Elena is out, I start gathering my stuff scattered all over the floor, I shove it all into the rucksack higgledy-piggledy, squeezing, creasing, crumpling everything, and when I'm more or less packed I peek out of the house, look around – the coast is clear, I set off down the path through the park leading to the main gate,

I keep turning back, is anyone following me? has anyone spotted me? with my seventy-kilo rucksack on my back I must stick out like a sore thumb, and now that stupid yellow mutt has joined me, he must be a part of the institution, he's trotting after me with his snout close to the ground, otherwise nothing, no one, the main building is slowly but surely disappearing from view, goodbye, it was nice to meet you, but there will be no next time, definitely not, forget it, I mutter under my breath, just a few more steps and I'm out, free again, out of this hellhole, and what then? the Slovak embassy? the first phone box? hitchhike via France, Italy, Austria all the way to the border? I don't care, all I care about is getting out of here, out of Bellevue, nothing else matters, only a few more steps and—

a figure appears at the main gate, I freeze, paralysed like a deer caught in the headlights of a car, the figure comes closer, it's Isabelle the nurse, yes, it's her, I can now make out her features, the crude make up, the curly hair tied with a rubber band, I should run away, hide in the park, among the trees, but at the same time I know – I'm screwed, it's too late, Isabelle is flabbergasted, she's now standing right by me, *tu plaisantes, j'espère*, she grabs me by the shoulder and drags me all the way up to the main building like a sack of potatoes, she's dumbfounded, she's swearing, cursing, fortunately I can't understand a word,

everyone glares at me for the rest of the morning, checking all the time that I'm still in my seat, on the chair in the dining room where I withdrew after Isabelle made a scene, because Isabelle shouted it from the rooftops when we got back to the centre, you won't believe this, it's beyond belief, she screams for everyone to hear, so she's on her way to work as usual, going up the hill and what does she see? there's Blanka! strolling down the path, cool as a cucumber, rucksack on her back, like nothing's happening, she might as well be whistling merrily along, she was almost at the gate, do you get it? she almost managed to run away! a few more metres and she would have been out! better not even think about that … … *elle est folle, cette fille! tu comptais aller où, hein? dis-le-moi,* she turns to me, but I keep firmly silent, I sit on the chair without moving for an hour or two, I don't stir even when preparations for lunch get under way, I'm not helping, that's the last thing I need, I just watch, Martina, Drago, Luca, Ingeborg carry trays, distribute carafes of water and wine on the tables, cutlery, glasses, napkins, they're giggling horribly the whole time, nudging each other in the ribs, shouting, probably to show me how they stick together, that they're as thick as thieves,

gradually the room fills up with wheelchairs, nurses, chatter, the clatter of cutlery, I'm still sitting there, I've stopped observing what's happening in the room, what could be going on, they're just eating, stuffing their faces, drooling, guzzling, farting, burping, spluttering as usual, aren't they? my eyes fixed on the ground, I can't block my ears, that would look like a provocation, mustn't overdo it, I parse everything quietly, just for myself, analyse what's happened, what it all means, the possible repercussions, why they're not letting me go, what their game is, how it relates to hatred, it takes me a while to notice that Drago is standing before me, the six-foot tall Drago has come up to me, he crouches down, embraces my knees, looks me in the eye from close to, Blanka, my dear girl, you're not having any lunch? I don't answer, I turn my face away, Drago insists, you've got to eat something, Blanka, you don't want your sister to find you all pale, skinny, sickly, surely you don't want *someone to worry* about you, he articulates the words *someone to worry* so clearly that I look at him startled, is he trying to blackmail me? humiliate me? is that why he's here?

he continues, well, so you really don't care that your sister will be worried about you? you don't care that your face has gone completely green? but I do care, Drago! can you hear me? now he's almost shouting, I curl up on the chair, subconsciously expecting the first slap in the face, I'm scared of him, I've always been scared of him, people shouldn't be six foot tall, people shouldn't have such powerful shoulders and piercing eyes, leave me alone, I mumble, I want to turn my back on him but he squeezes my shoulders, I won't, Blanka, you know what, I won't leave you alone, because right now you're going to have some lunch, I shake my head, I'm not hungry, but he just snorts, I don't give a damn if you're hungry or not,

he picks me up, drags me to a table like a rag doll, he puts me, or rather, shoves me onto a chair, the little scene has started to attract attention, astonished residents and volunteers stare at us from every direction, I sit at the table motionless, my arms hanging limply, Drago asks, what's wrong, won't you help yourself? OK, let me do it for you then! he flings a piece of meat on a plate and starts cutting it up, the residents at our table smile mischievously, Laurence giggles, in so far as her convulsions allow it,

and Drago means business, he begins to force the first bite on me, I clench my teeth, turn my face away, then I realise I'm only making things worse, so I open my mouth, Drago seems pleased at last, I'll do almost anything for you, Blanka, but you have to do your own chewing, I feel like crying, there's a lump in my throat but I chew, swallow with difficulty to stop them laughing at me even more, there is now an unmistakeable mood of elation at the table, even those in wheelchairs further away have turned to have a better view, some have buzzed closer to our table, everyone wants to witness this, everyone is keen to see what will happen, what's coming next,

I manage about six bites in this way, but I can't eat anymore, I stare at Drago imploringly, is that enough? I push the plate away but at that point Ingeborg hands me a glass, have a drink! you mustn't forget to drink! liquid intake is very important! especially in the south and in the summer, to avoid dehydration! she holds the glass to my lips but in my astonishment I don't open my mouth quickly enough, water pours down my chin, now the residents are laughing out loud, spluttering, sniggering, are they really so pleased to see me humiliated? actually, why am I even surprised, what else could I have expected than glee, vindictiveness, Martina bends down to me and dries my chin with a napkin, *to nic, Blanko, to se může stat každému*, don't worry, Blanka, it can happen to anyone, tears well up in my eyes,

Someone taps me on the shoulder, it's Isabelle, a phone call for you, she says, the call has been put through from Michel's office, she points to the receiver on the wall at the far end of the dining room, I dash towards it, grab the receiver, my mum is at the other end, I don't let her talk, I start babbling straight away, mum, I've got to tell you something, just don't be frightened, I heard voices and there was no one there, it's schizophrenia, I hear voices, mum, but that's not everything, everyone hates me here, they want to lock me up in a loony bin, I don't know what to do, they've taken my documents and won't let me out of here, mum is horrified, what's going on, Blanka, she shouts, for Chrissakes, what are you saying? a suspicious silence around me, I look over my shoulder, they're staring, of course, all eyes fixed on me, Martina is bending down to Drago, could she be trans- lating what I'm saying? was I so loud? now I'm trying to whisper so they don't hear me, I cover the receiver with my hand for good measure, I can't talk, mum, they're watching me, they don't believe me but you've got to, I've found out how much they hate me, I tried to run away today but they stopped me, I nearly managed to get away, if it weren't for Isabelle I'd be on my way home now, but don't worry, I will try again, mum screams, don't! don't run anywhere, Blanka! for heaven's sake, just stay where you are! stay at Bellevue! do you hear me? your sister is coming to get you, she'll fly over, you must hold out until she's there, I whisper, no, please don't, don't buy air tickets, they must be awfully expensive, we'll be ruined, my mum pleads desperately, but Blanka ... I interrupt her, I've got to go, these bastards are listening in, and I put the receiver down without further ado,

some of the residents are smiling, especially Ahmad, with that dumb beatific expression of his, Ahmad, who speaks Slovak, how could I have forgotten, Martina is holding her head in her hands and looks at me incredulously, Drago raises his eyebrows, he shouts across the whole room, well, Blanka, satisfied now? are you finally happy with yourself? I stare at the ground, march out of the dining room, Ingeborg manages to yell after me, don't you dare go anywhere! I don't bother to turn around,

I walk to my room, go to bed, close my eyes for a moment, a sharp pain pounds in my temples, I reach out to the fridge, pick up my mobile, stare at the three-dimensional butterfly for a while, it seems so long ago, the day I bought it, La Ciotat and the café and the terrace, *Memento*, Drago and I still friends through thick and thin, it's all so long ago and yet only two weeks have passed, I turn the phone round in my hand, look at the display, then write a message to Peter in Košice, I write to my Peter, tell him that I love him, am thinking of him, I've never wanted things to end this way, don't be cross with me, I press send, close my eyes, fall asleep,

it's still light when I wake up, I look at the mobile, I've slept for less than four hours, I'm not well, I feel numb, lumbering, infirm, *dead*, there's a text message from Peter, he asks what's going on, he doesn't understand anything, could I explain by email, my text wasn't clear,

I splash some water on my face in the bathroom, brush my hair and set out for the computer room, empty corridors, parked wheelchairs, silence, afternoon, the siesta, but when I throw the door open I see Drago sitting at a computer writing something, I walk in, he turns to me, our eyes meet, we look at each other for a long while, neither of us knows what face to make, neither wants to take the first step, in the end something in me breaks and I rush towards him, throw my arms around his neck, bury my face in his chest, I'm not crying although I would like to, I wish I could have a good cry, I tell myself, quite rationally, I wish he would say that he still loves me, that everything will be all right again, that he will look after me and won't let anything happen to me, but neither of us says anything, I just hold him tight, for long minutes, finally I look up to him and ask, is it all over? Drago smiles, nothing is over, you just have to eat and drink so that you don't have a total breakdown before your sister comes, can you tell me what those shenanigans at lunchtime were about? those hysterics? can't you take a joke? are you in such a state that you've lost all your sense of humour?

I pull away, I didn't think there was anything funny about the way you humiliated me at lunchtime! and the way you all listened in on my phone call. Drago shakes his head, who, Blanka, who listened in on your phone call? stop being paranoid, you were at the far end of the room, and even if I did hear what you said on the phone, do you really think that by some miracle I've learned Slovak overnight? or Laurence, or Thomas, of all people? do you think they want to know what you're discussing with your mother over the phone?

I interrupt, but Ahmad does speak Slovak! and throughout the phone call his wheelchair was right behind me, I'm sure he heard it all and told everyone else what I was saying, I'm sure he wouldn't have deprived himself of that pleasure, Drago stares in amazement, what are you raving about? Ahmad knows about as much Slovak as I do, hello, how are you? that's about it, just calm down please, the only people here who understand Slovak are you and Martina,

I go berserk, they're all just faking it anyway, they're pretending, playing games, how can you make head or tail of it, how do you know who to believe, how much of it is real and how much just humbug, camouflage to deceive the enemy, some of them just pretend to be wretched, powerless people who need wheelchairs! Drago frowns, he doesn't understand, I try to explain, I believe that everyone here, all the residents, all these so-called disabled, handicapped people, can actually walk normally, move and talk, they could leave the centre whenever they wanted to and take part in normal life, except that they don't want to, that's the problem, they're lazy, they want to be carted around (Drago makes a horrified face), all right, maybe not all of them, some are just scared, afraid to stand up on their own two feet, afraid to face life out there, like the rest of us, but whatever the reason, none of them would be here if they didn't want to be, I'm sure of that! Drago clutches his head, Jesus, Blanka, are you totally off your rocker? but I insist, do you remember the party the other day, when Luca burned the seafood risotto, and Olivier stood up, he was so pissed he forgot he's supposed to be wheelchair-bound, that he's supposed to be infirm, he stood up on his feet, I saw him, he was standing properly, you saw him too, we were there together, remember?!

but Blanka, Drago puts his arms around my shoulders and shakes me hard, Olivier propped himself up on the armrest if you recall, he managed to stand like that for about two seconds, then he slid back into his wheelchair, two seconds, do you get it? *capito*? he can't manage to stay upright longer than that, and that's him, just him! do you really think that someone like Laurence has been faking it all, those facial tics? the jerking limbs? or someone like Ahmad, who can't even articulate properly? Or Adam, yes, poor old Adam, with the alphabet board attached to his armrest, do you think he's just faking it, that it's because he's lazy that he pokes his finger at the alphabet board instead of making the effort to talk like everyone else? you think he's faking that swollen head and stick-insect legs? come on, you don't know what you're talking about, you're totally out of it, he dismisses me with a wave of his hand, turns back to his computer and starts typing,

I sit on the floor for a moment, dejected, resigned, battered, then I get up, sit down at the computer next to Drago's, log onto freemail and start writing an email to Peter in Košice, I've got to explain to him how things stand, but how do I explain it, too much has happened, too much is happening,

I limit myself to the absolute basics: hatred, revenge, my pathetic and theatrical escape attempt, humiliation, blackmail and hatred again, because I'm full of hatred too, I can't deny that, that's about as much as I can say, but he mustn't worry about me, really, although I know he won't, Peter won't be worried, Peter is more concerned about getting through all the Spanish novels in time for finals and about taking sensible notes than about some people in wheelchairs hating me here in Marseille, but I will tell him the honest truth anyway because he has the right to know what's happening to me,

I don't even say goodbye to Drago on my way out but later, when he joins me in the dining room – I'm watching the final episode of *The Thorn Birds* – he asks, why are you doing this, Blanka? can you explain to me why you want people to worry about you? is that the only way you know how to attract attention? you're like a child trying to stick her finger into an electric socket to make the grown-ups take notice of her! but you're old enough to know that emotional blackmail is a very foul way to fight, the dirtiest trick, I can't stand people who try to get what they want in this way, as he speaks to me I'm seized with horror, has he already seen my email to Peter? is he so internet- and computer-savvy that he's managed to hack into my email account so quickly? I start defending myself, but you don't know my boyfriend, you don't know Peter, the only thing he worries about is doing well in his Spanish exam, that concerns him much more than … than … me! I look at Drago but he pretends not to understand what I'm driving at, I don't give a shit about this Peter of yours, I'm talking about myself, Blanka, don't you understand? and stop looking for excuses, that's really annoying! he takes my hand, come on, let's go and help the Algerians serve dinner, I hope you're not planning to just sit here and watch the others work,

after dinner – tables cleared and residents back in their rooms – the volunteers decide to take a night-time walk in the area, Luca says, we've been here for three weeks and still don't know what this neighbourhood looks like, Martina asks if I'd like to come along but I know she's only asking in order to be polite while in reality they don't want me to come along, so I say no, thanks, I'll stay in my room, I'm quite tired and might have an early night, then I think, what's the point of this show, I can see right through you, you want your privacy so that you can badmouth me to your hearts' content, put your heads together and figure out how to get rid of me,

I turn in, lie on my back in bed impassively awaiting Drago's return, waiting for them to decide what to do about me, but it doesn't bother me for now, my head is empty, I'm not thinking about anything, I just stare at the ceiling, I know it so well by now, the crack above the bed, it seems to have grown, I must be imagining that, actually, wait a minute … I narrow my eyes, yes, it is getting bigger! I look away, a bit frightened, I don't really need this now, to look at the crack growing, I force my eyelids together and when I come round – how much time has passed? how long was I asleep? – there's a strange man standing in the doorway, I quickly sit up in bed but it's only Xavier, he's smiling, Xavier is going to stay the night, Drago says from near the wardrobe, he'll sleep in Luca's bed, I'll just clear up a little, I hope you don't mind, I wince, what, how do you mean?

I hear it as I open my eyes, it's still ringing in my ears, the sound of an ambulance howling, shrieking, ululating continuously, unbearably, unrelentingly, all night I heard nothing but the wailing of that bloody ambulance, steady, neither getting closer, nor moving away, it was just there, a few metres from me, flashing its lights and howling, I stay in bed for a while waiting for the horrid noise to subside but when it stops I remember the scene from another dream I had, another nightmare, I'm kneeling in front of Drago frenziedly giving him a hand job, the scene is brightly light, like in some amateur porn movie, it all feels disgusting, I turn my head to the left but it hurts to move,

Drago has propped himself up on his hands in bed, he is looking at me but isn't aware of what the two of us have been up to at night, and that's when I remember Xavier, he's spent the night in the room too, I lift myself up, I can't see anyone, the third bed is empty, and then a pair of legs, stretching upwards behind the bed, Xavier is doing yoga, callanetics, Pilates, whatever, or he's just getting the blood to circulate in his head,

Drago and I watch him intently, Xavier changes position, now he's sitting cross-legged and reaching up towards the ceiling, he smiles, jumps to his feet, shakes out his limbs, you can't imagine how good this feels first thing in the morning, it really wakes you up, it's like a cold shower, Drago sits up, Xavier's optimism visibly annoys him, he puts his feet down on the floor, shakes his head, I had a terrible dream last night, I shoot him a terrified glance, could it have been the same as mine? but he says, I dreamt about my mum, her blue eyes, she was looking at me so sadly in the dream, he sighs, it's been a long time since I dreamt about her, he gets up and shuffles over to the bathroom, but before he goes, he says, turning towards me, but my mum can't worry about me anymore, she's dead, as you well know!

I sit up on the bed, thunderstruck, what was he trying to say? it sounded almost as if he resented the fact that my mother was still alive, as if he envied me, as if I didn't deserve it, I can't get this out of my head throughout breakfast, his hostile tone, his words, *she's dead, as you know, dead, as you well know...* at one point I feel like getting up from the table, going up to him and saying: but it wasn't me who killed her, Drago! it's not my fault she's dead! but I stop myself, because just then it occurs to me that nothing is accidental these days, nothing that happens or is said, I have to delve into everything, take a close look at every seemingly insignificant comment, maybe he was implying something, maybe he let slip some of the things they had discussed last night on their walk, maybe what he wanted to say was that *my* mum could... soon... be dead,

as soon as that thought sinks in, as soon as I articulate this sentence in my mind, I'm swamped by a wave of horror, I'm still sitting at the table, in the dining room, next to the other volunteers eating their breakfast and chatting calmly, but I start to shake, can it be just my imagination, my thoughts are racing, but how, how could they have done it? remotely, from here? no, that's impossible, calm down, they can't reach this far, though their network is powerful, no doubt about that, but it can't reach this far surely... I keep repeating this to myself until I calm down, I try to take deep breaths, I tell myself, my mum must be all right, I spoke to her on the phone only yesterday, and anyway, they've all gone to Veľká Čausa, Michel has no idea where that is, and by the time he finds out...

I put my slice on the plate, push the plate away and plonk my glass down in the middle of the table, I've made up my mind, I'm not going to drink any more of their water, or eat any more of their bread, from now on I will do everything I possibly can not to get in their way, to take up as little space as possible, I won't get involved in anything, I'll make myself invisible,

I sit there biting my lower lip and ripping a paper napkin into tiny shreds, Ingeborg notices and leans over with a glass of water, here, Blanka, have a drink, dehydration can be really dangerous here in the south, you should drink more, I shake my head, no, no, thanks, it's very kind of you, I get up and start pushing my way out through the tables out to the terrace, but suddenly Amélie blocks my way, little Amélie, she is smiling, positively beaming with joy, her words come pouring out, her father the cab driver has just driven her up here, she will finally tell Michel her decision, she is quite sure now, I don't understand, what decision? what are you talking about? that I want to become a nurse of course, that I want to spend my life working with the physically disabled!

she stands there, Amélie, smiling like a living reproach, the prototype of the kind person who is dying to help her neighbour, as opposed to me, I see, that's what you were trying to say, because I care only about myself, I look around, which one of you has sent her? who gave her the task of telling me this?

to humiliate me like this? to point up my outrageous selfishness? and she adds with a smile, I'm off to help with the morning wash now, and she disappears somewhere in the building,

I walk over to the nearest chair by the pool, curl up on it, draw my knees up to my chin, grasp my legs with my arms, I suppose I should also help with the morning wash, I haven't done anything for a very long time, I haven't lifted a finger or wiped a bum, I can't even remember when my last shift was, that's why they sent her to me, the innocent little Amélie, as a discreet reminder of my obligations, of course, you fool, even if you don't eat or drink, you're still a parasite, a leech, as long as you're sleeping under their roof and breathing their air...

except they're not letting me leave!

I raise my head, the dining room door has opened, it's Drago with Ingeborg, Martina and Elena, they sit down on the chairs around me but pretend I'm not there, they're chatting, every now and then they guffaw, they pay no attention to me, although I'm sure they're watching me in secret, monitoring me, I can feel their stealthy glances, it's all just a show, a charade, I know full well that in actual fact they're only sitting here because of me! because they have to keep an eye on me, to make sure I don't run away, climb over the fence or set fire to the Centre, or push some defenceless resident down the stairs, they're nothing but cops, snitches, spies, although they look so calm, laid back, as if everything was hunky-dory, as if nothing special was happening, or – the horrible thought suddenly strikes me – as if they knew something I don't, as if everything has been resolved, mission accomplished and they no longer had anything to worry about,

Elena rests her feet on the edge of the pool, she moves her chair to catch the bright southern sun, she's evidently keen to get a tan, make the most of the last rays of the August sun and it is, in fact, quite hot although it's not even midday,

Luca comes out of the dining room, a rucksack on his back, he stops before us and has a word with Martina, then turns to me out of the blue and says out aloud, so that everyone can hear, Blanka, I'm off to town now, would you like to come along? I'm going to look at some books, in this bookshop in La Canebière, how would you like that… he pauses, or will you tell me go fuck myself again? he raises his eyebrows as if waiting for an answer although it's obvious he's not expecting one, we stare each other down for a moment without a word, then I turn away, from the corner of my eye I can see Drago grinning,

Luca walks down the tarmac road towards the gate, whistling away, I quickly glance at the others to see their reaction, what they've made of it, Elena studiously examines her fingernails, she makes no effort to look in my direction, Ingeborg is rocking back on her chair, visibly amused, only Martina watches me intently, as if expecting something from me, some kind of reaction, defence, repartee, anything, we lock glances for a while, is she trying to provoke me into doing something? then suddenly she gets up, she practically shoots out of her chair, everyone looks up in surprise, Martina walks over right up to the grey wall of the main building, stops by the parked wheelchairs, lifts her arms, and does a perfect handstand,

everyone watches her now, her perfect figure, her slim tanned legs, flat stomach under the rolled down T-shirt, Martina stays still for a few seconds then returns to her original position, first one leg down then the other, and she's back, she starts to fix her hair, staring at me all the while, then she says, as if in passing, my mum is a gym teacher, that's why I can do any exercise easily, including a handstand, I can do a handstand anytime I feel like it, easy-peasy, she really is looking at me and her face broadens into a smile, a contemptuous, condescending, knowing smile, and that's when I understand, Drago has spilled the beans, he told her everything I confided in him that night when we wandered around Marseille, he must have told her that I can't manage a handstand, he must also have told her about my phobia about my own body, my depressions, my father, I'm sure he also told her about my spitting semen out of the window, about Rachel and my lesbian tendencies, now she knows everything there is to know about me,

and she's not the only one, I look from one of them to the next, Ingeborg too, and Elena, and surely Luca and the two Algerians as well, they all know everything about me, they're all in on it, that's why these smiles, that's why they're so calm and relaxed, they know my weaknesses, they know where to hit me to inflict the maximum pain, they know how to wield the blade of the scalpel,

and suddenly all the dots connect in my head and it all begins to make sense, suddenly I get it, of course, it's blindingly obvious, self-evident: it's my family they've decided to destroy, not me,

they have my documents, passport, wallet, even my address book! I hadn't thought of that, my address book with all my contacts, all the people closest to me,

and all this time I thought they were out to get me, get rid of me, sell me off to a harem, but now I see that's not it, they've come up with something much more effective, more humiliating, better, the real revenge will be to keep me alive, not rotting in a harem, no, I will dutifully return home, to my family in Bratislava, to Peter's room in the halls of residence at Mlynská

Dolina and when I think it's all over, that it's safe to turn the page, that's when it will start, anonymous phone calls at three in the morning to mum's mobile, and a voice on the other end of the phone: would you like to know what Blanka was up to in Marseille? well? would you like to know what she looked like when she held it in her mouth? interested in hearing that? – hello, who is this? who's there? who's calling? then just a click and the engaged tone, more and more details about my behaviour will gradually emerge, how I humiliated the disabled residents, cheated on Peter with Drago, spat semen out of the window, things I said on the beach about Peter, that he can spend the rest of his life jerking off, the wiping of soiled bottoms, everything, they've got it all on record,

how they must secretly enjoy this, they must be laughing their heads off, be in stitches thinking about what they will do when the camp is over, they'll join forces and terrorise my mum, my sisters, Peter, for months, years, they'll keep phoning them and I bet they'll start blackmailing them,

the phone calls will be followed by letters, photos, videos featuring me, they must also have photos of me in bed with Drago, photos that show me doing it with him, I'm sure about that, surely that's why he slept with me, why else would he have done? just so they have it all documented, so that they can psychologically destroy Peter as well, humiliate him, Drago will take care of that personally, as I know him he'll throw in the odd detail of my anatomy, something about the way I moan when he's inside me to make it sound more convincing, to spice it up a bit,

didn't Xavier also take pictures of me, that day on the beach, someone's been taking photos of me all the time, they've tried to capture me in this state, in the middle of the routine horrors of the Bellevue Centre,

they won't rest until they've destroyed us all, one after the other, they'll stop at nothing, and if that's not enough, they'll post it all on the internet, accessible to all and sundry, here you are, take a look at Blanka, see how she abused the disabled in Marseille, and there won't be anything we can do about it, we won't be able to stop them, my mum will weep into the phone – I know, I know, but that's enough, don't call me again, for Chrissakes, why are you doing this? leave us alone, please, our whole family,

but no, mum, they won't leave us alone, they're after our skin, nicely flayed and dried like a rug they can rest their feet on, so much hatred that it horrifies me, I should do something, prevent it, I should fight, but I'm totally paralysed, I can't move, and I'm sure they've also noticed that I'm incapacitated, I'm sure they're filming me now, for later use,

I get up, spin around my axis a few times, where's that fucking camera, where is it so I can smash it into smithereens,

I take a few steps towards the swimming pool, come to a halt, Martina calls out to me, where are you off to, Blanka? don't go anywhere! and suddenly I realise that she's right, where would I go, it's too late to run now, this is the end of the road, there's nothing I can do, nothing I can do for my family, my family is as good as dead now, and it's all my fault,

I've murdered them,

suddenly this thought, these precisely formulated words, and the certainty that they're true, that their death can no longer be prevented, that it's not within my power, that it's just a question of time when it happens,

I take a few more steps, my legs give way under me, I crash into a chair, I have to sit down, but instead of sitting down I collapse on the floor, I can't get up anymore, I can't move, all I can do is shout, scream, yell at the top of my voice, everything around me is in a whirl, the world starts to spin, the sky becomes a blur, moves away, comes closer, as if wanting to rip me out of the earth, suck me in, the Bellevue Centre becomes a gigantic hurricane raging around me, the trees, the swimming pool, the main building, the residents, everything is one enormous vortex, especially Martina and Drago bending over me, holding me down firmly, shouting at me, I can't understand a word they're saying but I thrash out, kick, bite, spit, screaming dreadfully all the time, you've murdered my family! why have you murdered my family? you bastards, I hate you! do you hear me? I hate you!

and Marie, I'm sure that Marie in her wheelchair is also staring, smiling, rapturous, I'm sure she's at the gate looking out for the ambulance, the ambulance that I can hear again now, the one from my dream, it's howling, groaning, screaming, the ambulance is wailing continuously, unbearably, relentlessly, it's here, just a few metres from me, flashing its lights and howling, I can see it now and I can see two paramedics leap out, they bend over me, pick me up and start strapping me to a stretcher, into some kind of a straitjacket, they tie up my legs, hands, I fight back as best I can, but they're stronger, I scream at them to leave me alone, to have mercy on me, to not kill me, impenetrable faces, trained movements, real professionals, they don't under-stand me, I know Martina is the only one who understands me, I've been shouting at them in Slovak, but I don't know any other language, every other language has deserted me, I see horror in Martina's eyes, also in Drago's, the two of them help lift me into the ambulance, they hold me down although it's quite unnecessary, the paramedics have tied me up well,

Drago stays outside, Martina gets into the ambulance with me along with one of the paramedics, they keep an eye on me all the way, making sure I don't wrestle free, although I can't move at all even though I'm still fighting, struggling, but I'm tied up too firmly, I can barely breathe, Martina strokes my hair, comforts me and that winds me up even more, I would bite her hand if I could, I'd kick her in the face, I'd kill her, but that's the whole point, I can't, all I can do is lie there, ramrod straight, frozen, as good as written off,

the ambulance rattles along, we're driving through Marseille with the siren blaring, suddenly we come to a halt, they unload the stretcher, unload me, put me on some kind of a cart, I could run away now, this is the moment, but I don't have the courage, at least ten people around me, Drago, Ingeborg, Xavier, Martina, paramedics, doctors, everyone trotting alongside the gurney, everyone holding me as we hurtle down some kind of a lobby area towards reception,

at one point a piece of paper is shoved into my hand, Xavier says, sign here, down at the bottom, I look at him uncomprehendingly, there, the gurney stops, Xavier guides my hand, here, your signature, he's explaining something but I don't understand him at all, the meaning of his words escapes me, I'm not really listening, I just nod and sign, nothing worse can happen to me now anyway,

I'm in isolation: bare walls, the bed I'm lying in, a chair and a door with some kind of a window, through which someone comes to take a look at me regularly, about half an hour later a doctor comes in, starts asking questions in French about what has happened, do I know why I'm there, what was all that screaming back there at the Centre about, I would really like to explain it to him but I can't put it into words so I just keep repeating, they've murdered my family, they've murdered my family, do you understand? they have! I point to the door, the doctor smiles, he understands, oh, I see, take this, he shoves a pill down my throat, he waters me like a plant, you have to rest now, you'll feel better soon, you'll see, he leaves the room and I tell myself, he didn't listen to me at all, why would he have talked such rubbish otherwise, they've killed my whole family! how on earth could I feel better?

but the minute he closes the door I feel something surprising and very alarming at first, a kind of incredible relaxation, a pleasant tiredness, I resist it but soon I submit to it, I close my eyes slightly and realise that I feel incredibly good, as if on a good high, everything ebbs away, suddenly I don't care about anything, the thought is still there, somewhere at the back of my head, it still buzzes a little, like an annoying bluebottle in the stagnant air of the room, the thought that my family is dead, but it doesn't really bother me that much anymore, oh well, they may be dead but I feel fantastic now, I can't help it, if I could I would spend the rest of my life on a high like this, in this kind of stupor, feeling this carefree,

the door opens, Drago walks in, he sits down on a chair by the bed, I follow his movements with my eyes clouding over, I tilt my head towards him, he's silent for a moment, doesn't seem to know what to say, then he clears his throat, I asked them to let me see you before I go, I give him a smile, that's nice of you, Drago, everything seems sweet to me on this high, he's rather taken aback by my words, he looks at me, his brow furrowed, then he shakes his head, bloody hell, can you tell them to give me whatever it is they drugged you with, you look like you've just reached nirvana, you've got to find out what that medication is called, do you hear me? he grins, oh boy, you've really freaked out! I smile slowly, feeble-mindedly, all right, sweetheart, I'll tell the doctor to put a dose aside for you, Drago slaps me on the shoulder, there's my girl, he gets up, take care, Blanka, we've got to go back to Bellevue now,

when he's gone, I tell myself that I might never see him again but this knowledge reaches me as if from a distance, like the rest of the world around me in fact, as if through some kind of screen, I look at the little window in the door through narrowed eyes, every now and then someone passes by, white coats, hair floating, shiny bald pates, scurrying figures, evidently nobody is concerned about me anymore, after my dramatic entry in a blaring ambulance suddenly this unexpected silence, I close my eyes,

I'm in a different room, they must have moved me here while I was asleep, to this hospital room, a window on the left, I see trees, a park maybe, a door on the right, it's closed, a door at the back, I soon discover it's a toilet, what luxury, I say to myself, an en-suite toilet, almost like a hotel, except that everything here is white, the walls, the bed linen, the bedside table, everything white and incredibly clean, not like in the loony bin in Pezinok,

I've only been to Pezinok once, just before my dad died, all I remember of that day is an overcast sky and an open ward, formica, linoleum, everything grey, sad, dingy, then a walk in the adjoining park and my dad saying that one of his fellow patients on the ward keeps nicking his soap and toothpaste, that he's got to hide everything away, otherwise they'll take it away from him, he's complained to the doctors but they don't care, they don't give a damn, my dad, a wreck, an alcoholic, a madman, that's the last memory I have of him, and suddenly it occurs to me, what would he say now, if he were still alive? that I'm following in his footsteps, that I take after him, that I've become *daddyfied*, would he be proud of me? would he feel guilty? or would it not affect him at all?

a nurse brings a tray, lunch or dinner, I can't tell, I sit up in bed and put the tray on my knees, the nurse leaves and I remove the clingfilm, everything is carefully wrapped, every piece of food, I eat some, leave some, put the tray on the bedside table, fall asleep again,

it's dark outside now, I get out of bed, go to the toilet, sit down to pee, suddenly the door opens, my eyes like saucers, a nurse is standing in front of me, she stares at me for a while, then she closes the door, I'm stunned, what did she do that for? why did she come into the toilet? did she want to humiliate me? and actually, why can't I lock the toilet door? It occurs to me that when I was admitted Martina and the others told her what I'm like, what a bitch I am, how I spent three weeks hurting disabled people at Bellevue, how I humiliated them, watched them being washed, how they repelled me, and here at the hospital they've decided to make me pay the price, to avenge them, now that I have sunk to their level, now that I'm in the same place, dependent on nurses' help, totally at their mercy,

it's morning, there's a drip in my arm and a nurse is bending over my bed, she says I have visitors, what visitors, I wonder, what kind of visitors? but just then Martina and Drago burst in, with my rucksack, sleeping bag, handbag, they pile everything up by my bed, sit down next to me, I shift a little to make room for them, Martina pretends to be very busy, she doesn't even look at me, just opens my rucksack and starts pulling things out, it's a bit of a mess, there wasn't much time, but don't worry, we haven't forgotten anything, here's your passport, wallet, ID, address book, your clothes, the Camus book, oh, this is the charger for my own mobile! I put it in by mistake but you would have sent it back to me right, Blanka? she glances at me, or maybe you wouldn't?, I don't respond, I don't understand, Martina sighs, perhaps you'll understand one day, she gets up and says, let's go, and Drago, who hasn't said a word the whole time, gets up too and as he leaves he waves a timid good-bye,

I look down at the stuff carelessly tossed on the floor, I'd like to sort out the mess but am not sure the drip would let me, it's too short, I look at it with concern, the transparent liquid streaming into my body, what could it be? why have they given it to me? I don't want it, I see the needle stuck in my vein, I touch it, it doesn't hurt, I press it down, now I can feel it, and at that moment, I don't know why, I start jerking it up and down furiously, the needle in my vein, I don't stop until blood has risen halfway up the tube, until it hurts really badly, but the sight calms me down, this is my blood, I tell myself,

I'm in bed, sleep for hours on end, look out of the window, at the sad trees swaying in the wind, a nurse looks in on me from time to time, she doesn't talk to me, just checks the drip or brings some food, covered in clingfilm again, thoroughly wrapped again, I have to go to the toilet with the drip, but at least no one opens the door on me,

in the evening I take a walk around the ward, I don't know if it's allowed but it doesn't bother me that much, it's dark outside, this is the first time I've been hospitalised, everything is new to me, the long corridors, the half-closed doors of the wards, the neon lighting, the brightly lit nurses' rooms,

nobody takes any notice of me, I'm not in anyone's way, it almost seems that it's not really me, that I've finally become detached from myself, that I'm looking at myself from high up, dispassionately observing myself as I shuffle along the linoleum, I feel almost like the little blond girl traipsing down the corridors in Lars von Trier's *The Kingdom*, the drip in my arm trailing behind me like a puppet on a string, I tell myself, so is this what the end of the road looks like?

the loony bin is the end of the road, at least that's what everyone in my family says, the loony bin will change you forever, once you're in there you'll never be the same again, you're lost forever, to say nothing of the shame that will dog you till the day you die, at least that's what they inculcated in me at home, but in actual fact this place doesn't seem so horrible, I'd even say it seems almost better than the world out there, the frightening world full of people in wheelchairs, of Martinas and Dragos, this place is so calm, serene, peaceful, but it probably just appears like that because I haven't yet met my fellow patients, the beasts who nick soap and toothpaste,

so I peer into their rooms, pull doors open, gawp at the people who have ended up here with me, a black guy groaning, covered by a duvet with only his feet showing, an old man curled up into a ball on the side of his bed, a woman who begs me to call a nurse – please, *mademoiselle*, be so kind and tell them to come! a young man who's asleep breathing loudly, I look at them and wonder which one of them will write the words *Welcome!* in shit above my bed as my sister always promised me they would.

You can hear it but you can't see it, just an ambulance blaring again, you're being transferred somewhere, you're no longer strapped in but you're lying on a stretcher, you feel the ambulance bumping up and down as it drives through Marseille, with all due ceremony, the sound reaching you from a distance as if it didn't relate to you, had nothing to do with you, you listen with interest, the screaming, the madness, will you hear nothing but the wailing of an ambulance for the rest of your life?

Someone's touching you, you open your eyes, people are bent over you, undressing you, their sweaty palms, mechanical movements, well-oiled teamwork, they lift your arms so they can take your T-shirt off, you let them drop back feebly, they flop down like the wooden arms of a marionette, you have no strength or will, no control, you're lying naked on a table, your breasts still trembling, your body lissom, you're not embarrassed about your nakedness, you're not proud of it either, there's a mesh over your brain,

Now they're squeezing you into some kind of nightshirt, you don't protest, they're doing their job, you leave them to it, they wheel you down a corridor, you don't even need to close your eyes, you've stopped taking in what's going on around you, your mind is detached from your body,

Alone again, you're lying in a hospital room, whiteness, cleanliness, just a beetle on the far wall, its black carapace, its wing-case that grows and grows and grows, getting bigger and bigger, you watch it impassively, a black smudge on the wall, is it you, Gregor?

You sit up in bed abruptly, bolt upright, saying, I'm the devil, I've murdered my whole family, you say into the void, and that's when you notice there's a woman perched on a bed across from you, ordinary-looking, dark hair, dark eyes, plump, middle-aged, she just sits there and says nothing, she doesn't react to your words in any way although you did utter them and she must have heard you, now she knows you're the devil, she knows that you're capable of murder, isn't she afraid, how come she's not afraid? you could kill her, too, in her sleep, but she just stares at you apathetically, your roommate Patricia,

You look around, another anonymous hospital room, built-in wardrobes, bedside tables, windows with blinds, a view of the park, two beds, giant pillows, deep mattresses you sink into, you're buried in them, as if they were trying to swallow you, eat you up,

Somewhere at the back of your mind the awareness, I've murdered my entire family, the inability to feel it, relate to it, you know this is not right, you should feel something, something like pain, suffering, loss, and yet – nothing, no pangs of conscience, no emotional upset, just a void, just this white hospital room and your slow-motion movements, slow-motion thought processes, your fading gaze,

The first time the nurse has to support you, *courage!* you can do it, see, it's not that difficult, she urges you on, first one foot, now the other, she helps you walk down the stairs to the communal lounge, you grip the railing and descend slowly, shakily, where are the days when you could bound down, four steps at a time, when your sister mocked you for stamping about like an elephant, you move your feet slowly, it takes courage to go from the first floor down to the ground floor,

The communal lounge, a few drooling patients that you avoid, a TV switched on in the corner, crossword puzzles on the table, you do them with Patricia, a ping-pong table at the back, it takes you several days to memorise the layout of the room, the arrangement of the tables, the sofas, where the toilets are, the dining room, to get your bearings, get used to this new setting, but time means nothing to you, you take no notice of it, it doesn't flow, you live in the present, not even that, you don't live, you just exist,

She gives you a push because you stopped moving, you're a sluggard, you trip on the threshold and find yourself in the middle of a bathroom, the nurse thrusts you under a shower, she says something, something you don't catch, it's in French, you just stand there, not understanding what she wants you to do, you look around in surprise, you haven't been to this place before, blue tiles, white walls, she grabs hold of you, starts lifting your arms, pulling your nightshirt over your head, she's swearing the whole time, *putain!* and *merde!*, admittedly, you're not making it easy for her, you're not helping her in any way, a rag doll, keep those damned arms up! now you're getting a little scared of her, she's shouting at you, bad nerves, zero understanding for your slowness, she starts to pull the rubber band out of your hair, you bend down, it hurts, all that tangle, you haven't brushed or washed your hair for about a week if not longer, grains of sand come raining down on the floor,

She directs a current of cold water over you, that's when she notices that she forgot to close the door, she can't think of everything after all! you look that way, a curious patient is peering at you, beat it! get out of here! the nurse snarls at him and turns back to you, you can see that he's not gone but it no longer bothers her, he's still standing there with a dim-witted smile, and why shouldn't he get an eyeful if he gets a chance, look at your heavy breasts and hairy crotch, the nurse snaps at you, will you hold that soap or not! you want me to wash you down as well, or what?! she flings the soap down on the floor and leaves, fuming, you're still under the shower, in a stream of cold water, the door still open,

You're sitting in an armchair, the lounge, news, you stare at the TV screen, you can't understand that life hasn't come to a halt in this hospital, that things are still happening out there, that everything keeps functioning in a world that only slowly filters through to you, bears down on you, you're gradually becoming aware of things, you've slowed down, now you understand, it's the medication, always the nurse with a glass of water, she towers above you, night after night, you swallow the pills dutifully, it's the medication, thoughts emerge with great difficulty but at least you're taking things in, that's something,

It takes you a while to recognise him, he's materialized in front of you out of the blue, he's sitting next to you, you chat to him like patient to patient, then it suddenly dawns on you: why, this is Peter, it's Peter sitting on the bench beside you! he's saying something about Jack Nicholson and *One Flew Over the Cuckoo's Nest*, it takes you a while to get it, you laugh, slowly, you're right, this place does looks exactly like the film, with all the crazy people, it doesn't occur to you that you're one too, Peter seems absolutely fine with it, he says you've lost weight, you're beautiful, he puts his rucksack on his knees and, making sure nobody is watching, fishes out some Dru wafers, hazelnut flavour, I bought it in our Tesco, on Kamenné Square, I thought you might like it, you munch away in silence, chewing carefully, neither of you wants to attract attention and make the others envious, so that they don't come and ask for some, it's only for you, Peter smiles, then he disappears, just as abruptly as he appeared,

The food is disgusting, literally disgusting, you're pushing it around with your fork, moving bits of chewy meat from one side of the plate to another, you can clearly make out veined bits of onion in the sauce, you look up, your fellow diners are gobbling it all up obediently, some let bits fall back onto the plate, many are drooling, nobody bats an eyelid, neither do you, suddenly you think, this is punishment, yes, it's punishment for all the shitty things you've done there, at Bellevue, the way you treated the disabled people there, you will wolf this food down even if it makes you sick, you've murdered your whole family and you have the gall to turn your nose up some chewy meat? I want more, can I have some more, your fellow patients look up from their plates astonished, can I have more onions please, I need onions, you shout, the whole dining room is looking at you, everyone has stopped chewing for the moment,

Peter comes every day, Luca drives him over in the morning, in the evening Luca returns to pick him up, in the van, they stop in front of the hospital, you see them through the glass door, Luca usually comes in to say hello, he laughs at your nightshirt, look at you, aren't you stylish! he shouts, waving his arms, *che cazzo fai, Blanka, ma che cazzo fai?!* The other patients always gawp, especially a guy with a discman who likes to sit in an armchair in the lobby, you privately dub him Bob Marley because of his hair, his Jamaican hat, very often, several times a day, he stops in front of you in the corridor, blocks your way, you don't wait for him to leave, you don't ask what he wants, you try to walk around him without a word, it nearly always means you have to brush against him,

You're driving the nurses up the wall, every time you walk into the nurses' room and start explaining your problem, your situation, they shout at you and chase you away, but you don't give up, an hour or two later you launch another attack on the nurses' room, you have nothing better to do anyway, please do something, I've murdered my entire family, one of the nurses rolls her eyes, another points to the door, out! this minute! or I'll get nasty! you're standing there, in the doorway, you don't move, but they are all dead! you have to understand, something has to be done, there has to be a way! you beseech them, try to explain, you can't just leave it at that! a nurse who's at the end of her tether shouts, you think you're the only one with problems here, or what?!

You decide to turn to a higher authority, a doctor, one has caught your eye, a good-looking fellow, dark eyes, black hair, aquiline nose, tall, slim, you follow him, first with your eyes, then on your feet, across the lounge, he's running away from you, zigzagging away, he goes out of the building, sits down on the steps, takes out his cigarettes, you sit down next to him, gaze at him with dog-like devotion, he ignores you but you are nevertheless convinced that he will understand, he'll help you, you start explaining the story of your murdered family, he gets up without a word, walks into the car park, you know you can't follow him there,

At first confusion, doubts, you shout, occupied, *occupé*, you're standing in the cubicle, by the toilet bowl, you haven't even managed to pull up your nightshirt when someone starts battering at the door, they're yanking the door handle, knocking, kicking, you feel they'll kick the door down any minute, you no longer shout, just wait in silence to see what happens next, will he rape you? kill you? you have no idea, he gives up eventually, you hear shuffling steps, receding, you stand there frozen for a while, was it a warning? you get the shakes, have to sit down, it can't have been an accident, a simple misunderstanding, it was deliberate, you don't leave straight away, you stay there for about an hour to be on the safe side, you sit on the toilet lid waiting, not daring to breathe,

And then the certainty, the frightening certainty, Bob Marley bars your way, at first you don't mind, he's been doing it several times a day after all, you want to give him the slip as usual but this time he doesn't let you, he moves in to block your way again, you look at him, wonder what he wants and then come the words, in your native tongue, I will write it in shit above your bed: Welcome among us, how about that? would you like that? you turn on your heels, run away, Peter doesn't believe you, you're sobbing as you tell him about it on the bench, Peter caresses you, reassures you, try to be rational, it's not possible, this homeless guy, this nobody or whoever he is, it's out of the question that he would have said something in Slovak, you just imagined it, you misunderstood,

But you know that you haven't imagined anything, you understood him very well, now you know, now it's dawned on you, it's all interconnected, Bellevue and this loony bin, they know everything about you, Drago has told them, or maybe it was Luca, you don't know exactly but it doesn't matter, they've decided to punish you, to avenge Thomas, Laurence, all the others, you'll be brought to book, a just punishment, the toilet this morning was also a part of their plan to humiliate, humiliate, the word thunders round your head, that's all they want, and suddenly you see, you're the only one dressed in a hideous nightshirt, all the others are wearing normal, everyday clothes, shirts, jeans, T-shirts, suddenly you're aware of how you look, the disgrace of it,

But you want to take revenge, to punish them, kill those bastards who've brought it upon you, Drago, you picture his house between two motorways and yourself prowling under his window, at night, in the moonlight, you walk in, find his room, his bed, and smash his head in with a hammer, in his sleep, he won't even have time to notice, and not just him, the Swede and the Romanian woman too, the Italian guy, the Czech girl, everyone, despite the mind-numbing medication you feel hatred, it's muted but it's there, it hasn't gone yet, you cling to it, your only certainty, but then, one afternoon, the alarming thought, what if they've sussed you out, what if they know about your plans, here in the hospital, maybe that's why they've kept you here, they're scared, you're a dangerous criminal after all, you haven't tired of telling them yourself, grinding out the mantra like a hurdy-gurdy? I've murdered my family, I'm the devil, I've murdered…

You walk up to their table, a nice, sunny day, the siesta, the doctors and nurses under a parasol in the garden, biscuits, coffee, lemonade, a wooden table with chairs, they raise their heads in surprise, a nurse is getting ready to step in, she opens her mouth to say something, but you're quicker, please let me go, no one says a word, you go on, I promise I won't tell anyone about all the horrible things you did to me here, the medication, the nightshirt, nothing, not a word, to anyone, a doctor comments, amused, *elle est bien bonne, celle-là*, you go on, you implore, I promise I'll never return, I won't come back to take revenge, I won't kill you, two nurses suddenly get up, indignant, you add quickly, I'm no Monte Cristo, seeing the doctors burst out laughing, a nurse takes you by the hand, she wants to lead you away, but you're looking at the doctors around the table rolling about with laughter, slapping their thighs, shouting Monte Cristo! Monte Cristo! drying their tears, you stare at them, baffled, they're laughing at you, they're not listening, they won't let you go, you wrestle free of the nurse, run into the park, nightshirt, mussed up hair, useless slippers, they catch up with you almost immediately, three nurses, where do you think you're going, huh?

Ahmad, he's sitting in the van, Luca signals for you to come closer, he's driven him all the way here this morning, Ahmad likes you, he wants to say goodbye, you stand before him, at a loss, he's saying something, you're in sync for the first time in terms of speech and movement, but still you don't understand, you just catch something about *adresse*, does he want us to be pen-pals? you get your yellow notebook, he dictates his e-mail address, you don't understand, ahmadwhat? a few futile attempts, scribbles on paper, in the end Luca comes to the rescue, he writes it down, it's something like this, and once in the car he grins and adds, what does it matter, Blanka? you're not planning to be pen-pals with a guy like Ahmad, are you?

Peter says, how about a game of ping-pong, he's clearly bored, he's been sitting on the bench with you day after day until visiting hours are over, you get up, pick up a paddle but instead of getting into position you start ripping off the outer layer of the rubber, bit by bit, throwing it on the floor, well, what's up, have you fallen asleep? Peter is on edge, he comes up to you, why are you doing this? why are you ruining the paddle? you raise your eyes, I was unfaithful to you, what? yes, unfaithful, you must know what that means, Peter is doubtful, not sure if he should believe me, what do you mean, you snap back, annoyed: it means exactly what I said! want to know the details? now he believes me, he slumps down on the bench, muttering, I see, so this is how this guy Drago was helping you with your depression, nice work, very nice indeed, you look away, can't suppress a grin, he gets up, well, I'll be off, don't go! you want to throw yourself around his neck, but all you do is just take his arm, you're clumsy, it's the medication of course, he shakes you off, what do you want? tears in your eyes, disingenuous, theatrical, you should have been an actress, are you cross with me? no, but I need to be alone now, you catch up with him on the stairs, do you still love me? of course I do, he smiles, go on, prove it! his hand on your crotch,

As the nurse drags you along the ground-floor corridor, she keeps saying *venez, mademoiselle, vite*, you don't understand but you don't care, you let yourself be dragged, you couldn't walk so fast by yourself, you're almost running, you barge into a room at the end of the corridor, someone presses a receiver into your hand, you hold it without taking in what it is, like a brick, the nurse encourages you, go on, talk, say something! yes? you pipe up hesitantly, Blanka, it's me, are you all right? how are you? you start to tremble, mum! mum! I've murdered you all, you say, but even you sense a certain lack of logic, the incompatibility of death and the voice at the other end that's telling you, don't worry about anything, Blanka, just look after yourself, understand? we're coming to fetch you, by car, you just have to manage somehow until then, but mum, you insist, I killed you, I really did! it's all right, Blanka, we'll talk about it when you're back, please don't worry about it now, OK? you promise you won't worry about it, but back in the corridor you try to explain it to the nurse, how could I have talked to her if she's dead, if I've murdered her? the nurse laughs heartily, you're quite something, your folks are alive and kicking! you don't believe her, you stop on the stairs, but how is it possible? you shake your head, but if I didn't kill them, then why... why am I here?

You're sitting in an armchair, in the lobby, Bob Marley is across the hall, watching you with a leering smile, you wish Peter would come soon, he's late today, could it be because of what I told him yesterday? but he said he wasn't cross, he shouldn't leave me here, on my own, at the mercy of this guy, Bob Marley listens to his discman, in his indispensable multicoloured hat, he looks as if he knew something you don't, he's making you nervous, your right leg is twitching, you cross it over your left to stop the involuntary tic, Bob Marley takes his headphones off, I've heard you like semen, you spit it out of the window, someone said that, you turn your head away, panic in your eyes, you don't want him to see how much this has upset you, again, he spoke Slovak again, how could that be? you get up, walk to the glass door, the only person who could have told him is Drago, it's beyond doubt now, it's all one big web, everything is interconnected, an organisation, all-powerful, and as if in confirmation – Drago is walking down the gravel path with Luca and Peter, like in a nightmare,

You sit in the lounge facing each other, you're not talking, you don't understand why he's here, Drago, what it is he wants from you, the only explanation you can think of is that he wants to revel in the sight of your humiliation, of what you've been reduced to, the hideous nightshirt and slow-motion reactions, your fall from the very pinnacle of power, the very opposite of delirium, he says, how are you, Blanka? are they looking after you well? you nod slowly, it's fine, except for the insects, Drago doesn't understand, you explain, I've been plagued by insects, first the ants in the little house, and now a beetle on the wall, Drago nods as if he knew what you're jabbering about, I see, insects are still following you, he stops to think, I know what it is, it's the curse, you vaguely recall the picture of the basilica with the blood-red sunset, yes, that's probably it, it's obvious you have nothing to say to each other, Drago gets up, he wants to touch you, pat you on the shoulder by way of farewell, but changes his mind, withdraws his hand, says only, take care, Blanka, he waves a greeting to Peter, the two of you watch him walk towards Luca and the van, Peter couldn't care less, neither can you,

You write down in your yellow notebook, *Hello, Peter, my darling, I know I've made so many mistakes but please, if the test results are OK, just do whatever you like with me. Because I love you very, very much. Very much. Everyone gets bruises and bumps and that kind of stuff. But I love you very, very much, so much that I can't lie, so please. Understand. It's probably quite hard to understand. In the state I'm in. And maybe this state –* you cross out the final sentence, you don't know how to put your thoughts into words, you show it to Peter as soon as he comes, in the morning, he frowns when he reads it, he gives you the notebook back, I can't make head or tail of it, what do you mean it's hard to understand, in the state you're in, bollocks, you're the one who's in a state, not me, I understand everything very well indeed, you look at him, baffled, you don't understand what he's saying, why he's rejected it, your declaration of love,

You're sitting in the lobby again, deep armchairs, you've changed into your own clothes, finally in your own gear, you're leaving today, that's what the nurse said, this morning at breakfast, they're coming to collect you today, you feel less vulnerable in your jeans, T-shirt, a bra at last! Bob Marley sits across from you, minus discman this time, watching you intently, well, well, my darling, so you're off, home to your mummy, happy now? looking forward to it? you say nothing, what's the point of replying if he's so well informed, so will you give us a handstand or a somersault, as a good bye, you seem so supple, so flexible... you get up, they said you're leaving today, you don't obsess anymore about the fact that he is speaking Slovak, that he knows everything about you, you walk out of the glass door, it's raining outside, you're just in a T-shirt, you go out onto the staircase anyway, to keep an eye on the drive, look out for your murdered family, what's taking them so long, how can they leave you here, at the mercy of this bastard, suddenly a nurse at your side touches your bare shoulders, you've got goosepimples, aren't you cold? you shake your head, she gives a laugh, you're quite a weirdo,

the doctor takes you to his office, he claims to be your physician-in-charge, you don't believe him, you could swear this is the first time you've seen him in your life, your brother-in-law takes his psychiatry diploma out of his briefcase, the physician-in-charge just waves him off, doesn't even glance at him, I believe you, of course I believe you, he starts talking about you instead, your case history, considerable improvement, not so delirious anymore, Peter translates, my brother-in-law nods, you don't listen, you look at the doctor with fascination, you've never seen eyes this blue before, they seem to radiate light, *vous avez des yeux si bleus*, you interrupt him, he smiles, slightly embarrassed, yes, my eyes are blue, he turns back to your brother-in-law, as I was saying... Peter mutters through his teeth, you have some cheek, to hit on your psychiatrist, so publicly, you look at him, stunned, who's hitting on whom here?

You're lying on Peter's sharp knees, at the back of the car, rain pouring down the windows, it's getting dark, you're leaving Marseille, so it is true, you fall asleep instantly, your brother-in-law rouses you from sleep, he wants to know how to pay the motorway toll, he doesn't understand what it says in French, your brother-in-law is on edge, but before you manage to reply he figures it out by himself, tosses some coins into the net, the barrier goes up, you're back on Peter's hard knees, the whole evening, whole night, they wake you up only to put some tablets in your mouth, you wash them down with mineral water, *un petit traitement de sortie*, in the morning, still dark, somewhere in lower Austria, at a petrol station, Peter insists, he wants you to tell your brother-in-law about it, about being unfaithful, I'm sure he'll help you, that's what he's here for, isn't it, he's a specialist, right? you hesitate, Peter insists, Blanka, please do as I say, you're obviously not quite all right yet, you should tell him when he comes back from the shop, you stop him by the car, you tell him what happened, you jabber, quietly, your eyes cast down, staring at the tips of your shoes, your brother-in-law is extremely uneasy, he says just, well, you shouldn't have told Peter that you were unfaithful to him, and at that moment you know, you shouldn't have told your brother-in-law either, now the whole family will know, get out of the car, mum calls to me from the kitchen window, I look up, wave and slowly start walking across the courtyard to our block of flats, mum rushes down from the third floor, hugs me right there in the courtyard, next to the rubbish bins and a frayed armchair taken over by feral cats, she has a little cry, I barely notice, my movements and thoughts are still slowed down, I can't even smile naturally, Peter supports me all the way to the lift, we enter the sweltering flat, hugs and sweaty cheeks, a squeeze round the shoulders and little Klára, racing happily from one room the next, half-naked, I walk over to my room, it seems to have changed slightly, after a longer absence it always seems a bit alien, letters and postcards that arrived while I was away on my desk, wooden shutters closed because of the heat, a white fan behind the TV, a pink blossom on the cactus on the windowsill,

Peter and my brother-in-law hump the luggage upstairs, pile everything up in my room, it's all there, money, mobile, phone card, even the camera, the one from America, the one from dad, the shutter stuck on frame 35, looking at it makes me giddy, I realise it's all there, Drago, Bellevue, the hoists, captured in some form, preserved, without a second thought I open the camera, expose the film, rip it out, roll it out fully, destroy, destroy all tracks leading to Marseille, Peter watches me disapprovingly, what was the point of that, Blanka? I look at him, confused, then I realise he doesn't know, it's the only solution, the only right decision, he doesn't know anything about

Marseille, doesn't know that the film captured the evidence of my wretchedness, documented my failure,

I'm lying on the bed, Peter has gone off somewhere, no idea where, he didn't say, he just upped and went, the door is slightly ajar and I can hear sounds from the entire flat, a conversation between my two sisters, Klára's shrill childish voice as she asks for chocolate from the pantry, my brother-in-law's business calls with Prague, each time he takes one he walks down the hallway and closes the living room door behind him, I'm very tired, on the cusp of sleep and wakefulness, I fall asleep at some point and when I wake up, Klára is standing in front of me in a Winnie-the-Pooh T-shirt and pink shorts, she's standing by the bed, smiling and showing me something, I squint, can't make out what it is, my eyelids still sticky with sleep, Klára places the thing in the palm of my hand and exclaims happily, 'it's a birdie, a glass birdie, look Blanka, see the colours inside, isn't it pretty?!' and immediately adds, 'it's for you, a present, so that you're not so sad,' she dashes out of the room and I can hear her shout in the hallway, 'she likes it, I told you mummy, I knew she would like it!'

in the evening I try to get some food down, at the kitchen table I'm forcing myself to eat some potatoes and meat, cucumber salad, washing everything down with vast quantities of mineral water, I look out of the window, at the block of flats opposite, the people pottering about on their balconies, the open windows, the cries of swallows and the colourful magazines on our windowsill, mum has to help me with everything, including taking a shower, it's awkward but I can't even hold the soap in my hand, I'm so weak, my limbs won't obey me, I barely manage to step over the edge of the bathtub, in the end I let her, after all, it's been a week since that wretched incident with the nurse in the shower room, a week since I had a proper wash,

in the morning they take me to Tehelná Street, to see my psychiatrist, a veritable entourage, Peter on one side, my sister from Prague on the other, the lift to the fourth floor and as usual, the waiting room full of mad people, I don't even have to wait very long in the half-darkness of the corridor, squeezed between two patients on the rickety chairs, my sister makes sure I'm seen straight away, in view of my state, in view of the gravity of the situation, I sit in the consulting room listening impassively, Peter takes out of his bag the letter from the French psychiatrist, my so-called physician-in-charge, I catch only a few words, *verbalisations délirantes, phénomènes hallucinatoires, état dépressif sérieux avec culpabilité*, it all sounds interesting, but what's it got to do with me? my psychiatrist tries to talk to me, she asks questions, I don't understand, it's the medication, it's still preventing me from taking things in, talking, articulating normally, in the end she turns to my sister and together they agree on something, I don't know what,

in the afternoon my sister turns on the TV in my room, a documentary about Charles Manson and his murders, about Sharon Tate and her unborn child, I'm lying on my bed, face to the wall, I'm not asleep, I listen to an account of the events, I only turn to the TV screen when they start talking about the trial, how the women laughed, how they sang when they were asked some questions during the hearing, and about Sharon Tate, how she had pleaded with them to spare her baby at least, begged them to come back for her after she'd given birth, I wonder – is it a coincidence that this film is being shown right now? and just then my other sister walks in and says, it's for you and hands me the phone, I pick it up and hear someone speaking Czech at the other end: *'nazdar Blanko,'* hi Blanka, how are you, are you back in Bratislava? are you OK? I realise who's talking and my heart skips a beat, Martina, it's Martina, why is she calling me? what does she want from me now? so it has started now in earnest, the persecution, all my forebodings are coming true, I cast an unhappy look around the hallway in a desperate attempt to hold on to something, to escape somewhere, the simplest thing would be to put the phone down and pretend we were cut off, but in the end I mutter something along the lines of – yes, I'm back home, but that's not enough for Martina, Martina keeps asking questions, she persists, she wants to know how I'm feeling, what I'm doing, how I'm coping, I tremble as I answer her questions, am relieved when she releases me, when I can put the phone down, but later, when I tell my sister about Martina's evil plans, that she wants to take revenge for Bellevue, terrorise our entire family with phone calls and God knows what else, my sister just shakes her head, come on, don't be paranoid, she just wanted to know how you're doing, it's quite nice of her actually, I try to explain things to her, make her understand the whole situation, the circumstances, but I'm not getting through to her, my sister sticks to her version, she can't see anything suspicious in the fact that a friend from the camp has phoned me at home,

later in the afternoon Peter and I go to the Polus shopping centre, mum has given me a bracelet in the hallway, it's black, from a shop called Pink, my sister bought it but doesn't like it, she explains, she doesn't want it, I should exchange it, pick something I like, at the same price, for myself, here's the receipt, she shoves it in my hand, I don't understand, what do I need a bracelet for? When have I ever worn a bracelet? but she's not interested, she pushes me out of the flat, along with Peter, my mobile rings on the tram, it's mum again, the shop, Pink, it's on the second floor, she's telling me so we don't get lost, that's all she wanted to say, I look at my mobile, it's still there, the three-dimensional butterfly from La Ciotat, I peel it off and slap it on the handrail I'm holding on to, only in Polus do I notice that Peter looks somewhat run-down, there's a hole under the armpit in his T-shirt, he smells of sweat, there's several days' stubble on his face, he doesn't fit in with the crowd, the overdressed young ladies in heels skipping down the mall's Champs-Élysées, the young men with gelled hair, arms nonchalantly thrown around their companions' waists, but Peter doesn't care, Peter is preoccupied with something quite different, he seems upset, he marches ahead in mile-long strides, I can barely keep up with him, he's muttering under his breath, these people, they give you a ring, they ask how are you are, are you all right now? but has anyone thought of cancelling your bus ticket from Marseille, oh no, it hasn't occurred to any of them to get a refund, that would be asking too much, but I've sorted it out, while you were asleep, I went to the bus terminus, showed them the psychiatrist's report and they refunded everything, I gave the money to your mother, one less thing to worry about, Peter mutters, I nod vaguely, uhm, uhm, I'm not listening, I'm choosing a bracelet, I point to one, a metal one, with jumping dolphins, Peter shrugs, take it if you like it, and let's go now, tomorrow is registration at uni,

but for me it's out of the question, the state I'm in, surely I can see that, Peter will sort it all out, he'll sort out my registration, it's for the best, I don't need to worry, yes, everyone knows what's best for me, ever since I've come back home, a little household pet, no one asks me anything, they're all taking steps, making arrangements for me, I just do as I'm told, go with the flow, before slamming the door Peter whispers to me that he's going to look for Svetlana at uni and bring her over to see me so we can talk, surely I'll like that, won't I,

my sister comes back from the chemist's, she's picked up the post on the way, she hands me an envelope absent-mindedly, goes to the kitchen with some bills, I go to my room and close the door, three photos fall out onto the bed, a folded letter, it's from Xavier, he's sending kisses, yes, kisses, *bisous*, and a P.S. underneath, sometimes it's hard to talk but whenever you feel like it, you can write to me, anytime, my email address won't change, and at the bottom, right in the corner, another signature, in tiny writing, but there it is, Martina, what's Martina doing in Xavier's letter?

I hold the first photo closer to my face, recognise it immediately, it's the dining room, my first dinner, I'm sitting at a table at the back, my face partly obscured by Ingeborg's head, Martina in the foreground, she's sticking a fork into the mouth of a resident off camera, then two more photos, me in Cassis, the pictures Xavier took of me on the beach, with me turning sideways, to present my profile, this is the first batch, a second one will follow, then a third, it will show me being loaded into the ambulance, with Drago, it will get tougher, blackmail, they're all in it together, it's started already, yesterday the phone call from Martina, today the photos from Xavier,

but my Prague sister doesn't believe me, she's shaking her head, when I give her the full picture to warn her of the impending disaster my sister laughs, what are you on about again, just take a proper look at these photos, come on, just look at them, there's nothing compromising here, just holiday pics from a summer camp, a few snaps from the beach, a picture of the disabled centre where you worked, you're reading things into it, I'm sure this guy Xavier just wanted to make you happy, he thought you'd be pleased to see the pictures, my sister doesn't understand that it's coming, that the worst is still to come, the *real* pictures, this is just a taster, an overture, a who's who, the enemy has taken up position, and if we don't do anything, if we don't strike back, if we don't defend ourselves, things will get seriously out of hand, they can destroy us, our entire family, I try to explain, I jabber on, but my sister just rolls her eyes, listen, the medication doesn't seem to be working yet, I'm surprised that you're capable of such elaborate delusions, despite being so groggy and slowed down,

I spend the afternoon in bed, try to get some sleep but I can't, even though I'm exhausted, I keep waking up, to my numbed senses, yesterday I managed to wash all by myself, Peter says I've been walking a little faster, he's getting concerned, he laughs, I'll run away before he knows it, I mull over Martina's phone call, Xavier's photos, what if my sister is right? what if they wish me no harm? the thought unsettles me, it interferes with my painstakingly constructed certainties, it's hot in the room, the drawn shutters, the rumbling of trolleybuses in the street below, Klára has gone to Tehelné Pole swimming pool with my sister, mum must be at work, my other sister is sitting in the kitchen listening to the radio, I flinch, someone is here, I sit up in bed,

the door opens, Svetlana comes in, I greet her with a feeble smile, Peter gives me a friendly wink from the doorway and closes the door behind him, Svetlana walks across the room, sits down on the bed beside me, hugs me, holds me for a long time, whispering in my ear: Peter has told me everything, you don't have to say anything, it's terrible, the things they did to you there, it's lucky you got out of there, that they let you go in the end, they could have held you there for months, locked up, in solitary, on downers or electric shocks, these sadists, they don't understand anything, they won't listen, just stuff you full of drugs and pretend that's solved everything, they've done their duty, they would destroy anyone,

I glance at Svetlana, hesitate for a moment, but who else can I tell, if not Svetlana,

but, Svetlana, I heard voices, I heard voices although no one was there, laughter, steps, I ran out onto the balcony and there wasn't anyone there, I'm not making it up, it was hallucinations, I had aural hal—,

so what?! so you heard voices, is that a problem? did they tell you to kill anyone? and even if they did… come on, do you know how many people have hallucinations? and they live with it, they've learnt to live with it, what else is there to do! and they don't go all hysterical like you, or do you really think that everyone else is beautiful, together, zen?

you shouldn't have said a word to anyone, Svetlana goes on, if you'd kept it to yourself, nothing would have happened, you could have spared yourself the whole business, the hospitalisation, or do you think it's helped you in any way, has it enriched you in some way, are you better off now that you know what it's like to give up control over your life, to abandon yourself to the vagaries of *science*?

I keep quiet, then I start: but I couldn't stand the thought that everyone hates me so much, everyone at that Centre, the disabled people, the thought that they want to destroy me, they took my pictures to have compromising material for later, I'm sure they filmed me as well, look, the pictures have arrived already, the first batch that is, from Xavier, I pick up the photos from the bedside table and hand them to Svetlana, she doesn't even look at them, I continue: and yesterday I had a call from Martina, I think she wanted to take revenge, to blackmail me, but my sister says it's not true, the thing about hatred, that I'm just imagining it, that it's just delusions or something, a symptom of the disease,

Svetlana puts the photos back on the table, so people hating you is supposed to be a symptom of a disease? she chuckles, where does your sister live? in cloud-cuckoo land? of course they hate you, everyone hates you out there, surely you haven't imagined that everyone loves you?! and why should they? can you give them a reason? to love you? no, they hate you, they hate me too, but I've accepted it a long time ago, come to terms with it, and so has everyone else, you've got to learn to do that as well if you want to survive, welcome to the club, I'm glad you've finally worked out what it's all about, it's better to live fully aware of what it involves than to drift through life numbed by medication,

I feel like crying, I stammer, but I'm not up to it, I don't want to go on living if everyone hates me,

Svetlana squeezes my hand, not everyone, Blanka, not absolutely everyone, there are some people who love you, you'll gradually figure out who they are, don't worry, you'll learn how to tell the difference, in time you'll find a few people who will support you when you feel really down – and you certainly will – but you have to be on your guard with others, you have to be on your bloody guard, do you understand?! you can't be always open with everyone, that's what little children are like, but you're not a little child anymore, you have to keep things to yourself, bury them deep inside, let them settle like sediment at the bottom of a lake, you mustn't expose them to the light, let them muddy the waters, you have to wait for them to settle, become a part of you until you stop noticing them, that's what everyone else does,

I nod,

Svetlana sighs, don't worry, we'll get through it together, I'll keep an eye on you from now on, I give her a grateful smile, we sit in silence for a while, just gazing at each other, seeing the immense sadness in Svetlana's eyes sends shivers down my spine, Svetlana's eyes are resigned, inconsolable, they're blue like the azure of the bays, the *calanques* where you can see the tiniest detail, right to the bottom of the sea, her gaze is like an abyss opening before me, a whirlwind dragging me off the earth, sucking me into its depths, I hurtle down towards my centre at breakneck speed, suddenly this vision, plastic chairs and swimming pool with a hoist on the left, rustling trees and parked wheelchairs on the right, before me Martina and Drago and paramedics, suddenly I see, I feel, I know, that I am still, and will forever be, at the Bellevue Centre.

RECENT TITLES PUBLISHED BY JANTAR

In the Name of the Father *by* BALLA

Translated by Julia and Peter Sherwood

Balla's nameless narrator reflects upon his life filled with failures looking for someone else to blame. He completely fails to notice 'the thing' growing in the cellar. A hilarious satire poking fun at masculinity, the early years of the Slovak state and the author himself.

--- ISBN: 978-0-9933773-5-8

Big Love *by* BALLA

Translated by Julia and Peter Sherwood

Andrič and his girlfriend Laura have been seeing each other for a long time now but it isn't clear what each sees in the other. A critique of contemporary society, in which the triumph of liberal democracy has increased rather than diminished the Kafkaesque aspects of life.

--- ISBN: 978-0-9934467-8-8

Hear My Voice *by* DAVID VAUGHAN

International diplomacy has stopped working. A new breed of authoritarian ruler has emerged, contemptuous of the rules of diplomacy and collective security, and willing to lie and bully to build power and influence. Europe's democracies are confused and defensive. It is 1938 and Germany is putting pressure on Czechoslovakia. A young man has arrived in Prague. His job is to interpret and translate, but he finds himself literally lost for words as conflicting versions of the truth fight for the upper hand.

---ISBN: 978-0-9934467-3-3

For further news on new books and events, please visit
www.JantarPublishing.com